DARK MIN

COMING HOME

A DI TAVERNER AND DS WILDBLOOD NOVEL, BOOK 1

Published by Amazon, 2020

www.charliedeluca.co.uk

Proofreading by My Cup of Tea Press

To JKSC. The best father anyone could wish for.

Chapter 1

Gabriel Taverner stepped out into the city. It was a fresh
November morning, and he was here to explore the centre of York. It
was the first time since arriving as a detective in North Yorkshire that
he had had the opportunity to behave as a mere tourist, and he
breathed in the wintery air and faint smell of death and decay, with a
frisson of expectation. He looked up as the sun briefly glimmered
through the clouds, illuminating the honey coloured, ancient buildings
and began to walk, clutching his well-thumbed copy of a 'Brief
History of the City of York.'

He'd read that York dated from Roman times, known then at
Eboracum, and was the capital of the Anglo-Saxon kings of
Northumbria. It had become a staging post of the Plantagenet royals as
they attempted to conquer Scotland and was close to the site of one of
the bloodiest battles of the War of the Roses. In ancient times, the city
walls had been studded with the heads of murdered noblemen. He read
that the Knavesmire, now incorporated into the grounds of York
racecourse, had once been the site of public executions until the
townsmen decided to move it, feeling that the row of severed heads
which greeted visitors, made a ghoulish impression. Instead, the
execution site was moved to the grounds of York Castle, well within
the city walls, where hangmen plied their trade, killing thousands
including the notorious highwayman, Dick Turpin. In Mickelgate Bar,
the young King Edward IV rode into the city having secured the

3

throne for himself and the House of York. He learned about the bars or city gates which were used to control entry into York and were situated along the walls. They were known as Bootham, Mickelgate, Monk and Walmgate Bars.

Taverner walked on towards Pavement, an area where proclamations used to be heard and soaked up the atmosphere. If he half closed his eyes, he could almost see and hear the imprints of those who had walked these roads many centuries before. He pulled his collar up against the chill of the winter's day and glancing up at the sky, noticed the rare appearance of the sun. Ever since he had arrived in North Yorkshire from London, he had felt cold. He supposed this was something to do with the London smog which insulated the city and kept the heat from escaping, whereas in York, the skies were clearer, with much less vapour, so the temperature could quickly plummet. Small wonder that here, he always had to wear an extra layer of clothing to keep warm.

York was busy, tourists thronged the streets, of all ages and nationalities. There were middle aged couples, complete with hi-tech cameras slung round their necks and herds of twenty something young men who prowled in packs, eyeing similar groups of women. There were hordes of school children in smart uniforms on school trips, clutching quiz sheets, frowning as they attempted to complete their questions and several hen and stag parties even at this time of the morning. He even spotted a man dressed as a Victorian undertaker, beckoning visitors with a bony finger, to his Ghost Tour, which was advertised by an artificially aged sign, depicting times for excursions written in a shaky, Gothic hand. Taverner promised himself he would come back for a tour, as he imagined that the city was full of ghouls

4

and phantoms. Then there was the Chocolate Story, a museum which told the tale of the rise of the great confectioners in the city, Terrys, Rowntrees and Cravens, a guided tour around the city walls, the Railway Museum, the Minster and the Cold War Bunker. And when the sightseeing was complete, a trip to Betty's was in order, the iconic tea room which boasted the best afternoon tea for miles around, was highly recommended. Everyone, it seemed, wanted to visit York and Taverner had to concede that there was something for most.

As he walked down the market, into the hustle and bustle, Gabriel turned left onto the Shambles, which he'd learned from his guidebook, had been home to many butchers in its heyday. Now it was a narrow street where tall half-timbered houses bowed their heads above him, and cobblestones paved the walkway. In ancient times, the cobbles had run red with blood from animal carcasses and there were still ancient metal hooks outside the front doors where the cuts of meat were hung. The street wouldn't look out of place in a film set, he realised and was not surprised that it had become a celebrated part of York's history. He could almost hear the chatter of medieval folk, the padding of feet upon the cobbles and hum of daily life, today replaced by busy natives wrapped up against the cold, their flat northern vowels much in evidence and then the visitors, their faces looking up, entranced by the ancient architecture. The modern Shambles was an intriguing mix of shops, chocolatiers, jewellers, a Harry Potter outlet, shops selling exquisitely scented teas, gifts, book shops and chichi cafés. He took a deep breath. Knowing that his mother must had trodden these self-same steps made his heart race. The usual burst of emotion when he thought of her surged through his veins, hope

5

mingled with longing and trepidation, almost as if she was close by, within touching distance. Breathing deeply to steady his nerves, he walked on as the magnificent sight of York Minster rose to greet him. He stood for a moment, taking in the 200ft central tower and gazed in wonder at the huge stained-glass windows. The minster seemed to preside majestically over the whole city, dominating the landscape for miles around.

He was not a religious person, but the beauty and vastness of the cathedral inside, was enough to make him believe in a higher being, as he gazed at the vast domed ceiling, saw the light streaming through the stained glass windows and inhaled the faint scent of incense. The air was still, as faint particles of dust illuminated by the sunlight, darted around in front of him. It was incredible to think that mere humans had built such a building. His eyes scanned the roof which was supported by beautiful stone pillars and he marvelled as the light filtered through the ancient panes, and gave way to dancing rays of red, green and blue. He noticed the beautifully ornate Rose stained glass window, shaped like its namesake, high in the south transept, which was built to commemorate the end of the War of the Roses. Further ahead he noticed that there were guided tours of the minster and saw that one was just about to start. He glanced at his watch. He longed to go to join it and drink in the history. He didn't have time today but vowed to do so in the future. Yet, he wanted to mark the occasion of his visit and wondered how best to do this.

Then in the corner he spotted a small altar where visitors could buy candles, so he slipped a couple of coins into the honesty box and lit a pale white tea light. He looked into the flame and uttered a silent prayer for the family he had never known and his adoptive family, for Helen, Lawrence and for himself. For the son he was, and the son he could have been. He thought back to his time at the Met and the incident when he had arrested an infamous criminal and had been badly injured in the fallout. He had longed to get away from the Capital after that to find a sense of perspective and much needed inner peace. He stood in quiet contemplation for a few minutes concentrating on the flickering flame, breathing in the scent of the place. He could almost believe that everything would be alright, that he would be absolved from all guilt. A surge of electrical energy pulsed down his spine as he did so. It sounded fanciful, but he felt a jolt of recognition, almost as though he had been here before, as though he belonged in this quaint, historic city and that somehow it would heal him. The thought pleased him. He was so close; all his plans were coming to fruition. Then he felt a vibrating noise in his suit pocket and was brought back to reality, like an elastic band snapping back into its resting position. He dipped his hand into his pocket and pressed at the phone's buttons, anxious to stop it ringing out and disturbing the peace and tranquility of the Minster.

'Taverner.'

'It's Sykes here.' Taverner involuntarily straightened his back at the sound of his new boss's voice. Sykes was typically brusque. 'A body has been found in the River Ouse, reckon it's that missing student. We need yer 'ere if you can start a day early? Where are yer? The body has washed up near Holly Terrace on the banks of the river Ouse near the city centre. DS Wildblood can pick you up if it's not too far.'

7

Gabriel explained he was on a sightseeing tour of the Minster, so he arranged to wait outside the main entrance for his Sergeant to pick him up. He could have refused his superior's request, he supposed, but in truth, he'd been fed up with unpacking and sorting out his belongings as he settled into his cottage and found he was relishing the call to work. He had already been into the station at Fulford Road to meet his colleagues before he started his job proper. They had come across as a decent bunch, he'd had a cup of tea, though sadly they'd had no Earl Grey, only strong Yorkshire tea. He tried to remember what he knew about DS Wildblood who was picking him up. He'd had a fleeting impression of her; she was a capable, no nonsense type, with lots of dark curly hair and was attractive when she smiled, which he suspected was not often enough. He remembered that she had been recently promoted. His contemplative mood dispersed almost immediately. He glanced at the flickering flame and turned back the way he came, all thoughts of the past and his own demons forgotten. He was suddenly purposeful now, focused and intent. Questions about the missing student began to form in his mind. He was back on familiar ground and he had a job to do.

Chapter 2

The scene was awash with professionals, North Yorkshire Fire and Rescue personnel, uniformed officers and staff from SOCO. The row of handsome Georgian terraced houses stood about two hundred feet or so from the banks of the River Ouse which snaked through York. The body had surfaced in the riverbank nearby and had been found by a jogger, a middle-aged man who was sitting in the back of a police car, giving a statement. Pathologist, Dr Tony Ives was in attendance, Taverner identified him by his white forensic suit and air of authority. Ives' large stature gave him the appearance of a giant polar bear. He was peering over the body of a young girl. It was a pitiful sight; her green lace dress riding up her legs to reveal slender thighs, her chestnut hair strewn with fronds of an aquatic plant. Her skin was blueish grey, the body not yet swollen which meant she had only been immersed in the river for a few hours.

Taverner tried to remember what they knew about the missing girl. Her parents had contacted the police after she failed to ring them on Sunday and had been adamant that something was terribly amiss. She had been last seen on Saturday night and it was now Monday. Wildblood had briefed him as she drove smoothly around the bewildering one-way system in the city.

'It's a right shame you had to come in early, sir. Sykes is proper bricking it. If it is our student and it's foul play, then it'll be

9

bad for tourism, and the University, come to that. He'll want a result pretty quick, if yer ask me.'

'I'm sure he will. What do we know about the student?'

Wildblood drove deftly around a parked car. 'She went missing on Saturday when she was out with friends, got separated from her mates. The pathologist should be here, so we'll know more then.'

'What's he like?'

'Dr Ives? Alright. Very experienced and knows his stuff. Fancies himself as a bloody detective so he'll quizz yer, bound to. Given half a chance he'll be taking over the investigation, so mind what yer tell him.'

God, that was all he needed. Pathologists who were wannabe crime fighters.

'OK, that's good to know.'

As they arrived, Ives studied Taverner. 'I suppose you're the new chap?'

Taverner nodded his confirmation.

'Good to meet you.' Ives held up his gloved hands apologetically. 'I won't shake your hand. I'm Dr Ives.' His accent was a nasal Edinburgh burr. 'Poor wee lassie.' He nodded at the dead girl. 'Such a bloody waste. I suppose it's your missing student, is it?'

Another SOCO staff member, also dressed in a white coverall, was leafing through the contents of a damp handbag. 'This was found a few hundred feet downstream chucked into the undergrowth, sir. We're doing a fingertip search of the area, but the student ID reads Emily Morgan, so it looks like it is the missing girl.'

Taverner nodded at the young man. Emily was a student at York University and officers had taken down the details but had believed that parents were overreacting when they had insisted that she rang them every Sunday, and the fact that she hadn't rung that Sunday, was a sure sign that something was very wrong. They'd reported her the same day. Officers explained that parties, drinking and socialising, all the usual student activities, could easily disrupt this routine, except the parents had been right after all. Emily Morgan had certainly come to harm.

'Is it likely she simply had too much to drink and slipped into the river?' Taverner asked. In winter, he knew, that drownings were relatively common from cold water shock, where the body was so overwhelmed by the cold that death came quickly.

Ives shook his head. 'Och, I don't think so.' He gently rolled the body over to one side and pointed to a bloody mass of hair and tissue on the body's head. 'Look there's a large wound to the left temple, which looks like it occurred just before death. I say that because the injury is deep but the bleeding minimal. Then the lass was in all likelihood thrown into the river, almost immediately afterwards.' He pointed at slight abrasions on her upper arms. 'Look at these marks from where she was dragged.'

Anna Wildblood stirred. 'Are you sure that the head injury was not from the fall?'

'No, the injury is crescent shaped and across the temple. That area of the skull is actually the most vulnerable due to there being four bones which can fracture and lacerate the middle meningeal artery and cause an epidural hematoma. Aye, I'm pretty sure that this is what happened here. Injuries to that area of the head can easily be fatal.' He

11

prodded at the wound. 'I'll need to run further tests but it's pretty conclusive. The blow would have been severe enough to kill her.' Ives shook his head mournfully. 'I think our wee lassie was murdered.'

'So, we're looking for a murder weapon, some sort of blunt instrument?' asked Taverner.

'Aye, that's right.' Ives studied the wound more closely. 'I'll know more when I've completed the PM, mind.'

'OK, we'd better get down to where the handbag was found and examine the scene. We'll join you for the PM, Dr Ives.'

The pathologist nodded mournfully. 'You do that. I'll know more when I've run the usual tests, but who would want to murder the poor wee bairn? A boyfriend, robbery, a random attacker? Bet it's a boyfriend, it usually is.' He looked from one officer to the other. 'That would be as good a place as any to start if you ask me...'

Anna grinned, glad that Ives was behaving true to form. Taverner bit back an angry retort, irritated by the pathologist's assumption that he didn't know what the hell he was doing and tempted to reply that he hadn't asked him for his opinion. Taverner wouldn't presume to comment on anything vaguely medical. He sucked his teeth and strived for a more neutral response, after all, he didn't want to alienate his colleague so early on.

'Yes, yes, we will cover all bases. We'd better get on. See you soon.'

They walked the short distance to where the girl's handbag had been found. Members of SOCO were there now, raking over the earth. Taverner cast his eyes around the scene taking in the contents of the bag. All items were scrutinised and placed in evidence bags. He noticed a lipstick, hairbrush, powder compact, purse, a silver bracelet

12

and an eye liner. Taverner studied the bracelet and the girl's handbag, a large black leather variety, at length, pausing to examine the inner pockets carefully.

A white suited officer appeared. 'I presume there is no doubt about the girl's identity?' Taverner asked him.

'Her handbag and purse have her students' union ID and driving license in them, so it's pretty conclusive. Her purse was emptied of money, but they left the credit cards.'

'And her phone?'

'Missing unfortunately.'

Taverner brooded over this. Damn. Phones were like an Aladdin's cave in terms of evidence and revealed so much about individual's latest calls, lists of contacts not to mention GPS trekking information. They could get the data from the network provider, but it would take longer, sometimes several days. If it had been chucked into the river, then the likelihood was that it would be useless by now anyway. He looked at the sea of white, as staff scoured the area including the riverbank, where there may still be flattened areas where the body had been dragged. The divers would soon be systematically scouring the riverbed for any sign of the murder weapon. Hopefully, Ives would have a better idea of what type of item would have delivered the fatal blow and if they found the murder weapon, that could be a real game changer. He also had a high regard for police divers. He knew if there was something to find, then they would find it.

As they walked back to the car, Taverner scanned the street. 'We need to secure the scene and contact the next of kin. There might also be CCTV footage if Emily walked home and we need to speak to her friends too. I want to find out who she was with and who she met. We need to get some officers onto it right away. Someone must know something.'

Wildblood followed him as he made his way back to the car.

'I want the team assembled at eight for a briefing but before then we need officers to go into each of the local pubs. She went out with friends who may have noticed her missing at some point. We need to know what happened before she became separated from them.'

Wildblood agreed. 'Yes, sir. Poor kid. She can't surely have been murdered for her cash. Doubt she had a lot. She's only a poor student, after all.'

Taverner turned to look at her. 'Hmm. She had a Mulberry bag and a Tiffany bracelet which all looked pretty new, so not so poor, but which the murderer left behind, so I think we can definitely rule robbery out as a motive.'

Wildblood whistled. 'Are they genuine, do you think? How do yer know so much about designer stuff? There's lots of fake gear on the market these days.'

Taverner gave a ghost of a smile. 'The Mulberry bags each have an identity number near the inner pocket which that one does, and the bracelet has the right hallmarks.' He noticed Anna's raised eyebrows. 'My partner regularly asked for such things as gifts, that's why. She's my ex now and is with a richer man who can provide her with every bloody designer thing she's ever wanted.'

Wildblood blushed at this personal revelation, so early in their acquaintance. 'I'm sorry.'

14

'Don't be.' He frowned. 'We were never really suited anyway.'

'I suppose they could have been gifts?'

'Could be. We need to see her family. Do we have an address?' He looked at his sergeant consideringly. One of the team had rung through to the University and had supplied Wildblood with the address of the next of kin.

'Her parents live in Cottingham, in East Riding, sir.'

He glanced at his watch. 'It's four o'clock and it will take us at least an hour to get there and the visit might take ages.' He tapped his thigh with impatient fingers. 'I'll get a FLO on standby. Are you OK with that?' Taverner knew that Anna had toddler twins at home and had a lot of help from her husband and family according to Sykes. He was full of admiration for women with young children who worked in difficult jobs, he only had himself to look after and still struggled from time to time. He could only imagine how Anna managed to care for her little ones, run a house and still turn in and complete an eight hour shift day in day out, with great efficiency, from what he had been told. He wanted to give her an 'out', but not make it too obvious.

Wildblood frowned. He could see her bristling slightly at his assumption that she had to get home, that because she had children, he had to make allowances for her. Damn, he was trying to be understanding, but he could see that she had rumbled him. He watched her weighing up the situation, biting her lip abstractedly. Then she came to a decision.

'No, no. It's fine, sir. I'll just need to ring home. I can't leave yer to go on your own or ask one of the others to go. I mean yer not

15

even meant to have started and you've still had to come in. Besides, it's important.' She pulled over and turned the car round, her mouth in a tight, determined line. 'Can you navigate?'

Taverner nodded, pulled out his phone and typed the address into google maps.

Chapter 3

It was almost ten o'clock by the time Wildblood arrived
home. Rob was sitting watching the news, his face drawn with
tiredness, an empty glass of wine in front of him. Anna had managed
to text him from the Morgan's house to say she would be late and
knew he'd be relaxed about it. It was, after all, a very familiar
scenario.

He managed a smile as she came in.

'Drink? You look like you could do with it. How was it?'

Anna felt herself enveloped in his broad embrace as she took
the glass he offered.

'Oh, terrible as it always is. The new DI had to come in and
start a day early.'

'Oh right. What's he like?'

'OK, I suppose. He's quite posh, a bit aloof, I'd say. Not sure
what the others will make of him.' That wasn't strictly true, her
colleagues had been quite vocal on the point. She thought back to the
comments from Haworth and Ballantyne who couldn't forgive him for
asking for Earl Grey tea when they'd first met him. Haworth thought
he was a 'southern softie' and not likely to last two minutes and
Ballantyne had agreed. They both speculated as to why he had left the
Met and decided that there was some sort of scandal surrounding him.

'Aye, he'll be gone shortly,' Ballantyne had added darkly. She
wouldn't put it past the pair of them to freeze the man out. Anna

17

wasn't sure about their new boss either, but she had to admit he was certainly easy on the eye, tall, dark, with fine features, she could see how the other officers would certainly feel threatened by him. He was very well dressed, which was another surprise; his suit looked very expensive. DCI Sykes had given little away except to say that their new Inspector liked modern policing and was partial to psychological theories about criminology. He had a degree apparently, another mark against him, according to Haworth and Ballantyne, who thought he had probably been 'fast-tracked', promoted beyond his competence, would lack experience and 'wouldn't know his arse from his elbow.' Anna wasn't rattled by him having a degree; that was fine as long as he possessed some common sense. Academics seldom did, in her experience but she wouldn't judge him yet. He was so different to the usual bosses she had worked with. Still, he had been great with the grieving family, considerate and calm. She thought back to their pale faces, the mother breaking down into hysterical tears, the father crumbling before them. The pair were obviously hardworking, proud of their daughter and appalled at the news which no parents ever wanted to hear. She felt helpless as Taverner listened to them and explained the investigative processes. They had waited until the Family Liaison Officer had arrived. Then, somewhat guiltily she acknowledged, she had been glad to be able to leave.

She sipped her wine and tried to shrug off the tensions of the day. 'Anyway, how are the boys?'

Rob grinned. 'They ate well, had fun in the bath and have been sound asleep since seven…'

'OK, I'll just pop my head around their door…'

18

Anna mounted the stairs and made her way into the boys' room. She was desperate to see them. Jasper was sucking his thumb whilst Archie snuffled in the furthest bed. Her blue eyed, gorgeous little angels. She dropped a kiss on their foreheads, taking in their sweet smell and stroked their blond curls. What would she do if anything ever happened to them like it had to Emily? Fear clutched at her heart. Supposing something did happen whilst they were in the care of her mother-in-law and she was at work, worrying about other people's children who were after all strangers? Guilt gnawed away at her about her decision to work full time and apply for promotion. It all started when they saw their current house. She and Rob had set their hearts on the place, a beautiful barn conversion on the outskirts of York, as soon as they saw it. They had it all planned out. Rob had become a partner at the accountancy firm where he worked, and she had just passed her Sergeant's exams when she had become pregnant. As a couple they had worked out their finances, factoring in her maternity leave. It was going to be tight, but they decided that with good money management, they would cope. Then Anna had found out that she was going to have twins and the finances were stretched even further. Anna had thought that the mellow stone barn was the most important thing before she'd had the boys, but as soon as they were born, she knew that their safety and welfare were all that mattered. Today she'd have given anything to move back to their old terraced house, which was after all like a Tardis inside, then Rob could carry on working as an accountant and she could give up work, at least until the boys were at school. If she was at home, she'd watch them grow and flourish instead of relying on her mother-in-law, Marian, relaying tales of their escapades to Rob, which he then passed onto her third

19

hand. It wasn't that she disliked Marian, she didn't. She was very fond of her. She'd had to be co-opted into helping to care for the boys whilst Anna worked, a task she had approached with quiet efficiency. She ought to feel grateful to Marian and she did, but she also felt a crushing envy and awful feelings of guilt which pressed heavily down on her shoulders. She had thought that she would love being a police sergeant and she did, she had been delighted with the promotion, but she adored being a mother too. Anna laid on the floor between the boys' beds, watching shadows scud across the ceiling and listened to the soft breathing of her two little boys. She had been exhausted by her maternity leave, but she had also loved every minute of it. The problem was because of their hefty mortgage she'd had to go back to work. Initially, it had been a slow start as she got back into the job, then she had been promoted but now with a murder investigation, she knew how absorbed she would become, she anticipated the stress, the long hours, the emotional turmoil and sighed. Had they made a huge mistake? Their home was beautiful, but she felt frustrated that they had less time to enjoy it together. She wondered if the move had really been worth it. The boys mattered more to her than anything, she knew that now. By the time she came downstairs, she had it all worked out in her head.

'Look, I've been thinking, Rob. I just think I'll jack it all in, and maybe work when the boys are at school. I'll never get this time back with them. I'm missing all their firsts, I missed their first steps, their first words…' Her sobs caught in her throat. 'We didn't need to move to such a big house, we could go back to our old place or somewhere like it…'

Rob patted the sofa beside him and pointed at the wine. It was a well-worn topic.

'Come on, Anna, sit down here and have a drink. We've talked about this. It's just that you've had a crap day seeing that girl, breaking the news to her parents. You'd hate it at home if you were here all the time, besides the boys are fine. Mum loves having them, and we manage. Lots of women work and have children and their kids are fine, as ours will be.'

'Hmm. I suppose.' She knew it was true deep in her heart.

'Don't beat yourself up, it's a waste of time and energy. This is a great place to bring the boys up, it may not seem like it now, but it will as they grow older. They are in a much better catchment area for schools, far better than our old place, and it really will make a difference over the years. You need to look at the bigger picture. Come on, you're just tired and upset. That's all.'

Anna suddenly felt exhaustion seeping into her bones. It was a conversation they'd had on many occasions, but it seemed she needed to talk about it again. As usual, Rob was clear headed and logical in his thinking but was he right? The school catchment area, so the boys could attend a good school, was high on his list of priorities. Rob was adamant that education was vitally important for their children, so they could mix in the right circles with the right people. She was not so sure. If the twins were happy, then that was the most important thing. Rob had even hinted that he would send the boys to a private school and he was busily saving for them. It was something they had argued about with no real conclusion and she didn't intend debating the whole thing again after the day she'd had. Certainly, she was tired and emotional, so she did as she asked, drank her wine and watched something mildly amusing on the TV, as Rob rubbed her tense shoulders.

'Better?'

She nodded as she gazed at the blond Viking of a man. She was lucky, she knew she had it all really, just sometimes it didn't feel like it, especially today.

'You know you're a really special person, Anna. You're bright and talented, you were a great DC and you'll be an even better sergeant. Not everyone can do your job. You've only been a sergeant for three months and the boys have been fine. This family, this dead girl, they need you to find out what happened to their daughter. You're good at what you do, you'll find out who did it and justice will be done. And beside you'll be a great role model for the boys when they grow up. What job could be more important than upholding justice after all?'

Anna felt the horrors of the day receding as the wine relaxed her. He was right, of course. It was always like this when she was working on a high-profile investigation, especially a murder, she was just getting everything out of proportion, that was all.

'So, you don't think I should knock it on the head?''

Rob sighed. 'No, you just need to do your job, that's all. You'd be bored out of your skull otherwise, sitting at home cleaning. Then the boys will be at school and you'd go even more stir crazy. You're an outstanding officer and a great mother. You can be both, you know. Never forget it.' He kissed the top of her head. 'We have a good future ahead of us, lots to look forward to. Oh, that's just reminded me, you haven't forgotten about the fundraiser on the tenth of November, have you?'

22

Anna nodded. 'No. I haven't. I definitely won't be working late as it's my day off.'

'Marvellous. It's a really important evening for Domus and we have some influential clients. John Armitage is coming, and you know what a successful businessman and philanthropist he is.'

Anna smiled. Rob was a decent person. It was the kind of thing people said all the time but didn't really mean, but with him he really did care about his job as an accountant and loved his charity work too. He really did want to make a difference. She knew he was right about her situation and it did make her feel better. It was just that she felt like she was juggling everything and in serious danger of dropping the ball with potentially disastrous consequences. Rob was always looking out for her, that was the thing that had attracted her to him initially. He actually listened to her and took her seriously. In a family where she and her younger sister were mere bit part actors to her brother's lead role in their family, her mother still hung on his every word, this was a powerful aphrodisiac. Rob, with his Viking like good looks, charm and sophistication, had virtually rugby tackled her off her feet, such was the power of his attraction for her. He had a gift of making you feel like you were the only person that mattered, and that had been a revelation. She drifted back to the memory of a couple of Christmases ago, when she went home to her parents. Her mother only really came alive when her brother turned up, late as usual, as she insisted that Christmas was all about family. She and her sister, who'd been there days before and spent their time skivvying around cooking and cleaning, had been barely able to generate a smile from their mother. Her sister, Ellie, had remarked sourly that it was almost as though they were strangers who had wandered in off the street, surely, they were family too? She would never do that with her children. Of course, mum adored Rob too, so maybe it was just a male thing? She wondered briefly what Taverner did when he got home, how he coped without a partner to support him, how he would fit into the team and what had led him to come to North Yorkshire? He seemed to have an air of sadness about him, of vulnerability perhaps. She had wanted to snap at him when he suggested that she might not be able to visit the girl's family, but now she was glad that she hadn't. He was just being fair that was all and hadn't wanted to make assumptions. Perhaps they were on the same page after all. Then the baby monitor crackled into life and she was suddenly alert.

'I'll go.' She was filled with such a sense of longing to see her boys awake that she ran up the stairs as fast as her legs could carry her. It was time to assuage her guilt.

Gabriel Taverner was bone weary. He pottered around his house, made himself a toasted sandwich and flicked through the TV channels, letting the drama wash over him. His spirits had been lowered by the visit to the Morgans. It was one of the worst parts of his job, telling relatives bad news, watching them fall apart as they struggled through the shock and pain to make sense of the investigative processes. He had learned that Emily had been a model daughter, her parents were quite justifiably proud of her, even more so when she had been admitted to such a prestigious University as York.

'So, she just fell into the river, is that it?' Mr Morgan's expression was incredulous. 'We thought she'd be safe in York, why wasn't she safe? Why didn't you do more to find her when we

24

reported her missing?' Steve Morgan's eyes raked wildly over them both. The words were out of his mouth before he could stop them. 'I mean, are you sure it's her?'

Taverner ignored the implied criticism. It was just the grief talking. Besides no one could have prevented her death. The depressing truth was that she was already dead when her parents reported her missing.

'Emily's ID was found in her bag, so we are as sure as we can be,' he had added as gently as possible. 'It looks like she was physically assaulted before she went into the water, but we'll know more when she has been examined.'

Mr Morgan gasped for air. 'What? Are you saying that Emily's death was not an accident?'

Taverner nodded. 'We are treating it as suspicious.'

Mrs Morgan had begun to wail so much so, DS Wildblood had made tea, and rang a neighbour before the Family Liaison Officer arrived. DS Wildblood sat holding Mrs Morgan's hand in the dining room whilst Gabriel had spoken to her husband in the sitting room. There was a younger sister wearing a black school uniform, so similar to her sister that he couldn't decide whether that would be a comfort or a curse to her parents as the weeks unfolded. She was aged about thirteen, Taverner decided. Her eyes were red raw from weeping, her childhood innocence well and truly shattered. The house was a small, modern terrace in Cottingham, the furniture rather too big for the available space. There were piles of boxes in one corner and the smell of paint, as though the move was relatively recent.

'How long have you lived here?'

Mr Morgan frowned. 'Only about six months. We used to live in East Riding, Kirkella, had a much bigger place but we had to downsize.' He looked sheepish. 'I was made redundant you see, and now this...' His lips trembled. Taverner realised that he was a very proud man and appearances mattered.

'I need to ask you a few questions, Mr Morgan. Did Emily have a boyfriend? Someone she knew from Hull or York?'

'Yes. Dan. His name is Dan Charlton. They were at sixth form together.' Mr Morgan's face crumpled. 'You surely don't think this is anything to do with him? He's a nice lad, wouldn't hurt a fly!'

'No, no. We have to follow certain lines of inquiry, that's all. It's just standard procedure. Did he go to York Uni too?'

'No, no, he has an apprenticeship in Hull, at Siemens.'

'OK. Do you have an address?'

Mr Morgan called his wife, and DS Wildblood gently prised the details from her.

'Can I ask, did she have any enemies, anyone who may have wanted to harm her?'

Mr Morgan's aghast expression said it all. His eyes filled with tears. 'Of course not. Everyone loved Emily...'

Then the FLO had arrived and was busy phoning relatives and making sandwiches. She was PC Lambert, a sensible officer, mid-thirties, who was calm, kindly and efficient. Instantly, she took in the situation and set about helping. She telephoned for a GP to administer a sedative to Mrs Morgan, distributed tea and kindness even finding time to wash the dishes. Taverner was certainly glad of PC Lambert's homely, reassuring presence and hoped the family would be too.

He had taken some more details from Mr Morgan, promised to keep him in the loop and reassured him that they would find Emily's killer. There was also the difficult matter of a formal identification of Emily's body, which Taverner broached as sensitively as he could. Mr Morgan promised to come to the Mortuary tomorrow, lowering his voice so that his wife didn't hear. Taverner felt his own resolve strengthening at the man's wish to protect his wife.

'We will find out who did this, I will do everything in my power to find Emily's killer.'

The man shook his hand gratefully, his eyes blurry with tears.

'You do that, lad, you do that.'

Taverner could not get the family's distress out of his mind. He felt sorrow, which turned to anger which then settled into determination to help them and get justice for Emily. But it was not going to be easy. Being a detective was a bit like putting together a thousand-piece jigsaw without the aid of the picture on the box and with several vital pieces missing. Each fact had to be verified and checked, weighed and measured carefully and arranged to see if it fitted a pattern that led them to the murderer. Then, of course, the evidence had to meet the stringent thresholds of the CPS, which was another matter entirely. They needed patience, hard work and sometimes a bit of luck and it was all too easy to be thrown off course.

Most women were murdered by men they already knew, often someone they were in an intimate relationship with. He wondered about Dan Charlton and where he had been on the night in question. He would clearly be someone that they needed to talk to. Various theories began to form in his mind. Had the couple drifted apart, had

27

Dan been dumped and exacted his revenge on Emily in the most brutal way possible? Had he followed her and seen her with another man and had they argued? He had to keep an open mind though, as experience had taught him to pursue all angles and not get so fixated on one suspect so that he missed vital clues which could lead down another route entirely. He was a great believer that clear, logical thinking would bring results.

He opened a drawer in his sideboard and pulled out a brightly coloured album. His own life story book. He flicked through the pages which were very well thumbed. This was the book about his early life, the one his social worker had provided when he was adopted at the age of two. It told his own history and he read it avidly taking in the details, the names, the faces as the old longings resurfaced. He felt rootless and abandoned at times; the feeling was almost as though he had been hollowed out like a trunk of a tree which had been struck by lightning. He'd had a family, to external observers, a normal happy childhood but he had always felt like he didn't quite belong and as he grew up, he understood the reason for this. He remembered his friends maturing to be almost replicas of their parents, the likenesses were just so noticeable, except in his family. *Where do you get your height, your dark hair,* his friends would ask, comparing him to his mousey haired, modestly sized parents. He felt a prickle of guilt as he had made up a distant Italian relative, which his friends accepted. Then there was his sporting ability, the football skills which neither parent possessed, his father was a cricket fan, but had never played. *Where was that from?* The Italian relative, with Italian football being all the rage, had come in handy again because despite his parents' insistence that he should tell people about the adoption, he just couldn't bring himself to do it, worried about the way it made him feel and how others would see him. He sighed as he remembered his sullen adolescence, the wild years in Deal, after his father had retired from London, the rows, his parents' baffled hurt expressions and then determined stoicism. But he had no time to deal with it at the moment, the investigation took precedence. He studied the photo of a young woman, his mother, her eyes bright as she gazed at the baby she was holding, her expression tender. Soon, he told himself, soon. He put the book back into the drawer with care and gazed out of his dining room window at the stars for a long time wondering if she was doing the same, seeing the same constellations, the same inky black skies as he was. The thought gave him some comfort on what had been a trying and emotional first day.

Chapter 4

DI Taverner stood before the links board and cleared his throat. There was a photo of Emily Morgan in the centre of the board, her smiling, beautiful face beaming out at them. He surveyed the team and tried to remember what he knew about everyone from his initial visit and rushed conversation with DCI Sykes. Sykes would be acting as the Senior Investigating Officer and DS Wildblood was on hand to support him and help him manage a team of DC's. Sykes had been sparing in his description of the team, but almost effusive about Wildblood's skills, so that was at least positive. There was DC James Ballantyne, a blunt Scot with a dour expression, modest DC Raj Patel, who was a whizz at anything to do with computers or phones, complete with DC Paul Haworth, who was apparently the joker in the pack. Graham Hyde, a retired officer, was recruited as the office manager. Sykes had arranged for another DC to join them, but as yet they had not been released from their commitments. The team looked attentive and he suspected were much quieter than usual, possibly on their best behaviour, as they gazed back at him. Taverner felt a flurry of nerves at addressing them for the first time as their DI and decided to press on in the hope that any tension would recede once he began to speak. He had dressed well, a trick he had learned from school where he had often felt the odd one out. Wearing the right clothes, today a sharp navy suit, white shirt, blue jewelled cufflinks and of course his trusty Church brown brogues, had certainly given him a boost. He

30

thought it would be as good a time as ever to set out his stall, be clear about how he liked to run his team.

'So, it's great to be here and I hope we will all work well together. What are the odds on having a murder inquiry in your first week of work? And I thought it was going to be quiet in rural Yorkshire...' There was a polite ripple of laughter at this and at least some smiles, enough to encourage him. 'Anyway, for those who haven't met me yet, I'm DI Gabriel Taverner. I've relocated to York from London where I worked in the Met for seven years after studying psychology and criminology, which inspired me to join the police force. I have heard that you are a good bunch of officers and I do hope we will work together well. Work hard, keep looking at the evidence, use your emotional intelligence, keep me in the loop and we'll be fine.' There was a murmur of assent and a few nods and smiles. 'Now to the matter in hand, Emily Morgan's body was recovered from the River Ouse yesterday. A jogger alerted the police. She had been missing some twelve hours prior to that and was reported by her parents. Inquiries were just beginning as to her whereabouts. She was aged nineteen, a second-year English undergraduate at the University of York and viewed as bright and popular. I have read the notes of the police officer who was carrying out the initial inquiries. Officers have spoken to Emily's friends, family and her lecturers. A PM is being carried out later on today, but preliminary inquiries suggest that she was hit on the temple with a blunt instrument. This blow was enough to kill her. Then she was dragged a short distance and thrown into the water. So, we are looking at murder and as you all know, most women are murdered by men close to them, often those they are in an intimate relationship with. I am a great believer in victimology because research tells us that we need to find out as much as we can about our victim, to work out who murdered her. We need to know how she spent her time, what she was studying and more importantly, who she had relationships with, especially of a close, personal kind. This should help us find out why she was murdered and lead us to the perpetrator. In terms of inquiries, I want her family and friends interviewed, and Emily's boyfriend, of course, Dan Charlton. Also, city centre CCTV will need to be examined closely. We know that she was on a night out with friends on the Saturday but became separated from them. They assumed she had met up with a mate and stayed overnight when she didn't turn up the next day. She always rang her parents on a Sunday without fail, apparently, so they were immediately worried and reported her as missing. Someone must have an idea who she met on that evening, there may well be CCTV footage of the group in the city centre, pubs and clubs and we need to rule these people out. Any theories?'

DC Haworth stared at the photo of the victim. 'She were reight bonny, weren't she? Lass like that's bound to attract a bit o' attention from t'lads. Maybe, she got friendly with one, maybe they took a fancy to 'er. P'raps t'boyfriend saw, he followed her and bashed her o'er the head.' He shook his head sorrowfully.

Taverner frowned as he struggled to understand the thick dialect.

'What Paul means is that the boyfriend could have come to York and surprised her and found her with another man. If he saw her out and about with someone, then he could have become angry and hit her,' DS Wildblood translated. Taverner did not miss the scowl that she directed at Haworth.

'Aye, or it was a random attack? Could it be connected to any of the other drownings we've had?' commented DC Ballantyne, darkly. There had been a spate of drownings in the past couple of years, usually students either deciding to go on midnight swim or who had fallen into the river, which snaked through the city centre, when drunk and then found themselves in difficulty. Taverner hadn't been in the area then, so wanted to find out more.

'DS Wildblood, can you pull the files on the recent drownings and see if you can find any links with any of them and Emily?'

'Yes sir, though the coroner ruled misadventure in all five, as we all know.' Taverner noticed her glaring at Ballantyne.

'Five drownings? Over what period?'

'In the last two years, three in the Ouse and two in the River Foss. They were all students who had all been drinking, who fell in walking back after a night on the tiles and were not able to swim to safety because of the amount of alcohol they had consumed.'

Taverner had been a student himself and knew only too well the alcohol and drugs that students could sink, but even so, five drownings seemed excessive. Still, it would do no harm to read the files and see if there were any similarities or suspicions of foul play.

'Right, I want Ballantyne to continue to check out the CCTV and city centre pubs and clubs, Patel to liaise with forensics and see if the divers can find Emily's phone and more importantly the murder weapon, Haworth to interview the friends she was with that night, speak to the University and liaise with Ballantyne. Wildblood and I will go to the post mortem, visit Dan Charlton, Emily's boyfriend and find out what he has to say for himself. The first 48 hours are vital to any murder investigation as you all know, so let's get cracking and

33

leave no stone unturned. The death of a bright, beautiful young student is really going to hit the headlines and never forget, we've a grieving family who want answers, so let's get to it.'

'Right y'are,' muttered Haworth and there were nods from the others. It was important that they had a good start as Taverner really wanted to impress his new team.

Dr Tony Ives, pathologist, appeared to have an unfailingly cheerful disposition, which was just as well, given his job. He had been examining the body and talking into a dictaphone but broke off as soon as he saw the officers approaching. Taverner hated mortuaries, the familiar, medicinal scent of the place, not to mention the physical presence of the dead body complete with hastily sewn up scars where vital organs had been removed, examined and weighed, was most unpleasant. Thankfully, he'd had a light breakfast, and hoped he wouldn't be sick. That wouldn't do at all in his first week. He gritted his teeth and looked at the doctor inquiringly.

'Och, it's what I thought. She was hit over the left temple with a blunt instrument, something smooth and heavy. I'd say it was pretty big and curved in shape to make that injury.'

'Any idea what?'

'A heavy object with a specific man-made curved edge. Like a wrench with an inner curved semicircular shape.' He pointed at the large wound. 'You can tell by the injury and bruising. The blow fractured her skull so was wielded with some force and that area of the brain is where the skull easily fractures. The wrench would have been on the large side, but a common enough tool and I'd guess that our protagonist was right-handed judging by the injury site. She was then dragged to the riverbank and thrown in.'

DS Wildblood frowned. 'So, you can confirm that this blow caused her death, and she didn't just hit her head whilst in the water swimming?'

'Aye. Toxicology tests reveal that she had drunk a little, no more than two drinks, eaten several hours before and was otherwise in good health. The blow to her head would have been enough to kill her. Judging by the severity of the injury and the lack of bruising, her heart stopped shortly after, before she was thrown into the river.'

'So, it's not a simple case of her falling in and drowning?' Taverner clarified.

'No, the wound clinches it. This is definitely murder.'

Taverner almost smiled at the Scotsman's rolling r's in the word murder.

'Would a male or female have been able to deal the final blow?' asked Wildblood.

Ives studied her. 'Hard to say, probably either.'

Taverner gazed at the porcelain like skin and titian hair. She had clearly been a stunning girl. He only hoped that death had not been painful and drawn out.

'How can you tell it was definitely murder?'

Ives smiled. 'From the bruising and the amount of water in her lungs, which was a lot. Most people who fall into water hold their breath voluntarily, but it looks like she was not able to do that so that tells me that the lassie was already dead when she hit the water. It all strongly suggests that death followed fast after she was hit. So, it would have been very quick.'

35

Thank the Lord for that, Taverner thought. As a policeman, he had seen lots of tragic sights but the death of a young person or a child usually got to him because of the appalling and senseless waste. It was hard not to think about how they died. If Emily had died instantly, then so much the better.

'Anything else you can tell us?'

'Not at this stage. I'm awaiting further toxicology tests. I have looked at nail scrapings but don't think these will tell us anything. The lass had a contraceptive implant under her skin so was likely to be in a sexual relationship, but there's no sign of sexual assault either, no abrasions, or injuries consistent with forced intercourse.'

So that was something at least.

Taverner suddenly felt quite lightheaded, the pungent smell of blood and cleaning fluids made him want to keel over, yet he dared not show any weakness, even in front of Wildblood. He tried to breathe deeply, in as surreptitious manner as he could.

'So, who's in the frame?' asked the doctor. 'Boyfriend, student with a wee crush, perhaps? Was anything stolen? What are your theories so far?'

Taverner realised he was about to offer some of his own and decided it was time to make a quick exit. He met Wildblood's eye remembering what she had said earlier.

'There are several possible suspects, but we need evidence, so we had better go and find some. Thanks. I'll wait for your report.' With that he turned on his heel and walked off, closely followed by Wildblood.

He noticed that she was silent and extremely pale as she drove back to the station. He saw that she looked clammy and was sitting very still. She had the window wound slightly down and took deep breaths. Something was clearly very wrong.

'Are you OK?' Wildblood didn't answer but breathed deeply. 'Look, pull over and take a sip of water.'

Wildblood looked at her rear-view mirror, indicated and then stopped. She opened her door and promptly vomited all over the pavement. Taverner looked on helplessly. He climbed out of the car, careful to avoid the traffic and handed her a handkerchief. Wildblood gasped and heaved again, narrowly missing Taverner's polished brogues.

'You alright now?' Wildblood nodded, her face ashen. She stood on the pavement for a while longer before wiping her mouth and checking her clothes which fortunately had missed the spatter.

Taverner held out his hand. 'I'll drive just to be on the safe side, but you might need to guide me back to the office.'

'OK.' She handed him the keys. Once in the car, Wildblood sat in silence.

'Was it something you ate, or do PM's always have that effect on you?'

Wildblood smoothed down her hair and tried to make herself look presentable. She had pulled out some wipes from her capacious bag and seemed to be composing herself. She took several deep breaths.

'It's the bloody PM's, sir. Ever since I've had the twins, I've been like this, more emotional and upset. I suppose it's just thinking about me own little 'uns.' She shook her head. 'Christ, sir. I'm so sorry. I feel bloody awful. Look, you won't tell 'em back at the office, will yer? I'll never live it down if you do.'

Taverner laughed, sensing an ally. 'Course not. At least you weren't sick in the car. Anyway, how old are your twins?'

Wildblood warmed to her theme. 'Three they are. Double trouble but I wouldn't swap 'em for the world.'

'Well, it can't be easy looking after them and working. I mean, it's not the easiest job in the world.' Christ, how on earth did she manage, he wondered?

'No, it's not. But I get lots of help, my husband and mother-in-law are great.' She gave him a sidelong look. 'We all muck in and it works fine.'

'I'm glad to hear it.' He overtook a cyclist. 'Anyway, I'll let you into a secret. I hate post mortems too. Anyway, I don't think we should be too hard on ourselves. There's nothing wrong with good old-fashioned revulsion, as my old boss used to say. Shows we're human at least and haven't become too hard.' He slowed down and peered at the signs. 'So, is it left or right here?'

'Right, follow the road round. Not long now. Fishergate runs into Fulford Road. So, do you reckon it's the boyfriend then, sir? It's tricky keeping the relationship going if one of you is at uni, I suppose.'

Taverner was deep in concentration trying to navigate around the unfamiliar roads.

'The boyfriend would be our prime suspect if he was in the area. Hull isn't a million miles away, so he could easily have gone there and back. How far away is it?'

Wildblood considered this. 'Fifty miles or so, it would probably take just over an hour, so it's entirely possible. We need to do a police check on 'im. Wonder if his name comes up?'

'Hmm. Any offences or intel which indicate that he has problems managing his anger would certainly be a red flag.' He glanced at his sergeant who at least looked like her colour was returning. 'Are you sure you're alright?'

Wildblood smiled. 'I am. Thanks sir. I'll be fine now.'

He pulled into the car park and found a space next to a bright red Fiat 500. As they were walking back to the office, he fished out his car keys, unlocked the Fiat and dived in, pulling out a box of tea bags from the back seat.

'Nice car,' added Wildblood smirking. It was a smart car but one she could imagine a woman driving, certainly not a tall, youngish man.

Taverner shrugged, unperturbed. 'It belonged to the ex. I borrowed it and have sort of ended up with it.' He caught her amused expression. 'A bit girly I suppose, but the fuel consumption is so much better than my Merc.'

Wildblood eyed the box of Earl Grey tea in his hand and suppressed a smile. He was certainly very different to the usual macho guys she worked with. She found herself warming to him, especially when she remembered his kindness when she had vomited and his ready admission about his dislike of post mortems.

Taverner was thoughtful. A speedy resolution to the case would be a dream start, but he realised that cases were rarely that

39

simple. Yet, he was also relieved. He felt that he and Wildblood had definitely broken the ice and that at least was positive. He sensed that the other members of the team, especially Haworth and Ballantyne, were very set in their ways and could struggle with his more progressive approach. He knew he couldn't be best mates with his team, but it was always much better if they respected him at least.

Back at the office, Taverner updated his colleagues on the PM and they gathered together the information from the inquiries to date.

'Well, there's nothing coming up on the police national computer about Daniel Charlton, 'explained Patel. 'He's squeaky clean, not so much as a parking ticket.'

'OK. Here's the details of his car registration, so can you do an ANPR check?' Taverner passed over the piece of paper he had written the registration in Dan Charlton's name from an earlier check and looked the map. 'If he came to York, I guess he'd be driving on the motorway and there's bound to be cameras on that route. Check on the day of the murder and the days around it, can you?'

'Right you are.'

Haworth was hovering with a menu in his hand. 'Just off to get us butties, boss, if you want summat?'

Taverner looked puzzled.

'Lunch, sir. Haworth's popping over to the shop, Ma Bakers. It's our nearest café and is better than the canteen. It does pretty good sandwiches,' translated Wildblood.

Taverner felt his stomach rumble. He'd not eaten since yesterday, apart from a small cereal bar, having been too nervous this morning for anything more substantial. He felt the horrors of the PM and the familiar smell recede slightly like the tide as survival took over. He needed to eat.

'Do they do wraps? Anything with avocado or falafel, would be great, thanks.'

Haworth raised his eyebrows in confusion. 'Right.'

Wildblood tidied herself up and on her way back to the office found Haworth and Ballantyne in the small kitchen unwrapping the sandwiches ready to hand them out.

Haworth was in full flow about the new boss. 'Bloody southerner with his fala... whatever it is and his avocado and his bloody psychobabble theories. Don't think he'll last two minutes. All that 'barth' and 'carstle' and 'cap of tea'! And have you seen his car? It's reight girly. A Fiat 500! I wouldn't be seen dead in the thing. Why is he here, for God's sake?'

'Aye, he's a wee bit fancy for these parts. The smart suit must have cost a bob or two and those cufflinks and as for the bloody Earl Grey tea! Cat piss, is what it is!'

Haworth was warming to his theme. 'Fancy asking for a blooming wrap! What's the matter with a buttie?' He registered Wildblood's presence. 'What do you make of 'im, Sarge?'

Wildblood had been as perplexed by Taverner as the rest of them initially, after all, he was nothing like the usual Inspectors who under a thin veneer of political correctness, were as macho as cage fighters, underneath it all and still did the alpha male posturing. They leered secretly at the women in their teams but pretended otherwise. She thought back to their journey from the PM and Taverner's sensitivity. He had been very kind and empathic.

41

She felt mortified about being sick and utterly appalled with herself, yet he hadn't made her feel bad, quite the opposite. He had even confided that he struggled with post mortems too. He seemed that rare breed in her line of work, a man comfortable with his masculinity, so much so, he didn't need to keep continually reinforcing it. He had seemed impressed that she was juggling so many balls. She felt a sudden protectiveness towards her boss and irritation with her peers for their narrow mindedness. Taverner's approach made a pleasant change from where she was standing.

'Gi' over, you two, don't think I don't know what you're up to. Paul, since when was your accent so bloody strong? You were doing that deliberately,' she hissed at Haworth. 'And as for you, Jim, you know very well the drownings have all had verdicts of misadventure, so stop throwing in red herrings and gi' the man a chance, for God's sake!' She paused only to glare at them. 'How would you feel in his position in a strange city, with you lot taking the piss? And for what it's worth, you could all do with taking a few style tips off the boss. Now have some respect or you'll have me to answer to!'

With that, she scooped up her and Taverner's sandwiches, avocado and ham for him, and cheese savoury for her, leaving them open mouthed and stormed back to the office. Bloody bastards! She made a mental note to keep a closer eye on those two. They had form for this sort of thing. Patel has suffered the same sort of jibes, just because he was Asian, more so because he was on the same grade as they were, but he had won their respect when he showed what a fine officer he was. They were lucky that he hadn't made a formal complaint and she had been very tempted to make one on his behalf.

42

She sensed that Taverner would do very well given half a chance. What was wrong with a man who knew how to dress anyway or who liked fancy food and posh tea? Better than Haworth who favoured wearing a much washed old green fleece over his shirts, and Ballantyne with his old fashioned, grey anorak that had seen better days. She left them gaping in silence and she hoped, somewhat chastened. So, the Inspector was vastly different to the usual macho idiots she had encountered, but to her he made a very welcome change.

Dan Charlton was tall with mid brown hair and a handsome face. Wildblood would have felt more sympathy for him if it weren't for his rather soulless blue eyes, which raked over her in a rather practiced manner, not at all appropriate for someone whose girlfriend had just been murdered. Taverner was his usual urbane self and when he expressed his condolences, Dan's eyes began to tear up, although he was clearly trying to fight it, so perhaps she had misjudged him after all.

'I can't believe that anyone would want to murder Emily, I just don't get it.' Dan raked his fingers through his hair and gave a half gulp or sob. He stood up abruptly. 'I just...sorry, I'm just struggling with all this. It's awful, truly awful...'

Taverner nodded. 'We do understand this, but in order to solve the crime we need to ask you some questions, Mr Charlton, and the sooner we do this, the better.' Daniel sighed, but appeared to accept this. 'Emily went out on Saturday night and never came back, so I need to ask you, where you were on the Saturday? It's just routine but we do need to establish your whereabouts, so we can rule you out of our inquiries.'

Wildblood watched as all manner of expressions flickered over Charlton's face, shock with a hint of fear, followed by a nervous smile.

'Erm, of course, I quite understand. Well, I wasn't seeing Emily until the following week, so I was here all weekend. I went out for a couple of drinks in Hull on Saturday night after I'd been to the match. I was tired and went straight to bed when I got back at about half ten.'

'OK, which teams were playing?'

'Hull. I support Hull. We beat Sheffield one nil. I met some mates in the city centre to celebrate and came straight home.'

'Is there anyone who can confirm that?'

'Of course. My friends and my parents, though they are both asleep by ten these days…'

'OK, can you give me the contact details of your friends and we'll speak to your parents on the way out.'

Charlton rattled off the names of two friends and gave them their mobile phone numbers and addresses which Wildblood wrote down. Taverner took a deep breath.

'I have to ask you about your relationship with Emily. It can be hard when one of you goes to University and the other one doesn't.'

Dan flushed and shook his head. 'It may be for other couples but Emily and I, well, we were strong, you know, we were different. York isn't far away, I've been there lots of times, met her friends, it wasn't going to make any difference to us, we had it all planned out.

44

I'm at Siemens, and expect to do well, Emily loved reading and books so wanted to do English, probably teach, maybe journalism. She's talked more about that lately. She wasn't a party girl, she was more serious than that, she was really into the community and stuff. I suppose she wanted to save the world.'

'So, you planned to stay together?'

'Course. That's all ruined now…' Dan's face crumpled as though he had only just thought of this. Maybe he really did love her.

'When did you last see Emily?' asked Anna.

Dan blinked back tears. 'The week before last, I went to York.'

'How did she seem, was she OK?'

Dan nodded. 'Yeah, a bit stressed about an essay, she was something of a perfectionist. I came back early so she could get on with it.'

'Was there anything else? What did she like to do at York, did she mention she had any problems, anything or anyone worrying her?'

Dan sighed. 'She was involved in a youth group and came across some problems there. She was worried about one of the kids and I just told her to report it to the authorities and leave it at that. She said she did, but she couldn't let it go. She was like that, very caring, fretting about stuff, she felt responsible for everyone and everything.'

'Where was the group?'

'In York. I think it was something that the Uni were involved in actually. It was to do with literacy and that, for kids who were struggling. I think her tutor set it up. She thought that helping kids read simplified versions of the classics might really help their lives, that sort of thing.'

Taverner nodded. Wildblood made some notes, wondering at the logic of encouraging deprived kids to read difficult books, even if they were simplified. Ever pragmatic, Wildblood thought they needed more help with the basics and probably the odd food parcel thrown in. But of interest was what it told them about Emily Morgan. God, this girl was rapidly turning into some kind of saint, helping to run youth groups in her spare time and working really hard. Most students she knew spent their first-year drinking until they were semi-conscious and then pulling members of the opposite sex at rowdy parties. She hadn't been to University herself and didn't feel that she had missed out, but her brother had, and he seemed to spend the whole time pissed up. It was a wonder his brain wasn't pickled in alcohol.

'OK, what car do you drive?' Taverner asked with a smile.

'The Citroen outside, the C1. Why?'

Taverner smiled again. 'Just checking, that's all.'

On the way out, Dan's parents were asked to clarify their son's whereabouts on the night that Emily died.

'What time did he get in?'

His mother smiled nervously. 'Oh, about half ten or eleven, but I'm not sure. I think I heard the door then.'

His father gave her a hard stare and tutted. 'I remember, Sue, even if you don't. It was definitely just before half past ten because I checked the alarm clock.' He shook his head as though amused at his wife's poor memory.

As they left Taverner made a note of the black Citroen C1's number plate and on impulse took down the numbers of the two other cars that were parked on the driveway.

Back in the car, Wildblood began to debrief. 'Are you thinking what I'm thinking?'

Taverner pursed his lips. 'Trouble in paradise? It all sounds too good to be true, all that 'we were different' stuff. He could have left early last week because of an argument. And Dan's mother was telling the truth that she had no idea what time he got back, so Dan could easily have got to York and back that evening. We need to do an ANPR check and see if he drove there.'

Wildblood frowned. 'Yes, sir. I wonder what state the relationship was really in?'

'Not half as good as he said it was. We need to ask Emily's friends; she's bound to have confided in someone. Women usually do.'

Back home, a rural cottage a few miles outside York, Taverner poured himself a stiff Macallans, fed a grey tortoiseshell cat, a female, that he was sure had meals at every house down the street, but turned up every other evening at least, purring and snaking round his legs. He wasn't sure who she belonged to. He rather liked her demands for attention and insistence that he notice her. She wore a collar with the name Pebbles engraved on a metal tag, which suited her. He didn't have the heart to turn her away.

He popped a ready meal, a lasagne, into the microwave, took a gulp of whiskey and sorted through his mail, trying to brush off the stresses of the day. There were the usual bills and circulars for pizza shops and double glazing, but one envelope had a familiar logo on it. It was from the Adoption Agency. His heart stilled. The last time he'd had any contact from them it was to inform him that they had handled his adoption. He had asked for their help to find his mother and he wondered what their response would be. It had seemed like light years away at the time, but now the enormity of their response and the possibility that they might not be able to help, hovered over his head like a loaded pistol in a game of Russian roulette. He stared at the letter fingering it for a good ten minutes or so. He ignored the ping of the microwave, as he drank yet another glass of the amber liquid and heard Pebbles miaowing for more food. He felt as though his whole body has seized up. It occurred to him that he should not be alone for such a momentous occasion, but who could he talk to? Not his ex, or his adoptive father who was still mourning the loss of his wife, Taverner's adoptive mother, who had died last year. Taverner was still grieving for Helen too, but in a way, it had also liberated him by allowing him to think about his other mother, the woman who had actually given birth to him. The idea had taken root and developed a life of its own until he had found himself writing to the Agency who had overseen the adoption. He was amazed when they wrote back to confirm they had handled his adoption and outlined their other services such as locating birth parents. He had written back asking them to do just that. Now he began to wonder what he had set in motion and whether, so soon after his mother's death and his relationship breakdown, he could actually cope with the consequences of finding her. He wished he had someone to discuss the matter with, but who? His ex-partner, Georgia, popped into his head, but he dismissed the idea. He didn't want to listen politely whilst she rattled on about her own wonderful life. She wouldn't understand his situation at all. He remembered trying to talk to her about his feelings of being cast adrift, of not quite belonging as a child and her beautiful mouth had pouted in petulance as she told him that she couldn't see the problem, as she 'relly, relly loved Helen and Lawrence,' and blinking at him uncomprehendingly when he tried to explain that so did he, but that wasn't the point and then sulked because she did not have his full attention. He could certainly not discuss anything with his father, grieving as he was for his wife. His friends were busy with their lives and lived elsewhere. Then Wildblood came to mind with her reassuring, calm presence but then he had only just met her. It would seem odd to ring her now and he pictured her snatching every single minute she could with her young children and decided it was just down to him. He couldn't possibly burden her with all this. He steadied himself, took several more mouthfuls of whiskey, and as his throat began to burn, he finally opened the envelope, the sound of his heartbeat reverberating in his ears.

Chapter 5

Rob had already put the twins to bed by the time Anna came in. She kissed their cheeks as they slept and crept out as carefully as she could to avoid waking them. Again, she felt the guilt of the working parent pressing down on her like an Olympic weightlifter's bar, heightened by the stress of the murder investigation. She thought back to what Rob had said, that the boys would be fine and that in years to come they would really appreciate the fact that she had a worthwhile job. It helped, sort of. She'd whip up a nice supper and see the boys later if they woke. Her head was swimming from the case and the horrors of the post mortem and almost worse, her puking up in front of the boss. Talk about embarrassing! Thankfully, she had avoided being sick in the car and managed to clean herself up pretty well. Taverner had been good about it and not said anything to her colleagues and she felt she could trust him not to take the mick. The post mortem had really got to her, the sight of that beautiful young girl and the horror of her death. It made her more determined than ever to work tirelessly to find her murderer.

'So, how were the twins today?'

Rob was washing up and cleaning the kitchen surfaces.

'Fine. Mum said they slept at different times, so she was able to spend individual time with them both. Jasper was smiley but Archie grizzly. Both loved going to the park to play on the swings. They both ate well, fine otherwise.'

'OK great. I'll make supper, you go and sit down,' she added.

Rob grinned. 'I'll sort out the wine, then. How's your day been? Any breakthroughs in your case?'

'Oh, it's in the early stages, so we're interviewing everyone at the moment. There's no obvious suspect as yet. It's just a case of doing all the background inquiries and hopefully someone will emerge.' She started to pull ingredients out of the fridge. 'Chicken pasta, alright for you?'

'Fine. So, it's not the boyfriend then?'

Anna looked at Rob sharply. 'Not sure. Why do you say that? She might be between boyfriends or gay for all you know...'

Rob grinned and raked his fingers through his thick blond hair. He had the beginnings of a beard that suited him, and his eyes were cobalt blue. Every day she had to pinch herself to believe that a man such as him wanted her. She had never considered herself much of a looker. Her hair was too thick and curly, and she hated her slightly pointed nose and her wide mouth and she was always fatter than she wanted to be, though she scrubbed up quite well and was a decent person, which was what ought to count, but rarely did in her experience.

'Because it's always the boyfriend, isn't it? Most women are murdered by someone they know.' He looked apologetic. 'You've said so yourself often enough and I've recently done some reading for Domus. They are thinking of running some new projects, a Women's Refuge being the main one and another helping develop activities for kids over the summer holidays and another group to improve children's literacy. We're hoping to have a lot more money to play with from our fundraiser and what with John Armitage on board, we should be able to fund everything, along with the usual grants.'

'Good. You're right though. It is usually the boyfriend or some male they know well, but I'm not sure in this case. Anyway, the new projects sound good.' She wondered about the literacy group Emily was involved in and thought about mentioning it. It was unlikely to be the same one. There were bound to be loads of similar groups. Parts of York were quite deprived, but visitors to the city were often unaware of this. There was certainly a dark side to York. Anna had seen enough poverty and deprivation in her work to know this firsthand.

'You are still going to be able to come to the fundraiser, aren't you? I mean with the case and everything. All the women in the office are going crazy with their outfits, honestly, it's all getting a bit silly.'

Anna chopped the chicken. Damn, she'd been hoping to get away with wearing an old wrap dress that she could pair with black suede heels. It was smart but not too over the top and the heels were only an inch and a half in length, so at least she would be comfortable. It was not that she didn't like nice clothes, she did, but these days comfort was also an important factor especially around the waist. Perhaps she needed to think again? If everyone was making such an effort, then she didn't want to let the side down. She'd have a look for a dress on the internet later for something effortlessly glam, flattering and not too expensive if such a dress existed.

'Is it going to be smarter than usual? Do I need something new?'

'No, only if you want something.' Rob shrugged. 'You always look gorgeous, but everyone else is going all out.' That decided her,

52

she would definitely look later. Suddenly the baby monitor sprung into life and Archie, or was it Jasper, began to cry. Anna immediately turned off the burner and made to go upstairs.

Rob looked vaguely sheepish. 'Listen, Mum took the boys to McDonalds, they had a Happy Meal and really liked the toys they got. They were thrilled.'

Anna stiffened. 'McDonald's? Listen we spoke about that and how bad junk food is for kids. I really don't want them to get a taste for the stuff. They're only three for God's sake! Honestly, why didn't she ask me first?'

'Look, it's not the end of the world, once in a while, won't hurt them. Besides, they really enjoyed it and Mum was rushing out to Zumba, so it saved her cooking. You were working late and so was I...'

The crying began again. 'It's just not what we discussed that's all...'

Anna ran up the stairs taking them two at a time, her feet thundering on the carpet. Jasper was sleeping soundly clutching a bean bag toy she hadn't noticed before, no doubt from his Happy Meal and Archie was distraught, his face red, his knees held up to his chest. She lifted the little boy up and kissed his hot face. She blinked back irritable tears. How could Rob and his mother go behind her back? She knew she was tired and weepy and in danger of overreacting badly. She should be grateful for her mother-in-law's help but Christ, she was the twins' mother, and she should have the last say. She had read all the literature about the epidemic in childhood obesity and the fact that junk food was behind it, so why on earth introduce children under three to bloody McDonalds? It made no

53

sense whatsoever. Except that Rob was right. She had worked late and so had Rob. She knew how hard it was to look after toddlers, and Marian saved them a fortune, so instead of being grumpy she ought to feel gratitude. It was just not something that she wanted to encourage. She breathed in deeply and tried to calm herself. She would talk to Rob and make her views known so that Marian would be in no doubt that this was not what she wanted, then all would be well. She knew all of this rationally, yet deep down she couldn't help but feel betrayed and panicky, as if this one small act would lead to her sons developing type 2 diabetes and a lifelong dependency on junk food, to related health problems and an early death. And she also knew that if she was at home with the boys full time, none of this would have happened.

      The next day Anna made herself a coffee and sat back at her desk. She still felt tired and irritable. She and Rob had argued and then made up, but not entirely. Rob had conceded that he would have a chat with Marian about McDonalds and junk food in general. Then he had reminded her that Marian did so much for them, taking on the role of unpaid childminder, that she had felt guilty like she had turned into a harridan mother from hell. There had been an atmosphere and when Rob had snuggled up to her later, she had feigned sleep. A mixture of emotions ricocheted around her brain; annoyance mingled with an overwhelming sense of guilt that just wouldn't go away. She had returned to work expecting her life to go on as before, but how could it now that she had two little people to look after? She had given a lot of the responsibility to her mother-in-law, so she had to trust her.

54

Things would be better after the murder investigation had finished and it was back to drug dealers, thefts, burglary and domestic violence offences. Best to just get on with it then, she told herself. She brushed down her trousers and tried to concentrate on the whiteboard and the different strands of investigations that were in progress. The photo of Emily smiling at the camera in her party dress, eyes full of promise, pout at the ready, having no clue what lay ahead of her, should be her focus. She hadn't deserved to die, and she deserved justice. Anna was just thinking through the possible suspects, when Taverner walked into the office with a young woman.

'Ah, Anna. Can I introduce DC Natalie Cullen, she's been seconded to us for the duration of the inquiry.' Taverner turned to a pretty woman in her twenties, in a grey suit with dark bobbed hair and a ready smile. There was an expectant hum from the rest of the team as they noticed the stranger.

'Listen everyone. This is DC Natalie Cullen who has been seconded to the team. I thought she could work with Patel to look at the CCTV. I hope you'll make her feel very welcome.'

Anna smiled at the young detective and hoped the team would behave themselves. Haworth was looking at the woman with frank admiration and she didn't miss him nudge Patel who flushed. Still, DC Cullen looked like the sort of person who could handle herself and judging by the sidelong glances she kept giving the guvnor, Patel did not stand a chance.

Taverner frowned. 'Anna, a word?'

The guvnor looked different. He looked as well groomed as ever, but sort of wired. Something was up. Maybe he had a new line of inquiry, or maybe it was related to the new DC who had joined the team? Taverner motioned for her to follow him into his office.

'Listen, I've paired Natalie with Patel because I think they will work well together, and Haworth and Ballantyne seem a bit set in their ways.' Anna nodded and could have said a lot more. Set in their ways was a polite way of putting it. She thought back to their behaviour the previous day. She really hoped that they heeded her words. 'Anyway, I thought we'd go to the University to talk to her tutor and find out more about Emily.' Taverner frowned. 'Are you OK? You look shattered. I hope it's not a recurrence of the sickness.'

'No, it's nothing.' Taverner paused, waiting so patiently that Anna felt obliged to fill the silence. 'Well, I had a row with my husband if you must know. My mother-in-law took the children to McDonalds. I know it's stupid, but I don't want them to get the junk food habit so early on. Then I felt bad because she is so good with them and I should trust her.'

The words came out in a rush. God, what was she doing telling her new boss all her troubles? Yesterday, she had chucked up in front of him. What was wrong with her?

Taverner frowned. 'You said they were three, didn't you?'

'Just three. I mean it's mad to introduce them to junk food at their age, don't you think?'

Taverner looked at her consideringly. 'Well, I can see it from both sides. The occasional meal won't hurt, surely? Perhaps, you should just talk to her? How are the boys anyway?'

Anna felt like she had overreacted and was suddenly keen to make light of the whole thing. He would think she was a neurotic,

56

controlling idiot. Her concerns sounded ridiculously petty now she had spoken them out loud.

'Well, they liked their McDonalds and Rob is going to talk to Marian about it, so there's no harm done. Hey, look it's a storm in a teacup.' She took in Taverner's tired face. She suspected that his problems might not be so easily

overcome. He wasn't just tired, he was also sort of animated, as though he was in love, she realised, pleased with her sudden insight. 'Anyway, that's my tale of woe. How about you? Women trouble?'

Taverner grinned. 'Well, sort of, but it's not about a mother-in-law in my case.' He looked elated and suddenly more vulnerable. 'It's more like my actual mother...'

Anna frowned. 'I thought you said your mother had died quite recently...'

'She did, but you see, she wasn't my real mother, I was adopted. I've been in touch with the adoption agency about finding out about my birth mother and they are happy to act on my behalf, so the search is on...'

Anna gasped, guessing his tumultuous news. 'Well, that's brilliant news, isn't it?'

Taverner nodded, unable to stop himself from beaming. 'Yes, but it doesn't mean they can locate her, just that they are prepared to try.'

Wildblood could not imagine Taverner's mother coming from York. She thought any parent of his would be exotic, foreign and somehow mysterious. So, that was why he had come up North. It all made sense now.

'Brilliant.'

'Yep, it's just so sudden, and there's so many things that could go wrong…'

Anna wanted to give him a hug, he looked so hopeful yet woebegone, but felt it wouldn't be professional. She had read about this sort of thing, about adopted children never quite feeling right, never having the sense of belonging which other families had and found she had enormous empathy for this complex man. Her own family wasn't perfect, but she had never doubted that she was her mother's daughter. They both had thick, chestnut hair and big hips, for starters and tended to be plain speakers. Maybe that was nurture, though, when she thought about it. She took in Taverner's worried expression.

'And so many things that can go right too.'

Taverner shrugged his expression becoming shuttered. 'I suppose so. Anyway, we need to get on with the investigation.' He frowned. 'And Anna, this is not to be spread round the office. I'd rather this was kept between the two of us.'

Anna grinned. 'Course, no problem.'

Chapter 6

The University was situated in Heslington, on the outskirts of the city, and had a proud academic heritage being a member of the prestigious Russell group of Universities. The buildings were surprisingly modern for a historic city like York. Taverner had been expecting ancient buildings similar to those in the city centre, but this was a far cry from that. In fact, much of the campus was made of concrete buildings which Taverner thought would be described as being good examples of 'brutalist architecture.' They certainly lived up to the name, he decided. There was also a huge duck pond in the centre of the campus with corresponding duck droppings surrounding it.

Taverner managed to navigate yet another pile as they made their way to another concrete building. They had spoken to DC Patel, who had studied the CCTV and found some footage of Emily going into various pubs in the city centre, mainly in Mickelgate and Fossgate on the night she died. With her were her three housemates, all girls, plus two males of a similar age. Taverner had contacted the University as he thought they would be able to identify the two young men, as they could be students. Patel and Cullen would be studying the later images and hopefully would be able to spot who Emily left the pub with, if indeed she did leave with someone.

'Who are we meeting again?' Wildblood asked.

'Her tutor, Dr Niall Lynch and then we can pop around to her student house. Forensics have already been, but we can talk to the house mates. I want to clarify some of their statements.'

Wildblood nodded. 'OK. I have read them, what was it you weren't happy with?'

Taverner shrugged. 'Oh, you know, it all sounded a bit bland but real life isn't like that, is it? There must be something which started off the chain of events, some sort of jealousies, petty squabbles. There must have been some reason why they left her to walk home on her own.'

'So, you don't think it was the boyfriend, Dan?'

'Not sure. We're waiting on the statements of the friends and we'll see if he turns up on the CCTV footage or if we get an ANPR match. I'm not sure that everything was rosy in the relationship, but that doesn't mean he murdered her.'

Taverner sighed. He was sure that Daniel was putting a gloss on things, which could be suspicious. He found Wildblood staring at him consideringly.

'You know what you said about you meeting your birth mother. Are you really going to go through with it?'

'Yes, if they can find her and she wants to see me, but I'll wait until things calm down a bit here.'

'OK. Yer might need someone to go wi' yer, I expect.' Wildblood flushed and bit her lip. 'I'd do it, if yer wanted.'

'Really?' His face was split in two by his grin, like he'd been given an unexpected pay rise or two. He was utterly dumbfounded and touched. She really did seem to understand his angst about the whole thing. 'Thanks that's really great. I appreciate it. I'll let you know when it's planned.'

Wildblood smiled and nodded.

There he was thinking he was being all professional and hiding his inner turmoil, by just dropping it into the conversation, but she had realised that it was really important to him. He knew that he must not underestimate her, she could be rather insightful, he decided and actually very kind, two great qualities. Usually he was a private man, and thought blurting out his history showed a lack of professionalism, but now he was glad that he had.

Dr Niall Lynch was handsome in a rugged, intellectual way. His office was lined with books, an awful lot of them about Victorian Literature, his speciality apparently. He had small rectangular spectacles, wore his greying hair a little too long and his clothes were studiously modern and well cut. He spoke in a modulated, thoughtful manner with a hint of an Irish accent. His manner was solicitous and very polite, but this seemed rather controlled. Overall, Taverner thought he was rather too self-confident and smooth. He distrusted him on sight.

'So sad about poor Emily.' He shook his head mournfully. 'She was a very bright girl with a promising future. Are you any nearer to finding out what happened?' He looked from Taverner to Wildblood and back again.

'We're following various lines of inquiry at the present time but would like to ask you some questions. We are treating her death as suspicious.'

Lynch blinked furiously at this. 'So, I take it that Emily could have been murdered?' He looked momentarily non-plussed. 'God, who would do such a thing? Look, I have already given a statement to your colleagues about Emily.' His face fell. 'A lovely girl. I'm not sure I can help further.'

Taverner squared his shoulders and removed the two photos from his inside pocket. They were blown up from the CCTV stills, a little out of focus but hopefully the faces were still recognisable.

'Do you know either of these men?'

Lynch leaned forward and studied the pictures. 'Hmm.' He frowned and pointed at the photo on the right. 'This one looks familiar. In fact, it looks like one of my current students.' He rummaged in a filing cabinet draw and pulled out a sheet of passport sized photos. 'I am allocated about twenty or so students to supervise throughout their time at York and that looks like Ross McAllister.' He jabbed at the photo. 'In fact, I'm sure it's him.'

Taverner examined the images. The CCTV still was less clear, but he was sure too. Lynch read through his notes.

'He's a second-year English undergraduate. Doing OK. I don't recall hearing anything that raised concerns about him.' He leafed through another file and studied some figures. 'He passed everything last year, good grades actually. He would certainly know Emily, of course, as they were on the same course. As for the other young man, I'm afraid I can't help.'

'Do you have an address for McAllister?'

Lynch nodded and tapped away at his computer. 'Holgate Road, York.'

Wildblood wrote this down.

62

Lynch looked inquiringly at them. 'Is that all Inspector? Of course, we're all very sad about Emily, but I do have a lecture to give.' He made a show of looking at his watch. 'About now actually.' Lynch stood up.

'Yes, we'll just be two more minutes. I'm sure Emily's fellow students would be happy to wait just a short while if it means the murderer of their fellow student is brought to justice,' continued Taverner tightly.

Lynch had the good grace to look embarrassed, like a child caught out in a lie. He sat down heavily.

'Can I ask you what you know about the Literacy Group that Emily was involved in?'

Lynch blinked. 'What possible bearing could that have on anything?'

'Just answer the question please.'

'Well, it's a group that the University help run along with other community groups. It is funded by various charities, but the idea is that the University gives something back to the local area to help improve children's literacy levels. The Vice Chancellor is very keen on community impact, all that sort of thing. The students help local kids read at various schools in one of the more deprived areas, providing books and encouraging the kids to swap. Emily was keen to get involved and had the idea of trying to introduce them to simplified versions of the classics. She was so enthusiastic, the sessions were popular, and the kids loved it. She had a gift of making things accessible.'

Taverner could see how this could inspire youngsters. He had loved his teachers reading Moonfleet to the class as a youngster, in fact it had ignited a lifelong interest in literature.

'So, who actually runs this group?'

Lynch smiled. 'It's a retired vicar, Matthew Lawson. He's a very good chap, marvellous. Here, I have his card.' He rummaged around in his desk and handed it to Taverner. It slipped through his fingers onto the floor. Taverner dipped down to retrieve it.

'Thank you. And on the evening in question, where were you exactly?'

Lynch looked momentarily shocked but recovered well. 'At home with my wife. I have already spoken to your colleagues, as I said.'

'And your wife will confirm that?'

'Of course, Inspector, of course.'

Taverner nodded politely. Although Lynch seemed composed with an impassive face, tension had leaked out into his legs and feet, something he had noticed when he had retrieved the card from the floor. He crossed and uncrossed his legs and despite all the bonhomie, he was stiff with tension. To his way of thinking this was a sure sign that he was not comfortable at being questioned and trying to conceal it. Interesting, very interesting indeed. What did he have to hide?

Chloe Thomas was pretty, blonde and rather sleepy. She had clearly just got out of bed at almost midday. Last night's makeup was strewn all over her cheek. She brightened when she had had a good look at Taverner and disappeared to make coffee, rubbing the worst of

64

the mascara off her cheek as she did so. The house was a typical student place; it was messy and smelt of stale curry overlain with beer and fags. Chloe came back fully clothed, brandishing coffees and biscuits with a bright smile. She had even applied some fresh mascara and lip gloss, Taverner noted.

'Late night was it?' he asked drily, looking around at the empty wine and beer bottles that were liberally sprinkled over the floor.

Chloe pouted. 'Yes. There were a few of us up late talking about Emily, that's all. God, it's awful, I can't bear it. Have you found out who killed her?'

'We're following several leads at present. We'd just like to ask you a few more questions, if we can. I know you gave a statement to my colleagues but there are some aspects we'd like to clarify.'

Chloe nodded. 'Certainly.'

Taverner went through the main points of her statement which Chloe confirmed.

'So, we know you and your housemates went out with Emily into York on Saturday last week. Who did you go with?'

'Yes, there was me, Emily, Flora and Olivia.'

'Did anyone else go with you or did you meet anyone else in town?'

'Yes, Ross McAllister and Alec. Ross is on the course and Alec is his housemate. I don't know his surname.'

'How did they get on with Emily?'

'Fine. Ross knew her quite well. They left with us and we went into various pubs in the city centre....'

'How did Emily seem to you?'

65

Chloe shrugged. 'Her usual self, I suppose. She had just handed in an essay, so she needed a break. We went to a couple of pubs then wandered around Mickelgate to the Geisha Bar. She saw someone she knew from the literacy group, so she went to talk to her. She said she'd catch us up in the next bar, but she never turned up. I messaged her, but she said she'd make her own way back.' Her face reddened and tears began to fall. 'Now I wish I'd done more to find her and drag her back, so she wasn't walking on her own. I just feel so guilty.' Tears began to fall down Chloe's face as her nose and eyes reddened.

Wildblood handed Chloe some tissues which she produced from her bag. Taverner noted that she was always prepared for every eventuality and wondered what else she kept in there.

'Are you OK to continue,' he asked. Chloe nodded bravely. 'So, who was the girl she was talking to?'

'Lola, I think she said her name was.'

'Any surname?'

Chloe shook her head. 'She didn't say.'

'What did Lola look like?'

'Young, lots of makeup, blonde wavy hair, petite.' She screwed up her nose. 'A bit common, I suppose.'

'Anything else?'

'Emily seemed sort of tense, upset. I just thought it was Emily being Emily.' Chloe looked sorrowful. 'She would help anyone, you know. I thought that Lola had probably had a row with her boyfriend or something and Emily was consoling her.'

'Did Emily say anything else about Lola?'

66

'No, not really. She just talked about the aims of the group.' Chloe frowned as if remembering something. 'She had seemed a bit anxious about it, I'm not sure why. She worried about the kids, she wanted to save the world, I suppose.' She frowned. 'She was very kind…' She suddenly started to cry as though she had only just thought of this.

Wildblood sat up. 'Did she say what she was worried about?'

'Not really. I think she spoke to one of the organisers though, so it might be helpful to talk to them.'

Taverner made a note, 'speak to supervisor' and underscored it several times.

'What sort of age do you think Lola was? I mean if she was in the pub then she must have been older.'

Chloe shrugged, as though the thought had only just occurred to her. 'Same as us, or a bit younger I'd imagine, but I don't think she was a student. At least I hadn't seen her around the campus.' The implication seemed to be that Lola wasn't bright or middle class enough either.

'OK. What can you tell us about Emily's boyfriend, Daniel?'

'He came to stay every other weekend or Emily went there. He seemed alright.'

Taverner paused waiting for the 'but'.

Eventually it came. 'But I got the impression things were cooling between them. Em didn't always want to go back home so often. He went home early the last time he came. Em said she had an essay to finish but I know she'd pretty much finished it, so I did think that was strange.'

Taverner realised he was holding his breath. He knew it.

'Was she seeing anyone else?'

'Oh, no, nothing like that.'

'Emily had some expensive designer items, a handbag and jewellery.'

'Oh yeah. She said they were presents from her family.'

This seemed unlikely from a father who was almost bankrupt, but maybe it was before that happened. They did look very new though. Taverner made a note to ask the FLO, PC Lambert, about what she had learned about the family's spending habits and income.

'So, if she wasn't seeing anyone, did she like someone?' Taverner probed further.

Chloe shrugged and bit her lip.

'It's fine to give us your impressions, there is often some truth in them,' added Taverner, knowing full well that there was something on her mind which he hoped to tease out of her.

'I think it was more who was interested in her...'

'Like who?'

Chloe hesitated, clearly wondering how much to say.

Taverner decided to push her a little. 'This is a murder investigation, Chloe, so if you know something then you must tell us no matter how trivial or insignificant it may seem to you.'

Chloe sighed. 'Well, I don't know anything definite, it's just impressions really but I always thought Ross McAllister liked her and...' Taverner raised an eyebrow and waited. 'And her tutor Niall Lynch. Ross was in her tutor group and teased her about it. He was always all over her, praising her work, he gave her far more attention than any of the other students. She was very clever, English came easily to her, but I'm not sure it was all down to admiration for her superior mind…'

Strange that Lynch had been so cool almost offhand about the death of his star pupil given what Chloe had just told them. Suddenly three people had a motive to harm Emily, Taverner realised, just as he thought the field was narrowing. Charlton, McAllister and Lynch. They had all been drawn to her like kids in a sweet shop. Interesting and sad, though, that Emily's beauty may have been what killed her in the end.

'Mmm, thank you Chloe, you've been most helpful.'

Chapter 7

It was the evening of the Domus auction of promises. Anna struggled into her dress and pulled the skirt down, turning this way and that in the mirror so she could get a better look at herself. She had ordered the tight, red lace dress online as a last-minute replacement for her tried and tested black outfit and overall, she was pleased with the effect. It was slightly shorter than she was usually comfortable with, but she added a chunky black necklace and decided that people would be drawn to this rather than her legs. She hadn't quite managed to lose her baby weight and she had all but given up. She was self-conscious about her size. Her stomach had stretch marks and her thighs were rather wobbly, but the dress did a good job of covering any flaws, and on balance, she was pleased with the result. She squirted herself with perfume, 'La Vie Est Belle', ran her fingers through her hair and dabbed at her lipstick to remove a little, so it looked more natural. She was used to wearing minimal makeup and didn't want to overdo it. She stared at the glamorous face in the mirror. She thought she'd do, a view confirmed by Rob when she descended the stairs.

'Wow, you look nice.' Anna returned the compliment. Rob was wearing a dark grey suit and smelt of a delicious citrus aftershave. Marian was bathing the boys, so they shouted up to her and sneaked off rather than running the risk of having to peel the children off them.

It was something that they had planned earlier with Marian to avoid tears. Anna knew she'd never be able to enjoy herself if she had seen the boys upset and tearful before they went out.

'Have a good time,' her mother-in-law shouted down the stairs.

'We will,' they replied.

Anna eyed Rob and grinned as they escaped into the cool November evening, like kids going out on a first date. Anna felt a bubble of excitement as they settled into the taxi but wished that it was just her and Rob going out for a meal on their own, more especially when he had run through who was going to be at the fundraising event. He had invited some staff from the Accountancy Firm where he worked. She had met some of the staff before at similar events, but this promised to be even bigger and better, was at a swankier venue and had even more extravagant prizes.

'There are some unusual promises this year, I hear. There's a fortnight's holiday in Paris at some posh hotel which I'm thinking of bidding on.' Rob squeezed her hand. 'We could have a second honeymoon.' Anna nudged him playfully, but the idea thrilled her. She had been to Paris as a teenager and loved it. It would be great to go there as a couple.

'You'll be lucky! Anyway, what would we do with the boys?'

'Mum would be delighted to have them, I'm sure.' He swooped in for a kiss. 'Anyway, you look gorgeous. Lots of the guys from work will be there, so it will be great.'

Anna's spirits lifted. It was going to be alright, she decided. She looked great and felt her spirits soar at being out with her gorgeous husband. She was determined not to worry about the boys or the investigation and just let her hair down for a change.

The fundraiser was held in a grand room at one of the most prestigious hotels in the area, Principal York, which was decked out with flowers and banners with the usual Domus turquoise and yellow colours. As soon as she entered the room, she was glad she had made the effort with her dress as the room was full of elegantly clad women in a vast array of expensive dresses and fine jewellery, some of which would easily fund a homeless family for six months at least, Anna couldn't help but observe. There were also glasses of champagne on arrival and formally dressed waiting staff circulating with canapés.

Rob's eyes were roaming the room and it was clear that he was desperate to schmooze. He seemed to know everyone.

'Let me introduce you to some people.' A tall, elegant dark haired woman with her hair in a messy updo, wearing a tight, bottle green off the shoulder dress, advanced towards them, air kissing Rob noisily.

'Let me introduce you to Naomi, my PA, my wife, Anna. I'm sure you two have met before, haven't you?'

Both women shook their heads and following a quick appraisal from the PA, Anna found herself enveloped in skinny arms and her senses assailed by the heavy smell of Chanel No 5. She squashed back worries that Rob had never mentioned that he had a new PA, but had she been too preoccupied with work and the twins to notice? No, she didn't think so, in fact, she was sure he hadn't said a word.

Several other staff appeared, homing in on Rob, a middle aged man called Albert whose red hair was twisted into dreadlocks, and a couple of older women, who were office staff. They clucked affectionately over Rob.

'Rob talks about you and the boys all the time,' confided Maureen, a big bosomed woman with a purple rinse. Anna had met her before when she'd had blue streaks in her hair, so it took her a little while to place the older woman. 'He is a real sweetie and so good at his job. We couldn't believe it when he got John Armitage to sign up with us. He's so well known and rich he could really do great things for the charity, not to mention the firm.'

Another woman nudged Maureen. 'John is rather handsome too. In fact, talk of the devil…'

Anna followed their gaze as a silver haired, well groomed man, made his way towards them. Tall and powerful looking in a dark suit, he certainly cut a suave figure, rather like a younger looking Richard Gere. He was followed by a smart looking woman with blonde bobbed hair, dressed head to toe in Chanel, if Anna was any judge. Rob practically fell over himself to greet them and introduce them to Anna.

Bright blue eyes in a remarkably unlined face ran the length and breadth of her.

'Pleased to meet you. Rob and I get on famously, so I'm sure we will too.' Anna's hand was crushed in his grip. The accent was refined, which was a surprise as Anna had heard that John was a local man yet there was no trace of a Yorkshire accent. She wondered if elocution lessons were to thank for that, which seemed wholly unnecessary and smacked of pretentiousness to Anna's way of thinking.

The blue eyes held hers for longer than was necessary. 'I hear you are a police officer, so I'll just have to behave myself, won't I, before I get myself arrested.'

'I'm sure that Anna won't be required to arrest anyone,' added Rob, his face falling.

'I certainly hope not, but I'm always on duty,' replied Anna her eyes never leaving John's face. Oh God, he was one of those men who liked to wind up police personnel when they were off duty. She had certainly met a few of those in her life, men who struggled with women in positions of authority. She bit her lip and smiled tightly.

John nodded and grinned. 'Now what are you hoping to win in the auction of promises?'

Anna answered immediately. 'Oh, that's easy, the Paris holiday would be my first choice.'

'Excellent,' added John. 'We'll just have to hope that someone wins it for you, won't we?'

As soon as she said it, she noticed Rob's face. She knew what their finances were like with the twins and a huge mortgage and realised she mustn't be too greedy. Someone else came to talk to John and he and his wife were ushered off to meet the Chairperson of the charity. Rob had also left her side.

'Have some more fizz,' suggested Maureen helping herself to a glass from a smart waitress.

Anna watched as Rob was seen in the distance head to head with the beautiful Naomi, their discussions seemingly very urgent. Anna knew that Pam, Rob's old PA had retired, but she hadn't thought

74

about his replacement. Pam had been homely and easy going, and not a threat at all, unlike Naomi. She wondered what they were discussing, probably boring work stuff but nonetheless she felt a spasm of unease as if someone had dropped ice cubes down the back of her dress.

She sighed. Oh well, she may as well try to relax. 'I don't mind if I do.'

Rob popped back then disappeared just as quickly, but Anna found that she was enjoying herself anyway with Maureen and Christine. Albert, the dreadlocked staff member was busily quaffing champagne and keeping a beady eye on Naomi's every move, she noticed. He watched her hungrily, like a cat eyeing up a mouse.

'Hey, the auctions are starting. Rob's going to be busy,' added Maureen. 'He's brilliant as an auctioneer, your husband.'

Anna had seen Rob compere the auction of promises year after year and he was indeed in his element. There was a palpable spike in excitement as everyone took their seats in front of the stage where Rob was standing, microphone in hand. The atmosphere bristled, there was a hush of anticipation and the auction began.

'What am I bid for this first lot? Five nights babysitting, hours negotiable.' He winked at Anna. 'Think we're in need of this ourselves, Anna.' He coaxed and teased the bidding up to £200.

'Blimey, £40 a pop, reckon I'll be turning my hand to babysitting at this rate.' Maureen muttered. 'He could sell ice to Eskimos, that man.'

Rob had similar results for a year's worth of car cleaning, grass cutting, a free haircut at a prestigious salon, theatre tickets and a weekend in the Cotswolds for two. The prizes improved steadily, with

75

a weekend break at a Health Spa, a weekend break to Bruges, a night at the theatre at a West End Show and then it came to the big one. The crowd were at fever pitch.

'Now I have some bids already for the big one, a fortnight break at a five star hotel in Paris, all expenses paid. This is an amazing prize, perfect for couples of all ages. Picture Paris in spring, strolling along the Champs Elysée, a trip down the river Seine and climbing the Eiffel Tower, what could be more perfect, gentlemen, for the lady in your life? I'll start you off at £500...'

The bidding was fast and furious as Rob followed a trail of hands. Suddenly the bid was at £5000, then £7000, rising to £10000. John Armitage was certainly in there, bidding with a slight nod of his head, but Anna couldn't tell who won in the end, much to her frustration.

'Hey, someone's going to be as pleased as punch,' muttered Maureen. 'I think Rob wanted that one.'

Anna beamed. How like Rob to want to surprise her, but surely it was too expensive? She quelled her feelings of excitement. She knew as much as anyone how tight their budgets were, so it was just no good getting carried away, she told herself. She'd be lucky to win the evening at the theatre at this rate.

Gold envelopes were given to the winners and she was delighted when Rob approached carrying an envelope. Hope leapt like a salmon.

'It's the weekend in the Cotswolds,' he muttered.

'Great,' Anna lied trying to keep the disappointment out of her voice. 'Just the job.' She squeezed his hand. What had she expected? Christ, she was a ridiculous woman.

As they were leaving, Rob made a point of shaking everyone's hands and thanking them for coming. John and his wife appeared to have enjoyed themselves. He was clutching ten or so golden envelopes, so Anna was pleased that he had entered into the spirit and knew he had also made a large donation. The charity would be delighted. Rob had disappeared to sort out the proceeds with Naomi.

John handed an envelope to Anna. 'I couldn't resist buying you a little gift,' he explained. 'Just a little something.' His bright blue eyes were staring at her intently.

'Oh, that's so kind, but you really shouldn't have…'

'Think nothing of it.'

John winked and went off to join his wife. Anna shoved the gold envelope into her pocket thinking that she couldn't very well open it with him hanging around. She'd save it for later.

Anna was exhausted and snuggled up to Rob in the taxi on the way home.

'The best night ever,' Rob explained in delight. 'We raised nearly thirty grand. We can do so much with that money. Everyone gave so generously, we raised almost double what we did last year. It was amazing.'

Anna beamed sleepily and it was only when she had checked on the boys and Marian had left, that she remembered the envelope that John had given her. Rob was already in bed and snoring noisily, so she tiptoed downstairs and fished the envelope out of her coat pocket. She tore it open without expectation. Perhaps, it was for the babysitting, which would actually be quite useful, she decided. It would be great to have a social life for a change and not have to rely on Marian all the time. She pulled out a piece of paper from inside the envelope and gasped. It contained the tickets for the fortnight's long break to Paris in the five star hotel, but instead of feeling pleased she shoved the tickets back into her pocket, feeling perturbed. What the hell was that about? Why on earth would John Armitage give them that? It was far too much. Now she felt beholden to him. What was worse was that she had the inescapable feeling that it was almost like a bribe, but for what?

Chapter 8

Taverner was beginning to dislike being grilled by Sykes who was becoming increasingly frustrated at the lack of progress. He had formed the opinion in their short acquaintance that Sykes was old fashioned, inclined to look at the obvious and lacked any sort of flair or imagination. He also looked like an aging boxer with a broken nose and had the high colour of a drinker. How on earth he had been promoted to DCI was beyond him. He also had a truculent manner and little in the way of social skills. Sykes sat back in his chair and glared at him.

'So, what lines of inquiry are you pursuing?'

'We are considering that it might be a crime of passion. We have checked the alibis for everyone potentially involved, namely Emily's current boyfriend, a fellow student who liked her and her tutor. They all seem alright so far, but we need to double check them. She seems to have been a model student and daughter, even doing voluntary work in her spare time running a literacy group.'

'Bloody hell. Why wasn't she in the pub or getting stoned like most of the other students? That's all we need, the press going on about St Emily and moaning about the lack of police progress. We need a result on this fast. What else are you looking at?'

'A blunt instrument was used to hit her over the head and then she was thrown into the river. Ives thinks the murder weapon could have been a large wrench, something with a curve to it that matches the injury. She would have been dead when she hit the water. The force of the blow to her temple suggests she would have died quickly. We are trying to retrieve the murder weapon and divers are searching the river extensively. She has no enemies, but we do know that Emily was worried about a girl at the literacy group she volunteered at, someone called Lola, so she might know something. It seems that Emily got separated from her friends because she was talking to Lola on the night she died. We have officer's scouring the CCTV and going to the various pubs that Emily visited to see if anyone knows Lola. She could be the key to Emily's murder.'

Sykes composed his face into a disdainful scowl. 'Maybe Lola was used as a decoy to separate Emily from her friends? You need to find her to eliminate her from your inquiries, certainly and re-examine those alibis for the three men.' Sykes scowled. 'Also speak to the FLO to see if they have picked anything up about the family. Maybe they're involved, you certainly need to rule them out. We have a press conference planned tomorrow, so hopefully we might get further leads.'

'Do you want me there?'

Sykes blinked. 'Yes. it would be much better if you led on it, actually. I'll be around too, but you're more photogenic and can get the message across better to the public, to my way of thinking.'

It was sort of a compliment, Taverner realised but would also generate more work for him when he should really be making headway with the investigation. Taverner couldn't help but think that Sykes had been only too happy to off load a difficult task on him. At least he had experience of giving press conferences, so he was not too daunted by the task.

'OK. I'd better speak to the press officer, Claire Jordan, right away, to plan things. Are we going to be open about this Lola character?'

Sykes nodded. 'I think so. See what you can find out about her from someone involved in the literacy group and then appeal to her to come forward to talk to you.'

Taverner glanced at his watch. It was almost eleven which didn't leave him with much time for planning.

'OK.'

Sykes glanced at the pile of papers on his desk, a sure sign that he was dismissed but as he was leaving Sykes looked up and barked.

'Don't let me down, Taverner. The University is one of the gems of this city, it's in the prestigious Russell group you know, and we don't want students being put off with worries about a killer on the loose. It's one thing having the silly sods drown through alcohol or drug abuse, but a murder, that is quite a different matter.'

'Right, sir,' Taverner muttered through gritted teeth. He was aware of the reputation of the University but didn't find it helpful that Sykes felt the need to point this out to him.

Thankfully Wildblood had managed to track down the man from the literacy group and they decided to visit immediately.

'What was his name again?'

'That tutor gave you the guy's card,' Wildblood tutted. She was a bit tetchy today it seemed. 'It's Matthew Lawson.'

81

Taverner dug in his jacket pocket and retrieved the card.

'Yep, you're right.' He gave Wildblood an appraising look. 'Are you alright? Hey, how was the fundraiser?'

Wildblood sighed. 'Oh, OK I suppose, the usual thing. I met John Armitage, you know the rich businessman and lots of other people.'

'John Armitage? Oh, even I've heard of him, local boy made good. I read about him in the papers. Great. Anyone else interesting there?'

'Loads of people. Glamorous women, not least Rob's PA…'

Taverner shook his head. So that was the way things were, was it? Anna was so happy in her own skin that he was surprised that she was lacking in confidence and insecure in other ways. He tried to frame an encouraging response.

'Hmm. Well, my ex was beautiful but was not always a nice person and that's what counts. What is it is they say about horses? Handsome is as handsome does? Well, the same applies to people.'

Wildblood brightened. 'Yep. Anyway, we won a fortnight's holiday for two in a five star hotel in Paris.'

'Brilliant. Rob must have spent a fortune on that. You must be delighted.'

Anna nodded and bit her lip.

'Yep. I'm just tired. I'm not used to going out and coming in late these days.' She shook her head. 'God, how boring I must sound.'

Taverner nodded. 'I wonder what this chap is like. Ex-vicar, isn't he?'

'Yes. Well, we've all heard about the scandals in the Catholic Church, so we had better check him out.'

82

'Now, now. Besides, a vicar implies he's Church of England.'

'Hmm. Not much to choose between them and the bloody Catholics in my book.' She gave him a sidelong glance. 'Listen, I've been thinking. You said you were adopted from York, have you thought about contacting the social worker who arranged your adoption? Perhaps, they still live in the area?' Then she flushed. 'Sorry, just tell me to mind my own business, but it might help prepare you before you meet your mother…'

Taverner had already thought of that. He felt flattered and rather touched that Wildblood had spent any of her precious spare time at all thinking about his adoption. It was a relief to have unburdened himself actually. Now that he had set the wheels in motion, he was hesitant to meet his mother face to face, nervous, anxious and scared that she wouldn't accept him, and he would lose her all over again. The worries went round and round his head in an endless loop. Then there was the investigation; it just took too much of his head space not to mention the time and emotional energy required to run an investigation. Ideally he needed a clear period of time to set aside so he could deal with the emotional turmoil if the meeting didn't go well, but had no idea when that might be, not in this line of work.

'No, it's fine, don't worry. It's just finding the time…'

Wildblood studied him. 'You are going to meet her when they find her, aren't you?'

Taverner avoided her eye. 'Course, when things have calmed down a bit here. I just need to get this job done, that's all.'

Wildblood shook her head and studied him. 'There's always time and it obviously means a lot to you. What was your social worker's name? I bet it was mentioned in your Life Book or whatever social workers call it, wasn't it?'

'Life Story Book, you mean. I'm not sure…' Of course, he did know. Children who were adopted had a book put together by their social worker, that explained the events leading up to their adoption in simplistic language. It also contained lots of photos of key people and places and a family tree. It helped him understand his past but also raised a lot of questions. He didn't even know who his father was. He had read the damned thing cover to cover, so much so, it had fallen apart, and he'd had to strengthen the whole thing and some of it was in A4 plastic covers. He was aware that Wildblood was looking unconvinced and had the uncomfortable feeling that she could see straight into his mind and clearly see the mass of insecurities which swirled around within it, beneath the polished exterior. It was an unnerving sensation like being in the presence of a psychic.

'Gi' over. I can't see it. You wouldn't forget a thing like that, surely?'

'OK. I haven't really. I think it was Green, Jennifer Green.'

Wildblood set her mouth in a firm line. 'OK.'

'Why?'

'I know some social workers, that's all.' He was sure there was more to it than that, but her expression was inscrutable.

Matthew Lawson was a salt and pepper haired, youthful looking man with a beatific smile and booming voice. He lived in a smart three storey townhouse within walking distance of the city centre, and was casually dressed, in a polo shirt and trainers. He was slim and fit and looked far too young to have retired. The house was

84

spotless, tidy and comfortable with lots of bookcases some with ecclesiastic tomes and sporting books amongst others. There were lots of family photos in the hallway showing a young boy and girl playing on a beach, the pair a couple of years later walking in full hiking gear with a fresh faced woman, presumably their mother and lots of a handsome young man playing football in various youth teams and then professionally in a kit Taverner recognised as belonging to Sheffield. He looked very like his father. Taverner warmed to him immediately and thought he looked serene, calm and someone who parishioners could really trust. He was also intrigued by the photos.

'Who is the footballer in the family? He's clearly a professional.'

Matthew grinned and flushed with pride. 'Oh, my lad, Nathaniel. Yes, he is, plays as a striker. He's just 21, he should really go places. He played at international level for the under 21s.' The pride in Lawson's voice was unmistakable.

'Well, he's certainly a chip off the old block, he looks just like you.'

Matthew beamed, clearly pleased.

Taverner had had hopes of becoming a footballer himself as a young lad and felt his interest sharpen. He had vaguely heard of a Nathaniel Lawson who was garnering a reputation, now he thought about it.

'Great. Is he still with Sheffield?'

'Yes, for now. He has lots of interest from other clubs though. I can't keep up, but he is injured at present.'

Taverner fought back envy. 'Sounds good, not the injury obviously…'

Matthew smiled, offered them tea and showed them into an airy, bright room with red coloured sofas and French windows looking out into the leafy garden. He served the tea in china cups and had no problem in producing Earl Grey, Taverner noted approvingly together with fancy, buttery biscuits. Matthew studied them with inquisitive blue eyes.

'So, it's not often I have police officers visit me. How can I help? Do call me Matt, by the way.'

Taverner kicked off. 'It's about the literacy group you run, we are investigating the murder of Emily Morgan and following several lines of inquiry. We understand that she volunteered at the group.'

Matt grimaced and composed his face into a solemn expression as if he was preparing to conduct a funeral.

'Yes, poor Emily. She was such a lovely girl. I was dreadfully sorry to hear about her death. I have prayed for her, of course.' He gave a brief smile. 'But what on earth could it have to do with the literacy group, I really don't understand. I presume her death was a horrible accident, surely?'

Taverner shook his head.

'No, I'm afraid we are treating her death as suspicious.'

Matt frowned as he took this in. 'Really? That's awful. How can I help?'

'She seems to have been worried about a girl called Lola who she met at the group. Just before she died, Emily was talking to her. We just want to talk to Lola, just as a matter of routine, of course. Can you tell us about the group?'

Matt sighed. 'Emily volunteered along with some other English undergrads from York University. We have groups in local primaries and secondary schools in some of the more deprived areas. The idea was that the students could put something back into the community, encourage, educate, that sort of thing. The University was very keen on the publicity and the young people were marvellous. I used to work as a vicar but retired when my wife departed. I was depressed for a while but then decided I needed to give something back and it was the best thing I ever did. And I volunteer doing tours around the Minster which is great, but I wanted to do more. Running the literacy groups was ideal and the kids got so much out of it. It was hard to believe that the volunteers could get them interested in literature, but they were able to communicate on their level somehow, make it relevant to everyday life.' His face clouded. 'Emily was especially good at that part. I did the initial training, processed the DBS checks, that sort of thing, liaised with the schools, all the admin stuff. I remember Emily very well. I have a supervisory role and popped into the sessions once they were established and liaised with the schools about the progress. I'm afraid that I don't know any of the young people very well as the schools selected the pupils. The criteria used was for those that were underachieving in education with social and emotional issues.'

'Which schools are involved?'

'Oak and Mortimer C of E Primary schools and Mortimer Secondary. You
might want to contact them about the pupils who attended. The schools selected the pupils.' He frowned. 'Who did you say you wanted to talk to again?'

'Someone called Lola,' Taverner reminded him.

Mathew looked blank. 'I'm afraid I don't know anyone called Lola.'

DS Wildblood stirred. 'So, Emily never mentioned anything about Lola, about any concerns she might have?'

'No, certainly not. I did lots of Safeguarding training in the Church, I still do some work in the children's homes and know many of the social workers. The initial training covers how to deal with any safeguarding concerns. From my work, I know how important this is and if there were concerns then the volunteers were instructed to gather basic details without conducting an inquiry then discuss the matter with both myself and the designated teacher to see if a referral should be made to the council.'

'And she never discussed anything like that with you?'

'No.' Matt looked thoughtful. 'Could Lola be known by another name?'

'Not that we know of so far. Did Emily talk to you about another girl?'

'No, I'm just trying to picture who she might be. How old was she?'

'Well, someone who was able to pass off going to the pub, so secondary age certainly.'

'Hmm. Best to contact Caroline Dennis then at Mortimer Secondary. She is the designated teacher so she'll certainly know about Lola, in fact she will have nominated her.'

'What books did the group cover?'

'Some Austen, Dickens, that sort of thing. I think the group at Mortimer were studying Jane Austen's Emma and Robert Louis Stevenson's Treasure Island, more for the lads. The idea is to summarise the plot, get the kids interested and help them to read simplified versions, to encourage them to read more. It really does work too. Emily read them the stories initially, got them interested about what was likely to happen next and this encouraged them to read further. We hope to develop a lifelong love of reading.'

'So how long was Emily involved?' asked Wildblood.

'Right from starting her course, I think. The students run a stall at Freshers, and she signed up, so she had been with us for well over a year.'

'So, you're not aware of any problems within the groups?'

'No, nothing at all. Emily may have gone straight to Caroline Dennis I suppose, but I would have expected her to talk through any concerns with me first and she didn't.' Matthew sighed.

The door opened and a young man popped his head round.

'Oh, sorry dad. I didn't know you had company. I'm just bringing your stuff back.' He took in the scene. 'Is everything OK?'

'Yes, Nathaniel. Don't worry.'

Taverner got to his feet. 'We were just leaving anyway. Thank you, you've been most helpful.' Wildblood hovered.

Taverner found himself waiting for her in the vast hallway with Matthew's son. The hallway was like a homage to the boy with pictures and photos of the man as a gappy toothed child kicking a ball about and later in the shirts of professional teams. Beneath was a large bookcase filled with biographies of footballers, Gerard, Ronaldo, Messi, Beckham and Crouch amongst them together with books on sport psychology, football training techniques and strangely enough a couple of weighty volumes on The Psychology of Sexual Deviance. Still, he supposed there were sometimes sex offenders who joined the

89

Church in search of acceptance or fresh victims to those of a more cynical disposition. He remembered having to speak to a Dean about how the congregation was to be protected from a recently released sex offender who had joined them.

The lad was blond and blue eyed and had the really healthy gleam of the extremely fit. He was also very like his father. Taverner felt slightly tongue tied, sure that he was in the presence of a rising star. He tried to play it cool and resolved to look the young man up on Google later. He nodded at the photos which adorned the walls.

'So, you're a pro, your dad said. Great. Sheffield are doing well, aren't they?'

A strange expression flitted over the young man's face, a combination of puzzlement and embarrassment.

'Oh yes, we are. But I pulled a hamstring, so I'm injured. I've just come back from an ankle injury so it's not great timing. It's healing well though, so I should be back soon.'

'Oh, that's bad luck. What position do you play?'

'Striker. Yes, injuries are par for the course, sadly.' He gave a grim smile. 'I'll leave you to it. Are you from the police?'

'Yeah, we just needed to speak to your dad, that's all. It's just routine. I think we're done though.'

A wary expression flitted over Nathaniel's face.

'What about?'

'Oh, just about the group your dad runs.'

'Oh, right. OK, I'll let you get on.' He seemed to shut down, probably losing interest, Taverner decided.

He waited for Wildblood who was saying her goodbyes to Matt. As she walked through to the hall, she turned to him.

'Listen, I wanted to get in touch with an ex-colleague, I used to work with her years ago. Jennifer Green, I just wondered if you know her from your Safeguarding role?' she asked.

Taverner's head was spinning. What the hell was she playing at?

Matt smiled. 'Jenny Green, Mitchell now, of course. I remember her well. She's still around, she's Head of Service now.'

'Wow, that's brilliant. She was always very good, of course. Where is she working now?'

'Here in York. She oversees all the children in care services.'

Wildblood glanced at Taverner. 'Great. I'll get in touch then.'

Taverner could hardly bring himself to speak.

'What a nice chap,' Anna said when they were safely in the car. 'Looks too young to have retired though. His son was the dead spit of him.'

'Yes, he was. Nathaniel is certainly the apple of his eye, there were photos of him all over the hallway. Anyway, I'll get on to DC Patel and ask him to contact the school to find out about Lola,' he replied stiffly. He fished out his phone from his pocket. He refused to look at Anna. How could she? Anna cast him an anxious sideward glance.

'So, are you going to see Jennifer Mitchell?'

Taverner shook his head. 'I can't believe you asked him just like that!'

Wildblood was unrepentant. 'Well, you just needed a little push. Besides, he doesn't know it's anything to do with you, I made out I wanted to get in touch with her...'

'I know, but...' Still he felt stiff and angry, out of sorts as though she had blundered into an emotional minefield and she had no idea of the consequences for him. He was aware of her looking at him anxiously.

'I just thought if you see Jennifer first and see what she remembers about your mum's case, it will help prepare you to meet her. That's all,' she added in a small voice.

Taverner shrugged. He felt awkward and as surly as a teenager. Even worse, he was horribly anxious and terrified now the subject was out there. He hated been pushed into something before he was ready and Anna had done just that, pushed him past the point of no return, where nothing would ever be the same again. He knew she meant well but he was still seething.

'Surely, it can't help to meet your old social worker?'

'Enough. Anna, you really have the sensitivity of a bloody rhinoceros! I need time to get my head round things, clear the way in case it all goes horribly wrong.' Anna opened her mouth to explain further. 'Just leave it!'

Wildblood continued the journey in silence, her fingers were white as they gripped the steering wheel. Taverner vowed not to say another word as they made their way back to Fulford Road Station, all manner of emotions flooding through him. Then his phone rang. It was DC Haworth. Taverner put the call on loudspeaker to save having to relay the details to his Sergeant.

'Guv, Ross McAllister turns out to have form for stalking a previous girlfriend under a different surname.'

'Right, we need to bring him in then.'

'And there's more. You know that girl you asked me to check on? There is no one called Lola in the school, but the teacher thinks she might be a girl called Lauren Jackson. She had the nickname Lola because there were three other Lauren's in her class. Lauren Johnson was in t'literacy group. Get this, she's not been in school for three days and when the staff went to speak to her, her mother said she'd gone to stay with her father who lives in Hull. I wonder why she did that? Sounds very fishy to me. Fishy, in Hull, get it?'

Taverner rolled his eyes, glancing at Wildblood in spite of his earlier irritation with her. He was delighted to have some leads at long last. Haworth was obviously a joker, but he was an experienced officer. He could cope with banter as long as it didn't impact upon their work. He had known several officers like Haworth, and he found that the ridiculous humour actually helped in a bizarre way. It gave officers some light relief from some of the darker things they had to encounter in their job. This may just be the breakthrough they needed. He even managed a smile as he caught Wildblood's eye as he included her in the conversation.

'You're right, it certainly does sound very fishy indeed.'

Chapter 9

Anna felt tired and emotional. She felt guilty about pushing Taverner about the social worker but exasperated at the same time. She pictured his hurt and upset expression and felt remorse flood over her. Oh God, it was such a huge deal for him, and she had no idea how he really felt about meeting his birth mother. He was bound to be full of trepidation. Guilt gnawed away at her. She should have tread more carefully, but she had seen the light in his eyes when he first spoke about her and knew how much it meant to him. Still, at least the case was moving forwards and they had a few more leads and with the press conference tomorrow, hopefully, more would be forthcoming. Then there was the other matter to attend to. She had to talk to Rob about John Armitage's gift and make arrangements to return it. For some reason, she had not yet broached the subject with Rob, and the envelope lay shut away in her dressing table drawer, like an unexploded incendiary device. It was such a generous present and Armitage was clearly so grateful to Rob, she began to wonder exactly what he had done to warrant such treatment and felt very uneasy. The copper in her sensed that something unwholesome was going on. Unscrupulous accountants could help businesses hide large amounts of tax legally, and frequently did. She had never thought of Rob being anything other than totally honest and above board in his professional life, but could he be taken in by someone as charismatic as Armitage? Possibly.

By the time she'd arrived back home, Rob was bathing the twins, so she dashed upstairs to take over, thrilled to be able to see them. Jasper and Archie loved their baths, so she spent an age with them. Their faces had lit up as soon as she walked in, Jasper holding out his arms and Archie mouthing, 'Mummy, mum, duck,' and Jasper, 'look oc'opus,' as they played with the bath toys of yellow ducks, a tiny dolphin and an octopus. Their speech was really coming on. She hugged her boys tight as she inhaled their clean, sweet scent and read them nursery rhymes and stories once they were in bed. Jasper played with her hair whilst Archie giggled and burped in her arms. They loved 'this little piggy' and squealed with delight as Anna did the actions and tickled their toes. It was great to be able to put them to bed and give Rob a breather. When she came downstairs the delicious smell of carbonara emanated from the kitchen, made the Italian way with lots of eggs and parmesan. Rob was standing away from her chatting on his phone. She'd pulled out the Paris tickets from her dressing table drawer. Accepting gifts was always difficult in her line of work and though John thought he was just being generous; she knew it would not look that way to others. She was used to dealing with hardened criminals and it was the sort of thing they might give you, so you turned a blind eye to their misdemeanours. She had learned a long time ago that there was no such thing as a free lunch.

Rob hastily ended his call and turned to greet her.

'Boys all right?'

'Yep. Sound off. Who was that you were speaking to?'

'Oh, it was just a work thing, a diary clash that's sorted out now.' He smiled a bright smile that instantly dispelled any doubts she might have, even though she knew he would have been speaking to his PA. 'Did you have a good day?'

'So so.' She went on to tell him about Taverner and her asking about his old social worker.

He listened intently.

'Poor guy. It must be very hard for him. All you can do is be supportive.'

Anna raked her fingers through her hair.

'That was what I thought I was doing. But I shouldn't have tried to find out his old social worker's name, should I? No wonder he got mad. I'm such a bossy cow, aren't I?'

Rob laughed and poured her some wine.

'Look. You didn't breach any confidences as far as I know and now Taverner can make his own mind up about whether to visit his old worker or not. So, what's the problem?'

Anna instantly felt better. He was right but she did still need to apologise to her boss just the same. The next matter she needed to speak to him about might not be so easily resolved.

'Listen, I need to talk to you about something else.' She waved the gold envelope at him. 'You know at the Fundraiser, well, John Armitage gave me a gold envelope as he was leaving. I didn't think any more about it but when I went to open it, you'll never guess what was in it?'

Rob was frowning. 'No, you're right, I'll never guess.' Anna handed him the envelope and watched as he opened it.

He gasped. 'Bloody hell, Anna. I remember him bidding for them. I thought they were for him and his wife.'

'I know he probably just thought he was being nice, I suppose, unless there's something you're not telling me. But I am a serving police officer, and it would look really dodgy not to mention compromise you. It's the sort of thing we have to be very careful about in my job. I would need to declare it anyway. So, there's nothing for it, you'll have to give them back.'

Rob looked at her and for a split second she thought he was going to contradict her or argue his case. He shook his head, a strange expression flitting over his face.

'No, of course, you're right. He probably didn't think it through. He's just such a generous guy. Don't worry, I'll talk to him.'

Anna nodded, relieved by Rob's response. For a second, he had been about to refuse her request, she was sure of it.

The Press Conference went as well as could be expected with Taverner emphasising Emily's parents' distress and how the murderer, who had ended the life of such a young and promising student, needed to be found without delay. The parents were supported by the FLO and Mr Morgan tearfully explained that 'the light of their lives had been snuffed out' and that anyone with any details about what happened on that evening, no matter how inconsequential, needed to come forward and speak to the police. Emily's boyfriend, Dan, was also present looking suitably ashen and upset. Taverner looked sombre in a dark grey suit and emphasised that someone must have seen something on the evening in question even if they were not aware of its importance at the time. He urged friends or relatives who might suspect loved ones, to come forward.

'We are particularly anxious to speak to a girl named Lola or Lauren that Emily was talking to on the night she disappeared in the Geisha Club. She was involved in a literacy group run at Mortimer School. If anyone else is aware of any information that will help us bring the murderer to justice, then please contact us without delay. You might think that the information you have is trivial, but it could really help in our inquiries.'

Wildblood suspected that with Taverner's undoubted sincerity and dark good looks, there would be lots of phone calls. Many members of the public enjoyed helping the police but when they were helping someone as handsome as Taverner, the trickle of calls was likely to become a torrent. Of course, they would need to sift out the cranks and nutters, probably there would be more of these than usual. Taverner had the sensitivity and gravitas to carry the media contact off and people wanted to please him. She was fascinated by how he spoke to people, the ease of his social interaction and his respect for others. He certainly had the likeability factor, except with certain members of his own team. Cullen and Patel seemed to like the boss, especially Cullen, who studied him with rapt attention. Haworth and Ballantyne were more cynical and muttered to each other, only stopping when Wildblood glared at them. She made a mental note to monitor them. Prejudiced idiots. She remembered the post mortem and how understanding Taverner had been. Somehow that and the revelations about his mother had helped them bond and she felt rather protective of him.

Wildblood reviewed the evidence from Forensics, there had been interesting finds in Emily's handbag and from her internet searches that could prove useful. She met up with Taverner as he swept upstairs in his grey suit and long black coat. He was holding a cup and a brown paper bag.

'Come and grab a drink and join me in my office. We need to prepare. I've got McAllister coming in voluntarily and Haworth and Cullen are going through his alibi with a fine-tooth comb before he arrives. Ballantyne and Patel are on Lola's trail.' Taverner grinned, shaking the paper bag at her. 'And I have doughnuts.'

There was no trace of the sullen attitude from yesterday, in fact he looked positively exhilarated, yet she knew she had to say something.

'Listen, boss. I was out of order yesterday. I was far too headstrong, and I had no right to do what I did. I'm sorry.'

Taverner shook his head. 'It's fine. I was being a bit precious. Listen, I have rung Jenny Mitchell, actually so it's me that should be thanking you. I did need a push.'

'You have? How did it go?'

Taverner beamed. 'Well, I'm meeting her tomorrow, so I'll tell you then. Now, we have McAllister coming in. Do you want to do the interview with me?'

'Great.'

Anna went on to tell Taverner about the findings from Emily's handbag.

'Look, she had a business card for the Geisha Club in York city centre and was in the bar on the night she died. It has a normal bar downstairs but a member's club upstairs. It markets itself as high class, but it is really just a sleazy club with pole dancers and strippers. We have been keeping an eye on the place for years but the owner, Mark Fenchurch is very clever, and we've not been able to pin anything untoward on him apart from drugs being dealt in there which he claimed to know nothing about. Sadly, we couldn't prove otherwise. Interestingly, Emily had done several internet searches about the place, I wonder why?'

Taverner studied the transparent evidence bag which contained the card. 'Mmm, curiouser and curiouser. What was her interest in a place like this? Maybe wasn't a saint after all? Do you think she was working there and maybe got done over by a punter? Or maybe McAllister fancied her and followed her there. Perhaps, he is the possessive type and didn't want loads of blokes leering at her?'

'Could be that because of her father losing his job, she had to supplement her student income.' Wildblood thought back to her parents' small house in Cottingham and Mr Morgan's embarrassed explanation for the move. 'Or maybe it was something to do with Lola?'

Taverner glanced at his watch. 'Now, McAllister aka Ross Kirkby should be here in ten minutes.' He bit into a doughnut and handed Wildblood a file. She had noticed that he seemed to eat everything and never gained weight. It was just so annoying. She only had to so much as sniff a Danish pastry and she ballooned, and it always went on her hips first.

'Have a read of this before he comes in. I have asked Haworth and Cullen to interrupt us if they find any holes in his alibi, which there could be. At last I think we're really getting somewhere.'

Ross McAllister aka Kirkby eyed Taverner with some degree of truculence. He was a tall blond youth with a smattering of acne and an air of not quite belonging. Wildblood could see him hanging around more socially skilled students but being on the fringe, awkward and alone.

'Do you confirm that you are also known as Ross Kirkby?' he asked.

'Yeah. That's the name of my father but my mum remarried so I used her husband's name, my stepfather's. His name is McAllister.' He shrugged. 'It's no big deal. My stepfather was around whereas my dad wasn't, never has been.'

'So, changing your name didn't have anything to do with the incident that occurred a last year?' countered Wildblood as she watched the colour drain from McAllister's face.

'What incident?'

Taverner leafed through some papers. 'That on the 10th of December, you were convicted of harassment and a non-molestation order was made against you, after you stalked an ex-girlfriend, bombarding her with texts, repeatedly following her and threatening suicide if she didn't go back out with you. Then you breached the order. It's all here.' Taverner pointed at the printout of the charge sheet. 'Your ex-girlfriend, Tania Cross, lived in fear of her life for a six-month period. You terrorised this young woman, Ross.'

Ross hung his head and looked tearful.

'Have you anything to say?' asked Wildblood.

McAllister sighed.

'Listen, I did do that but so what? I had to do Probation as I was just eighteen. I did loads of work and I'm a different person now.

101

This has nothing to do with anything. I didn't harm Emily, why would I?'

Taverner sat back on his chair and stared at him.

'Are you sure about that? From where I'm standing it proves that you've an aggressive streak and that is very significant. Is that what happened with Emily Morgan? We know you liked her, you were there on the evening that she was murdered, we have CCTV of you going into the same pub as her, drinking with her and her friends. Did you chat her up? Did she reject you, is that what happened? Did you follow her and then hit her and push her into the river? Maybe it was an accident and if it was then perhaps, we can help. All you have to do is tell us what happened on that evening.' Taverner paused. 'We're waiting.'

McAllister bowed his head. When he looked up, his eyes were red rimmed, and he had lost a lot of his earlier composure. He looked so young and boyish that Wildblood almost felt sorry for him. Almost, until she remembered Emily Morgan's lifeless, grey body being hauled out of the river, wrapped in bindweed and mud, lying in the mortuary.

'Alright, but I'll need my solicitor here before I utter another word.'

Wildblood eyed Taverner. At last, she thought, at last.

'So, what have you guys come up with?'

DC Haworth and Cullen flicked through their papers.

'McAllister was on Probation for a year. His probation officer is going to ring us back. He hasn't committed any other offences since. But his friend is now saying that they went back to Izzy's nightclub after the pub closed but that Ross wasn't with him all the time. His friend Mick was getting very friendly with another student, Hannah, in the nightclub toilets, would you believe!'

Wildblood snorted. 'Well, it's nice to know that romance isn't dead! Jesus Christ!'

'So, how long was Mick busy with Hannah?'

Haworth grinned broadly. 'I think he may be bigging himself up but he says for an hour or more and that did include snorting some cocaine, so it probably did give Ross time to follow Emily, murder her and then come back as though nothing had happened.'

A pulse was throbbing in Taverner's cheek.

'Right, check the CCTV to see if you can spot her and then him following her. They were walking through the city centre so there must be some footage. Check through Emily's phone records too and see what calls she made and received in the days leading up to her death.'

'Right.'

Wildblood filled Cullen and Haworth in on the interview so far. 'He has asked for a solicitor and has form for harassment.'

Haworth grinned. 'Hey up! Do you think he's our man, guv?'

Two pairs of eyes studied him, DC Cullen's gaze was most intent, as Taverner pondered this. It would be a real feather in his cap if they solved the case so early on, it was too much to hope for.

'Possibly. Come on, let's see what McAllister has to say for himself.'

As soon as they walked back in, Wildblood sensed that McAllister had regained some of his swagger and was much more relaxed. His solicitor, Giles Simpson, was a well known defence lawyer whom the team had clashed with on many occasions. He was known for his adversarial approach and he liked nothing better than getting one over on the police. Taverner greeted him politely enough but was wary as Wildblood had advised. She'd had lots of previous clashes with the man, as had DCI Sykes.

Simpson cleared his throat. 'My client wants to say something, detectives.' It was clear from Simpson's expression that this was against his advice. Taverner and Wildblood leaned forward in expectation.

McAllister took a deep breath. 'OK. When I was sixteen, I started seeing Tania, but we'd known each other for years. It was the first serious relationship for both of us, it was all great, our families were friends, we lived in each other's pockets and then things started to get weird at home. My parents started acting oddly, there were strange undercurrents, then one day my dad just walked out. Turns out he'd been seeing his secretary for ages. Mum got sad, I was taking my A levels and Tania announced she wanted out too. My dad came back once to see me and that was it, he said it was better that way.' McAllister raked his fingers through his hair, his eyes becoming red rimmed again, and there was a catch in his throat. His acne looked far more prominent too. 'When Tania said she wanted to end things, I couldn't handle it. My dad had gone, my mother was depressed, and I suppose I just wanted things to be back as they were. I felt like I had no control over anything, so I tried to control Tania. I did hassle her, followed her, rang her all the time and threatened to harm her and myself. I didn't really mean it, I just wanted her back. I breached the order a couple of times. It was wrong, I know that now. I got a community order. I went to Probation, had a really good officer and he helped me see it, how horrible it had been for Tania. They even ended my order early. I was ashamed of my behaviour. I had no idea how scared Tania was. So, when I came to Uni, I changed my name. I didn't want this following me round like a bad smell.' He looked from Taverner to Wildblood, imploring then to understand. 'I swore I'd never do anything like that ever again and I haven't. I did like Emily but so did lots of blokes. On that night, me and Mick had a drink, we saw Emily then we went to Izzy's Nightclub. I danced and chatted some girls up, Mick was busy with another girl and was worse for wear. He disappeared with her but came back later completely smashed. I ended up taking him home at about 2, like I said. Ask anyone, ask the bouncers.'

'So, you never left the nightclub all evening?'

'No, never.'

'And other people they that night can vouch for you?'

'Of course.'

Giles Simpson raised a sardonic eyebrow. 'My client has been more than cooperative, Inspector. He has been at pains to explain the circumstances around his one and only offence, against my advice. I assume you have no actual evidence that he was involved in the murder of Emily Morgan otherwise you would have charged him. Therefore, I suggest you release my client forthwith and go back to the drawing board.' He curled his lip in distaste.

Haworth and Cullen were under strict instructions to interrupt if they found any further evidence. Now would be a good time to make an entrance, Wildblood thought, unless they couldn't find anything, of course, which looked increasingly likely as the minutes ticked by. Taverner nodded to Anna, which was her cue to leave and ask them. Minutes later she came back shaking her head. After a couple of minutes, Taverner made a decision.

'Right, you're free to go, Mr McAllister.'

Simpson glared at them both as they left the room, leaving them in no doubt as to his true feelings.

Wildblood watched them leave. 'So, what did you think?'

Taverner sighed. 'Hmm, he could easily have left the nightclub and gone back to pick up his friend to give himself an alibi, but it's unlikely. We need to find which bouncers and staff were on duty that night, get statements then double and triple check the CCTV and keep tabs on him.'

Wildblood nodded ruefully, Thinking about Simpson's triumphant expression with distaste. They'd get the arrogant bastard back one day, but not without evidence. They would just have to work harder to get it.

'OK, boss.'

Chapter 10

The Social Services office was in the centre of York, not far
from the railway station. It was a distinguished looking, ivy covered
Georgian building, but inside it had been tastefully modernised and
still retained many original features. Jenny Mitchell eyed Taverner
curiously and showed him into her office. She was wearing a smart
black suit, chunky jewellery and leopard skin loafers. She was slim
and wore subtle makeup. Taverner acknowledged that she was
wearing well given what age she must be, about mid fifties, he
guessed. He found that he was slightly wrongfooted by this, and so he
had forgotten what he wanted to say.

'Aren't you the Detective leading the investigation into the
death of that poor girl, that student? I remember you from the TV the
other day...'

'Emily Morgan,' Taverner supplied. 'Yes, but that's not why
I'm here.'

Hazel eyes appraised him.

'Right. OK...'

'You see I've come about something that happened thirty
years ago, more actually...'

'A historic crime? I'm intrigued.'

Taverner felt utterly tongue tied and idiotic. His head was so
full of the murder that he had contacted Jenny and made the

appointment without thinking it through properly. He decided that it was probably best to be open and up front.

'Well, it's about an adoption…'

Jenny frowned. 'Yes?'

Taverner took a deep breath. 'Specifically, my adoption. You see, I believe you were the social worker involved then. I still have the Life Story Book and you are mentioned in it, in fact you wrote the book. You see, my name was Michael, Michael Brady…'

Jenny gasped and stared at him as her hand clutched at her mouth. She studied him closely.

'Wow, I see it now. You are Michael.' She shook her head. Then she extended her hand to clasp his. 'The last time I saw you was at the celebration hearing, just after the adoption order had been made. 'I'm delighted to meet you again, DI Taverner. Yours was the first adoption case I'd dealt with. I spent ages on that Life Story Book and debated about whether to put my details in or not, but in the end I did. I assume that's how you found me? You have turned out very well. I bet you have lots of questions.'

She smiled and it was a smile full of warmth. Taverner felt his misgivings melt away like snow on a sunny winter's morning.

'Yes, if you have the time, that would be great.'

Taverner was buzzing as he drove back to Fulford Street Station. Jenny remembered his mother and him very well. He found out lots of things, but the most important fact was that his mother had been just fifteen when she found out about the pregnancy. She had had a strict upbringing. She never revealed the name of his father probably because she knew that her family, her father and brothers would go after him. She had no choice from her parents' reaction but to have him adopted; it was either that or lose her family. Taverner remembered Jenny's words.

'She was completely overwhelmed, I think. She'd found out she was pregnant, had been abandoned by her boyfriend and ruled out having an abortion. That was out of the question for her. I think she hoped that her parents would relent but they didn't. Even then, having a baby at her age was considered shameful for such a family. So, she decided she wanted you to be cared for by a couple who couldn't have children, who could offer you far more than she could.'

Jenny bit her lip. 'She looked after you for two weeks, then some adopters came forward who were perfect. She handed you over to me, but it nearly broke her heart, Gabriel, it really did. I'm sure she has thought about you every day of her life since.'

Taverner felt wretched for his mother, for her torment, but elated that she had cared, enough to try and give him a good life. That really meant a lot to him. Jenny looked thoughtful.

'There will be records if you want to access them...'

He told her about his adoptive parents, how they were so delighted with him that they had renamed him Gabriel because he was like an angel to them. They had kept Michael as his middle name. He explained that his adoptive mother had died and now he had finished grieving for Helen, he'd felt that the time was right to meet his birth mother, the woman who had given him life. The longing to meet her was so strong, that it almost swept him off his feet in a tidal wave of emotion. Once his interest had ignited, it had become an obsession. His adoptive father had given him his blessing, he had set the wheels

109

in motion with the Adoption Agency, but he felt meeting Jenny first, might help prepare him for what was to come.

'Your mother will be delighted, I'm sure,' Jenny exclaimed, clapping her hands together. 'But it may be a shock at first. She is probably married, and her husband might not know about you, so you do need to tread carefully. I'm not sure how her life turned out.'

'What do you mean?'

'Just that. There might be other children who don't know about you too.'

'Oh, I see.'

Jenny frowned, taking in his expression. She appeared to be on the verge of saying more. She opened her mouth then appeared to think better of it.

'What are you most worried about?' she asked after a pause. Her gaze was intent.

'I'm not sure.' Taverner struggled to articulate his fears when asked a direct question, but something about Jenny made him open up. 'I suppose I'm worried that when we do meet, she will be disappointed in me,' he muttered in a small voice.

Jenny grabbed his hand. 'Gabriel, Gabriel, I doubt that very much. Look how well you have turned out! She will be delighted.'

Taverner realised that she was completely genuine, and his heart soared with wild, uncomplicated joy. Soon, he thought, soon.

Wildblood grinned as soon as Taverner came into the office.

'Hey up. Listen, the appeal went well. The phones have been red hot, we've even got some psychic who wants to talk to us.' She studied him intently, taking in his expression. 'What's happened? Are you OK?'

'What do you mean?' So much for thinking he could fool her. Taverner had deliberately composed his face into a blank expression as soon as he came into the office, but clearly, he was not as convincing as he had thought.

Wildblood narrowed her eyes. 'Ah, I get it. So how did the meeting with Jenny Mitchell go?'

'Useful. She told me loads of stuff and it feels good.' He was aware of sheer joy breaking through his supposed sombre expression. 'My mother was very young; she didn't have a choice but to give me up. She found it hard as her family would have disowned her.'

'I thought you knew that from the Life Story Book you have.'

'Yeah, it did say that, but I thought it was something the staff just said, to soften the blow, but to hear it from Jenny, who was the actual social worker at the time, it made it real.'

Wildblood patted his arm absently. 'Great. I'm really pleased.'

'Thank you, I wouldn't have contacted her, if it wasn't for you.'

Wildblood blushed. 'Hey, what can I say? I am a bloody genius.' For the first time, he noticed that she was clutching an armful of papers.

'What did we get from the appeal?'

'Loads of stuff, obviously the usual cranks who claim they saw something but can't possibly have. We have even had a psychic ring. I'm handing the contacts out to the team to go through.'

'Anything of interest?'

111

Wildblood beamed. 'Oh yes. A caller says that Emily was seen frequently in the company of an older man who was described as middle aged, smart and educated. Now who does that sound like?'

Taverner felt his pulse race. 'Niall Lynch?'

Wildblood nodded. 'The very same.'

'Right, we'd better take another look at him. It was his wife who was his alibi, wasn't it? Perhaps Cullen and Haworth could have a word with her on her own.'

'And there's been lots of calls about Lola. Several callers believe she was a regular at the Geisha Club. Ballantyne and Patel have spoken to the school as you know, and she is believed to be a girl called Lauren Jackson who is said to be vulnerable. She calls herself Lola to differentiate herself from other girls with the same name. They sound like they could be the same person, the descriptions match. She's not at her mother's or father's, so she's missing.'

'How do we know Lauren and Lola are one and the same person?'

'It's guesswork at present. Lauren went to the literacy group and seemed to get on really well with Emily.' Wildblood had an air of suppressed excitement about her. 'Anyway, you can ask her yourself because a girl called Lola has rung asking to speak to you and you alone. She refused to leave a number but said she would ring back.'

Taverner was impressed. 'Did we not trace her phone number?'

'Well, yes we tried, but she rang off before we could get a location, but she was adamant she would ring you back.'

'And did you say something about a psychic?'

Wildblood grinned. 'Yep. Woman called Maggie Malone. Actually, she didn't call herself a psychic. It's just that DC Cullen knows of her. She came across her in her old team, reckons she might be worth listening to. I think she's more of a clairvoyant or healer or summat.'

Taverner nodded. He knew that sometimes psychics did actually have information on cases but in his experience it was because they knew the perpetrators or had some knowledge of them and the psychic role could sometimes be used as a ruse to pass this on to the police. He was sceptical but felt that he shouldn't just dismiss the woman out of hand.

'Suppose it won't do any harm to see her.'

'She's in the waiting room downstairs.'

He was in a good mood, so what harm could it do? The case was changing rapidly. OK, so McAllister was no longer a suspect, now Lynch was, but the question was, how exactly did Lola fit into the equation? Prickles of alarm crept down his spine like mild electric shocks. Now Emily was dead, did that mean that Lola was in danger too? She certainly was if she was missing in the city, or was she hiding and if so, why and from whom?

Taverner spent some time shifting through the evidence and looking through the information that had been gleaned from the appeal. He rearranged the links board moving Niall Lynch closer to Emily and took a call back from Lauren Jackson's social worker, Kelly Stones. She was also concerned about Lauren

'Lauren's parents are separated. Her mother is a drug user. Her father is pretty sensible but has another wife and children so there are tensions there. I am beginning to suspect that neither know exactly where she is half the time. Her father lives in Hull, but he says he hasn't seen her for a few weeks and she's certainly not at her mother's, so I want to report her as a missing person.'

Taverner thought it was pretty self-evident that she was at risk if neither parent had bothered to report her missing and the job was left to her social worker. He filled Kelly in on the call from Lola. 'So, assuming that Lola and Lauren are one and the same, are there concerns about sexual exploitation?'

Kelly sighed. 'I'm beginning to think there are. We didn't have any actual evidence of exploitation, but I think we have to look at the case differently now. We do need to arrange a strategy meeting and share information because of the safeguarding concerns, maybe hold a case conference too. She will usually pick up my calls and I meet her at a set time at McDonald's, but she's always vague about where she's staying and spends the odd day at her dad's just to keep me off her back, but we don't know where she is day by day. I need to meet her and confront her with what her parents are saying and see if she will tell me where she's staying.'

'I presume our missing persons officer will deal with this and suggest tracking, but we do need to liaise closely.'

'Will do.'

'How did she seem when you last saw her?'

'OK, she was however, very upset about Emily, but she never told me that she saw her on the night she died. Do you think she's involved?'

'Not as a suspect, but I think she knew something, and we really need to talk to her. She has rung me as a part of the appeal, so I'll try to meet her to take a statement.'

They agreed to keep in touch. Taverner signed off and kicked his heels waiting for Cullen and Haworth to report back from their meeting with Mrs Lynch. He went through the calls and evidence again but found it hard to concentrate. Then they walked in.

'How did you get on?'

Haworth was beaming. 'Interestingly, Mrs Lynch is now saying she cannot be sure that her husband stayed in all night. Apparently, he stayed up to watch a film and she was in bed earlier and was asleep when he came to bed, so he could easily have gone out.'

Funny that she didn't mention anything earlier.

Haworth looked admiringly at his colleague. 'Natalie played a blinder, guv. Asked if she were worried about her husband teaching a load of young, attractive females. Let's just say that Mrs L looks her age and a bit more besides. Reckon she is quite insecure. That seemed to set the cat amongst t' pigeons.'

Cullen grinned. 'It definitely hit a nerve, boss. She clammed right up and suddenly had a doctor's appointment that she hadn't mentioned, but then opened up after I talked about the students her husband teaches, their ages and how he might be tempted to have an affair. I gave her a card so she can ring us at any point if she thinks about anything else. How about we check with the witness who rang in about seeing Emily with an older man so we can positively identify Lynch? Then we can visit her again with that bombshell!'

Taverner thought that Cullen was enjoying her role as tormentor-in-chief a bit too much. What did that say about the girl? Still, if it got results, it was all well and good, he supposed.

'Great, you do that. Hopefully you have planted a seed and it will start to grow.'

At that point Patel came bursting into the room, his expression urgent.

'Quick, boss. It's her, Lola, she's on the phone. Try and keep her talking for as long as you can, and we'll try and track her.'

Taverner nodded hoping he was up to the job. His fingers gripped the receiver.

'Hello there. It's DI Gabriel Taverner. How are you? People are worried about you, your parents especially, and Lauren…'

The girl sucked in her teeth. 'Me name's Lola. You wanted to speak to me? Meet me at 4 at Clifford's Tower. Come alone, just you. I'll run if there's more of you. Got it?'

Taverner's heart was racing, but he managed to modulate his voice.

'Fine. I'll be there alone. Listen, I can help you, if you're in trouble, being held against your will, or scared. All you need to do is tell me. Your mum and dad are worried. They just want you home.' Taverner wondered if the call was being recorded and monitored by whoever Lola was with, Chloe had mentioned an older boyfriend, so he had to be careful. 'Did you enjoy the literacy group with Emily?' he asked, hoping to prove that there was a link between Lola and Lauren, but there was a click, and the line went dead.

'Damn! Did you manage to get a location?'

Patel shook his head. 'No. Looks like she was using a burner phone, so no go there. Never mind. We'll give you a tracker you can put on Lola's bag or something belonging to her when you meet up later.' He held up a tiny plastic rectangle. 'You can attach it to her bag, clothing anything really.'

Taverner wasn't sure it would be that easy, but he had to try.

'OK.' He glanced at his watch. 'Christ, I nearly forgot. Better go and see that psychic woman then if she's still here. You coming?'

'Wouldn't miss it for the world,' replied Wildblood drily.

The woman had dark, wavy hair and was wearing a long green coat, boots and an eager expression. She wore a lot of rings and bracelets and studied Taverner intently with pale green eyes.

'Guv, this is Mrs Malone. Mrs Malone, DI Taverner.'

Mrs Malone smiled at them. 'Do call me Maggie or Magpie, like my friends do. I think I might be able to help you. I sometimes see things that other people can't.'

'I'm sorry about keeping you waiting,' he added quickly.

She inclined her head graciously. 'No worries, I'm sure you're very busy.'

Taverner considered telling her to come back later, he needed to prepare for the meeting with Lola. Now the psychic was here, he wasn't at all sure that this was going to help. She looked so earnest and other worldly, he couldn't quite turn her away and maybe, just maybe, she might know something from the real world not the mystical one. Perhaps, she actually knew the murderer and wanted to pass on information without revealing her connection to him or her. He'd heard of this tactic before.

117

'I won't take up much of your time,' she added, as though reading his mind.

Taverner nodded and led her into his office, followed by Cullen and Wildblood.

Maggie sat down and rummaged in her handbag.

'So, what can you tell us?'

'Look, I've been having dreams about Emily. Sometimes they're premonitions, sometimes they replay something that's happened. It was after I saw the appeal.'

Taverner listened, there was something compelling about the woman in spite of everything. 'Go on…'

She consulted a notebook. 'I keep seeing Emily running, I can feel that she was scared, as though she was running away from something, then there was a splash as though she'd fallen into water.'

Wildblood leaned forward. 'Anything else?'

'I see Emily very clearly. She has a good aura; she was a good soul. She had a passion for justice.' A faraway look swept across Maggie's face. 'It was almost as though she had uncovered something, something very bad. I just get this feeling of urgency and alarm from her as if she was just about to do something about it…'

Just then Ballantyne knocked on the door. 'Ready for the off, guv?'

Taverner stood up. 'Thank you Mrs Malone. Is there anything else?'

She looked hurt and shook her head.

'OK. We'll bear what you said in mind.'

118

She smiled. 'I could help you more if you let me touch the dead girl's things. And with my pendulum I may be able to help you with which areas to search, where to find valuable clues...'

'Sadly, I haven't got time today. I've got to go. Maybe another day. Thanks, bye.'

Maggie looked bewildered and upset. 'Oh, OK. I'll come back, you'll definitely see me again Inspector.'

He felt annoyed and irritated that for a second, he had expected something useful. It was an old trick, to pick up on the obvious and state it in a different way. Everyone knew that Emily's body had been found in the river and that she was a decent human being. All those facts were mentioned in the press conference by him and Emily's parents who were keen to praise her. The woman was a total fraud as far as he was concerned, a time waster.

Chapter 12

Wildblood and Ballantyne were dispatched to follow Taverner when he met Lola in person. The plan was that he would be able to get close enough to her to plant a tracker on her. Their instructions were to follow her if this failed, so they could get an idea of where she went and where she was staying. The meeting point was at the foot of Clifford's Tower on Tower Street. This was an impressive structure, which was all that remained of the old York Castle, and had been used as a treasury, law courts and even a prison. It commanded panoramic views of the city as well. They had parked and were following Taverner at a discreet distance, in an effort not to draw attention to themselves. It was a bitingly chilly November afternoon, but the city was still busy as the pair had made their way through the crowds towards the tower.

'Och, damned tourists,' muttered Ballantyne under his breath. 'It's always the same in York, too bloody busy. Too many tourists.' He pointed at a gaggle of Americans complete with baseball caps and cameras and a hen party, a group of twenty something young women wearing pink tutus, the bride to be, singled out by her 'L' plates and the fact that she was clutching a giant inflatable pink penis. 'God, bloody hen parties. Why do they always have to come to York? Just look at them!'

'Hey, you miserable sod, give them a break.' Wildblood nudged him. 'Come on, the boss thinks he's in the Olympics judging by the way he's striding out. We'll lose him otherwise.'

'Yep, you're right. We'll turn our headsets on as we get nearer and keep our distance from each other. Alright?' Ballantyne studied her. 'You look exactly like a tourist yourself.'

Wildblood grinned. She was wearing what Rob liked to call her hippy clothes, a Peruvian style hat with a pattern of red and purple llamas around the rim, a huge scarf and a red padded coat, whereas Ballantyne looked exactly like the middle aged, slightly overweight and grumpy police officer he was in his grey anorak which covered his navy fleece.

'And you look like a mardy copper. Here.' She removed her scarf and wrapped it around his neck, felt in her pocket for a beanie hat and handed it to him. 'There you look more like a tourist and it will hide your earpiece.'

Ballantyne sighed. 'Aye. Anyway, it's a good call, it's fair freezing out here.'

They made their way along Friargate, past the Quaker Meeting House and along to Tower Street as they followed the tall figure of Taverner, his long black coat swinging as he strode on with his collar up. Ballantyne nodded at him.

'Why isn't Taverner dressed up like a clown?'

Wildblood rolled her eyes. She was beginning to wish she had come with the much more cheerful Haworth, rather than the dour Scottish detective.

'Because Lola needs to recognise him, so he has to look like he did in the TV appeal.'

'So, what do we do, just follow at a distance and see where she goes?'

Wildblood nodded. 'Yep. it should be easy, quite straightforward. We don't have to stop her, one of us has to follow her to see where she goes, so we can gather more intel about the address she's living at. Easy peasy.'

'So, one follows and the other one?'

'We need to observe and take some photos of the scene and the girl to see if there is anyone with her watching what's going on. What do you want to do?'

Ballantyne sniffed. 'OK, I'll take the photos. I reckon you'll do a better job of following the lassie. Besides, I don't want to look dodgy chasing after a young girl. Look sharp.' They lost Taverner for a moment and picked up the pace. The crowds were thinning as they strode on under the grey, unforgiving sky.

'Right, earpieces on,' hissed Wildblood fiddling with the switch. 'Can you hear me?'

Ballantyne started at the noise. 'Aye, loud and clear.'

He scanned the horizon and squinted. 'Look at the wee lassie, 10 o'clock. That's her, I'll bet.'

Wildblood followed his gaze to a small, slight figure dressed in jeans and a grey hoodie. The girl, for the figure was slight enough to be a girl, had a watchful, hesitant air, as though she was waiting for someone. Wildblood scanned the streets, looking to see where the girl had come from and crucially where she might go. They saw Taverner advancing and realised that he was heading towards her.

'You get close enough to take the pics and I'll keep on her tail.'

Taverner was carrying a plastic bag and clutching a cardboard cup holder with two hot drinks. As he approached, he handed a drink to the girl together with a sandwich. Hopefully, she would hang around long enough to drink and eat, which was something. Taverner had no doubt planned it so that he had more time with her, thus giving him more opportunity to plant the tracker and gain her confidence.

Wildblood observed the pair and decided that things must be going fairly well judging by the body language. There was clearly a discussion taking place. Taverner was doing his best to charm her. She could see how that would work. Her friends had teased her when they realised that she was working with the good looking inspector they had seen on the TV appeal. He had a slightly aloof air about him that made him mysterious, which was very appealing. Now she knew him better, Wildblood guessed that the aloofness was partly due to vulnerability about being adopted. Haworth had made some inquiries via a friend of his who worked in the Met to see if there was any gossip about their new boss. He had shamefacedly admitted that his contact had found out nothing suspicious, just that he had been shot in the thigh after an incident with a criminal and that he was generally very well thought of. Still, Ballantyne and Haworth struggled with him, and were convinced that there was some misdemeanour which had led him to York. Anna had wisely said nothing about his adoption to anyone apart from Rob, it would be unfair to betray a confidence. Wildblood wandered up and down the street, trying to look like a tourist and then abruptly spotted the girl striding towards her.

Wildblood waited until the girl had passed her. She came so close that she was able to catch sight of her white face under her grey hoodie. She had an impression of blonde hair scraped back and a pale complexion. The girl was thin, had a spotty complexion and seemed preoccupied. The poor kid could do with a good square meal by the look of it. She was heading for the western part of the city and Wildblood dodged tourists as she followed her towards the river. Occasionally the girl turned around to see if she was being followed. Wildblood managed to peer into a shop window on one occasion, and dipped down to pretend to pick something up, on another. She continued walking over Skeldergate Bridge to where the crowds were thinning. The girl had picked up the pace and disappeared down a side street on to Ebor Street. Wildblood jogged now into a narrow road with old buildings on each side but realised to her horror that the girl had vanished. Wildblood ran on looking around her, startling an elderly man putting something in the bin outside a row of houses.

'Have you seen a girl about 5'2'' in a grey hoodie, jeans and white trainers, come this way?'

The man eyed her suspiciously. 'No, I haven't seen anyone. Who are you?'

Wildblood fumbled in her pocket for her warrant card. 'Police.'

The man relaxed. 'No, officer, I haven't seen anyone come this way.'

Wildblood nodded. 'Thanks.' The girl must have gone on ahead. Wildblood ran on to where the street split in two and looked one way and then the other, panic mounting. To think she had described the task of tailing her as easy! How wrong she had been. She thought she saw someone in a grey hoodie passing a parked car in the distance, jogged on ahead only to find that it was a young man who was substantially taller than the girl. Anna ran on wildly, in the

124

hope of finding her, but the girl was nowhere to be seen. She jogged further to look down both streets, but there was no one. Shit, then she backtracked and peered in driveways, under cars and hedges. The girl must be somewhere but where? Disconsolately, she looked everywhere the girl could have conceivably hidden, every driveway, alley and doorway but Wildblood had to admit defeat. She had clearly been onto her and dived off somewhere. Lola had simply melted away like ice cream in the sun. Damn. How was she going to explain that to her colleagues? Her earpiece crackled into life.

'Any joy?'

'No, sorry I lost her.' She heard Ballantyne's irritable sigh.

'Och no, Anna. This was supposed to be easy. Bloody hell.'

'I know, I know. I think she knew I was following her.'

Bloody hell, indeed. Wildblood felt frustration bubbling. She knew that she was going to struggle to live this down. She hoped that Ballantyne might have taken some good photos or that Taverner had planted the tracker on the girl, anything that might let her off the hook.

Taverner was scowling when he joined them, so the omens did not look good. He explained that he hadn't been able to fix the tracker either, so they were none the wiser about where the girl was living.

'She didn't have a bag so that wasn't an option. I toyed with the idea of popping it in her jacket pocket but thought she was bound to notice and in the hood of her top but that was no good either as she pulled it up. Where did she go?'

'Out over Skeldergate Bridge,' explained Wildblood sheepishly. 'I lost her though. I think she must have clocked me and gone off somewhere.' She held up her hands. 'Sorry, boss. Anyway, what did she say?'

Taverner sighed. 'Nothing that would help us with our inquiries. Just that she did go to the literacy group, that she is Lauren Jackson and is also known as Lola. She said that she really liked Emily. She said that on the night in question, Emily saw her in the Geisha Club and asked her what she was doing in the pub. Lola said she had fake ID and was there with a friend. She told Emily not to worry, that she was fine. She also said she was staying with a friend in York because she is sick of her parents and told Emily not to worry about her.'

'Did you believe her?'

'No, of course not. I told her that her parents were worried and how easy it is for girls to get sucked into relationships with older men that are not what they seem. She told me to stop worrying 'grandad' and said that home was crap and her parents 'didn't give a shit' and told me to stop pretending they did. She said she was happier than she had ever been and that I couldn't make her come back with me.' Taverner shrugged. 'She was upset about Emily, but said she had no idea how or why she was murdered. She wanted to meet me to tell me that. I offered to take her to her social worker, told her they could find her somewhere safe to live where she would be looked after, and it was then that she ran off.'

Wildblood shook her head. 'So, what do you think? Is she being exploited?'

Taverner nodded mournfully. 'I'd say so, I am worried about her, but she seemed genuine when she said she had no idea about who killed Emily. I gave her my card and tried to get a name and address

126

for the friend she was staying with, but she just clammed up. We'll need to do a trawl through all the likely suspects who have form for exploitation, liaise with Probation and probably pass it onto Social Services. They could threaten whoever is harbouring her with an Abduction Notice, that usually works.' Taverner noticed Wildblood's raised eyebrows. 'Sykes will insist on the case being passed on. We have no evidence that she had any information about Emily's death. She came forward to speak to us of her own volition, so I suggest we pass it on and leave it at that.'

Ballantyne chewed his teeth as he scrolled through his photos on his phone.

'Any good?' asked Wildblood, desperate to salvage something from their mission.

'Nothing so far. She seemed to come on her own, there was no one hanging around, but I'm just not liking this, boss. We can't just leave the wee lassie.' Wildblood knew that he had two teenage daughters of his own and she had to agree, but also knew that Sykes would not allow their staff to work on Lola's case when they had a murder to solve.

'How about I liaise with the child sexual exploitation team, I do know some of the coppers in there and impress upon them the link with Emily? I can speak to Lola's social worker too.'

Taverner nodded. 'Brilliant. Now we need to focus on Niall Lynch.'

Wildblood felt irritated with herself for not tailing the girl successfully and wanted to make amends, not just because of Emily but also because Lola was highly vulnerable, and she knew how the

127

older boyfriend scenario could play out. Soon, Lola could be given drugs and alcohol and start having sex with 'friends' of the boyfriend, who would start to resemble a pimp and before long she would be used and abused by hundreds of blokes. Rotherham was not a million miles away and the same thing could be happening here in York. She felt her resolve strengthening. She had a very good friend who worked in the multi-agency sexual exploitation team who could help Lola/Lauren. There was no time like the present, so as soon as she arrived back, she rang Rebecca.

'So, how's life treating you as a married DS with two gorgeous boys, living the dream, hey?'

'Yep, it's hard leaving the boys but it's great having Rob's mum looking after them, so I don't feel so bad.' As she said this, Anna wondered at the truth of the matter. Sometimes the longing to be at home was overwhelming.

'Anyway, I'd like to refer a girl we were dealing with in connection with the murder we're investigating.'

Anna went on to explain their concerns and what had happened that day. She could hear Rebecca typing up a referral.

'I'm not sure if this girl is known to you. She's only fourteen. The social worker will refer her too. Her mother is an alcoholic and she went to live with her dad, but I don't think either of them know exactly where she is half the time. She says she has an older boyfriend. She was seen talking to our victim on the night that she died and went to a literacy group Emily attended. Our DI went to meet her, and she says she saw Emily in the pub but had no idea why she was killed.'

'But you're not convinced?'

'No. Of course, we are also worried about Lola being involved with an older boyfriend. It might be something and nothing, he might just be seventeen and a perfectly nice bloke, or he might be in his thirties and part of an organised gang. Do we have such a thing in York?'

'So far we haven't found a gang but there are quite a lot of kids being exploited by older males acting alone. Actually, I have just checked, and it looks like her social worker has referred her already so the first thing we'll do is pull together a meeting to share information. I've added the stuff about Emily so if anything comes to light, I'll get back to you.'

Anna felt marginally better. Even though she had lost the girl at least she had made the right call and help would be available for Lola. There would be someone looking out for her and checking out where she was staying. It made her feel slightly less incompetent.

By the time she arrived home, the twins were asleep, and Rob had put on a pasta bake and was working in his office. It was past the boys' bedtime. Rob looked up and came through to the kitchen as they caught up with each other.

'Good day?'

'So so. I managed to lose a girl I was trying to trail, so not so good. Boys OK?'

'Exhausted, but fine. They went straight off.' He took in his wife's tired face. 'I'm sure you did your best with the girl, so don't worry.' Rob smiled and began to dole out the pasta. 'Oh, I managed to hand the tickets back to John without causing any offence but there is a catch.'

The pasta bake was delicious, and Anna found that she was actually famished. She had forgotten about the blasted tickets and still felt embarrassed and confused by John's actions. Rob looked ill at ease.

'OK, what is it?'

'Yeah, he invited us for a meal on Friday but don't worry, he understood as soon as I explained that we couldn't really leave the boys with anyone and you know Mum and Dad go out every Friday, so that rules them out. I did wonder, though, if we should invite them round here. What do you think?' He watched her anxiously. 'I thought I should speak to you first, but it would solve the baby sitting problem.'

Anna swallowed down her annoyance. Damn. She was looking forward to a lazy Friday night, feet up, takeaway and watching some trashy programme on the TV, playing with the twins and maybe even getting romantic with Rob. Having a dinner party was not on her agenda at all, but he was right, Marian and Ken's Friday night outs were sacrosanct, and she didn't trust anyone else to look after the boys.

Rob studied her. 'He is a very important client and I need to go through some figures with him about the new projects. Don't worry, I'll do everything.'

Anna took in the house, seeing it through dispassionate eyes. It would take some tidying and cleaning which would take some time, time that she didn't have. There were the children's toys which no matter how they tried to confine them to boxes, all seemed to overspill into the living room and beyond. There were bricks and playmats, cars and teddies all over the place, double what you would expect. Damn. Perhaps there was another way she could preserve her sanity?

'Look, why don't you go out with them? I'll make sure I'm back at a reasonable time and then I'll stay at home. You go and have a nice time. I'll be knackered with this case anyway, and no use to anyone, but you should go. Alright? You deserve it.'

'Are you sure? I suppose he is a very important client. I hate to leave you, though.'

She took a sip of wine. 'Look, it's OK. No problem.' She saw his relief and realised she had said the right thing. At least she was off the hook.

'OK, that's settled then.'

Chapter 13

Taverner tried to shake off the frustrations of the day as he made his way home. He felt decidedly flat and dejected. God, the case was going nowhere fast and Sykes had asked to see him tomorrow before his interview with Niall Lynch. He was disappointed that Anna had lost Lola and dismayed by the scant information that the young girl had given him. He felt that he should have been able to get more out of her. She had been guarded, wary and his attempts to reassure her had failed. He had seen her type before; her eyes were all over the place and she looked exhausted from being permanently on her guard. It was a good idea to bring the drinks and sandwiches, but Lola had just taken a small sip of the drink and politely refused the food. He just hoped that the other officers working through the information from the appeal might find something concrete to go on. Police work was painstaking and laborious, but the dedication and diligence were necessary in order to find the evidence to put to the CPS, so that charges could be brought. However, at the moment they had very little to go on apart from an edgy, restless feeling that she knew more than she was letting on.

Back home, he fed Pebbles who miraculously appeared at his door the minute he arrived back, ate a quick sandwich and pulled on his football gear. It was training tonight at a floodlit ground near York. He had gone along in his first week, had missed training since, but he hoped he could be an asset to the local Sunday League Club. The manager, Adrian, had been understanding of the demands of his job and impressed at his credentials so they were prepared to make allowances for his hit and miss attendance. As a youngster, when they lived in London before they moved, he had been selected for the Chelsea Academy and had been kept on hoping to be professional until damage to his cruciate ligament in his knee had cut short his promising career. Although he had made a good recovery, he had lost his place in the team and all the momentum he had built up. He never recovered his pace either after his injury, which had been the mainstay of his game, and eventually he'd had to admit defeat when he was released aged sixteen. He hadn't wanted to play for Sunday League teams, it seemed such a letdown after his lofty aspirations. His family had moved to Kent and bitterly disappointed he had decided to do 'A' levels and then opted to take a psychology degree instead; later joining the police. He still felt the sting of disappointment, but it had been a particularly bad injury that required physio and extensive rehabilitation. His knee still ached on occasions but at least he had recovered full mobility which was the main thing even though he'd had to have a rethink about his career. Then there was the incident when he worked in the Met. He was a DC when he was shot in the thigh when he was in pursuit of a particularly vicious drug dealer, who he managed to jail for 10 years. The criminal was out in five years and thankfully Gabriel had taken his Sergeant's exams, and after several years in the role had applied for promotion then moved to North Yorkshire as a DI. His leg had healed but it still did not stand up to excessive activity, but he could manage a full game at a lower level without too much trouble.

The usual crowd were there stretching and dribbling around cones.

'Hey up, nice of you to join us. Hope you're keeping the dark streets of York safe and not slacking,' said the coach, Adrian.

'Oh, I am indeed, but my nose has been so stuck to the grindstone that I needed a break.'

The other lads piped up. 'Bloody hell, we thought you'd done a runner,' said Harry the goalie.

'Hey t'Angel Gabriel,' muttered another. 'Well, let's hope you play on Sunday, we could do with your heavenly skills.'

'Anyway, twice round the pitch then twenty press ups,' ordered Adrian.

Taverner joined the lads as they began to run. It was great to be back amongst them doing something physical and not obsessing about the case for a change. At the end of the training, they all tumbled into The Poacher for a drink, undoing all their good work, but at least it was good to be able to chat.

Taverner ordered the drinks. The barmaid was young and brightened as soon as she saw him much to the amusement of the other lads.

'Someone's luck is in,' muttered Harry. 'Milly can't take her eyes off you, lad. I reckon you're well in there.'

Taverner flushed. 'Well, I'm sure you're wrong. She probably just recognises me from the police appeal.'

'How is the case going? 'asked Adrian suddenly serious. 'Good looking lass like that Emily murdered, right bad, that were. Hope you catch the bastard.'

'We will. We have several lives of inquiry we are following.'

'That poor girl, her parents must be out of their mind. Still, you'll get 'em, won't you?'

'Of course, he will,' muttered Adrian. Taverner wished he had the same conviction as their coach. Investigations always went through peaks and troughs, but they usually came right in the end, it was just a question of patience and hard work, that was all. Still, he decided to change the subject. People were always curious about the details of investigations, but for obvious operational reasons he couldn't say much at all. Vital information might seep out uncontrollably otherwise.

Later they chatted companionably about the age old things, the football league, work and women.

'Yer married?' asked Harry.

Taverner shook his head. 'No, nearly was but it didn't quite work out.' He thought back to the blazing rows he had with Georgia. The relationship had been intense, initially fun, but had very quickly turned toxic. He still missed Georgia but knew they had been right to separate before they hated each other. Love shouldn't be so painful, surely? Anyway, he could not see her coping with him working late nights and having to miss loads of social occasions, which would have been inevitable. She would have wondered why he couldn't delegate and not understood that was not always possible or desirable.

'Footloose and fancy free then. Good on yer,' replied Adrian enviously. All the other lads seemed to have partners, although some of them did not seem too happy about it.

'That Milly is still giving you the eye,' added Harry nodding towards the bar. 'Go on, ask her out.'

Taverner looked at Milly's beautiful chestnut hair and fair skin as the girl took away their empty glasses. She tossed her hair and cast surreptitious glances at Taverner from under thickly lashed hazel eyes. In his present mood, the distraction of a pretty girl and warm smooth flesh was hugely tempting.

'Maybe. It's not the right time to start a relationship,' he added.

'Who's on about a relationship?' asked Harry, nudging him, his eyes gleaming. It seemed as though his teammates wanted to live vicariously through Gabriel.

Later Milly served Taverner another round.

'Haven't seen you in here before,' she said. 'Are you in Adrian's football team?'

'Yes. I've not been here long but used to play a lot where I lived before.'

The girl studied him beneath her long eyelashes. 'Might come and see you play on Sunday then.'

'Yeah, you'd be more than welcome.'

She grinned revealing perfect teeth. 'Didn't I see you on the TV the other day?'

'Maybe...'

The girl did a double take. 'I know, it was the appeal for the girl that died, wasn't it?'

'Yes, that's right. You've got a good memory.'

'I never forget a face. Awful that was. There are posters all over the Uni. I'm studying for an MA, so I'm there a lot.'

'Great. What are you studying?'

'Law and criminology, actually,' she flushed prettily as she handed him his change. 'Might see you Sunday.'

Taverner smiled, his heart flipping. It was an unusual experience these days. She clearly had brains as well as beauty but thought it would be crass to say so. He decided to take the bull by the horns.

'Listen, I'm very busy at work at the moment, what with the investigation, so if you can't make it on Sunday, can I take your number? I will ring you, but it may take a while.'

The girl flushed and hastily scribbled her mobile number down on a beer mat and passed it to him. She smiled. 'You do that.'

Harry nudged him as he came back to the table, noting the beer mat. 'Good lad, tha's well in there.'

Taverner said little but suddenly felt his spirits rise.

Sykes was on the warpath the next day and despite Taverner pressing for the team to pursue Lola's case as it might be related to Emily's, he was predictably dismissive and bullish.

'We need results and you're not going to get those chasing around doing the work of other teams. Leave well alone, pass the girl's case onto the sexual exploitation team and social services and concentrate on finding Emily's murderer. Now how about this Niall Lynch character? When are you interviewing him?'

'He's coming in this afternoon. Our caller stated that she had seen Emily in the company of a man meeting Lynch's description, and she has now positively ID'ed Lynch. The only problem is that we don't have any evidence that he was around on the evening in question, so although his alibi is weak and he may have had a relationship with Emily, we can't yet place him at the scene. Forensics are busy working away and we're going through the CCTV again and conducting door to door inquiries at the businesses nearby to see if he was there.'

Sykes sighed. 'Keep at it. If he was in a relationship with Emily, then he definitely had a motive to kill her. She could have threatened to disclose the relationship to his wife.'

'I suppose so. We've already ruled out the student Ross McAllister who did have a thing for Emily and was there on the evening but has an alibi from a friend. He was at a nightclub, Izzy's, until late and so far, no one is saying that he left.'

Sykes looked thoughtful. 'He could easily have slipped out and then got back undetected. Check the CCTV again. I suppose it runs out near the river?'

Taverner nodded. 'Sadly, yes.'

'What about the murder weapon?'

'The police divers are still searching in the river. She was hit by a blunt instrument, like a wrench. If we could find it, it could provide crucial evidence.'

'What do forensics say about the likelihood of fingerprints still being available?'

'Well, submersion in water may have removed them, the longer it goes on, the worse the odds. We can but try.' Taverner had known of cases where guns have been thrown into lakes and still yielded some partial fingerprints. Murderers often panicked and threw the murder weapon away, so odds on it was in the river. If they were lucky, it might still have fingerprints. It all depended on the sebaceous secretions of the skin, which varied from person to person. The secretions were oil based and less likely to be removed by water.

'And what about Emily's laptop and possessions. Her phone was missing, weren't it?'

'Yes, so we are looking at her network records and her laptop. She also had a card for the Geisha Club in her purse.'

'Did she indeed! Hmm, well we've never been able to pin much on them but between you and me there are a lot of suspicions about what goes on there. Do you think she was a working girl?'

'I don't think so. Probably more likely she was looking out for some of the kids from the literacy group, Lola even.'

Sykes tutted. 'But you've spoken to the girl and she's not given you any information that suggests she has any idea why Emily was murdered.'

'But there could be a million reasons why she might not say anything.' Sometimes Sykes was so old school he didn't always appreciate the subtleties of child sexual exploitation and the control and fear involved. 'She might be being threatened, terrorised, traumatised, anything really. You know what pressures these victims can be under. If you think back to the victims from Rotherham…'

Sykes sniffed. 'Yes, well, I don't think we have anything like that in York, maybe in the bigger cities…'

Privately he thought it was arrogant to be quite so complacent.

'I still think we should keep an overview of the case. Wildblood has referred her to the CSE team and she has pointed out the links to Emily's case.'

'Well, an overview is fine, but leave the work to the CSE team. They will tell you if there are any concerns, won't they? Now get on wi' it. We need a result on this soon. Don't let me down!'

Taverner gritted his teeth. It was clear that Sykes was not going to bend on this one, so with that, he had to be content.

Cullen and Patel had been working on the case specifically with the interview in mind and had been dispatched with a photo of Lynch to the pubs and clubs visited by Emily on the evening of her death. They were also waiting on further information from the University. Taverner and Wildblood were to conduct the interview.

'Though, I wouldn't mind being good cop this time,' added Wildblood.

Haworth shook his head. 'It's not a role that you'd be good at. You've just got to be true to yourself,' he quipped.

Wildblood ignored him and turned to Taverner. 'So, how was Sykes?'

'Not happy and not prepared to accept that Lola/Lauren has any information that could be valuable to Emily's murder.' He frowned. 'Sorry, I did try, but he wanted the relevant department to deal with her. He thinks we have enough to do.'

'OK. I have referred the case on and spoken to my contact.'

They discussed how to play things with Lynch.

'Do you think he's the one?' Wildblood asked.

Taverner shrugged. 'He's smooth and I have no doubt he fancies his chances with the ladies, but a killer? I'm not really buying it and we have nothing to say he was anywhere near the city centre or the river on the night that Emily was murdered.'

Wildblood nodded grimly. 'My feelings exactly.'

The case was beginning to go cold. Taverner could feel the motivation and enthusiasm of his team starting to ebb away, as each passing day the case the clues began to dry up turn out to be dead ends like ruddy cul de sacs. A great lead would appear and then fade away into nothing. It was a bit like trying to unravel a large ball of wool with several loose threads, but as he was the boss, he felt he had to lead by example and try to look optimistic. What was it his father had said to him, the harder you work, the luckier you get? The same was true of police inquiries. All they had to do was press on and never give up.

He stood up and beamed at everyone. 'Come on, I feel like we're on the brink of a breakthrough. Are you ready, Anna?'

Niall Lynch looked suitably urbane and unruffled as they entered the interview room. He was certainly a cool customer, thought Taverner, suddenly keen to rattle him.

'So, we have issued an appeal for information from the general public and would you like to guess what a reliable source has told us?' was Taverner's opening salvo once the introductions were dispensed with.

'Sure, I've no idea,' replied Lynch though he was looking marginally less confident.

'We have been informed that you and Emily Morgan have been seen in various pubs in the area, notably The Deramore Arms in Heslington.' Taverner let this sink in. 'A caller has given us a positive ID that you and Emily visited at least three times in the last few months. I can think of no good reason why you should be drinking together other than you were having an affair, and I'm damned sure that such behaviour would be very frowned upon by the University not to mention your wife.'

Lynch paled. 'OK. I suppose I owe you an explanation.'

'We'd love to hear it.'

Lynch pursed his lips as though undecided how much to reveal.

'You see Emily was an exceptionally bright student but lacked confidence. She sought me out for advice during her exams. She was feeling very worried and stressed, so I suggested that we discuss the matter over a pint.'

Taverner was aware of Wildblood's incredulous expression.

'Really, so is that usual? Surely the University have rules about that sort of thing?' she asked.

Lynch nodded. 'They do.' He chewed his lip. 'I suppose there's no fool like an old fool. Let me explain. My marriage is pretty much a sham, we haven't shared a bed for ages and sometimes it's a real temptation when you like some of the students and they seem to reciprocate. You see my wife has ME. Myalgic encephalomyelitis or Chronic Fatigue Syndrome and sex isn't on the agenda. Some day she can barely clean her own teeth. So, it's hard to carry on sometimes and when a pretty girl shows an interest in you, it's difficult not to react, I'm sure you understand.'

Lynch was eager for understanding from Taverner, but he was not in the mood to give it.

'No, not really. I am aware of my professional standards at all times.' It sounded priggish even to his own ears.

142

'Carry on,' prompted Wildblood, ignoring her boss.

'Well, she did want advice and that was it really. I went to the pub, the local pub near the University, I suppose to test things out, to see if she wanted anything more. I thought if I went there, then it would be safe. I could retreat if I'd misread the signals. At first, she spoke about anxiety, feeling homesick and she was struggling with expectations, but I reassured her.'

'And how many times did you visit the pub in order to reassure Emily?' It was hard to keep the sarcasm out of his voice. Taverner despised people like Lynch who preyed on young girls and used their position to their advantage.

Lynch looked up to the left, a sure sign that he was trying to recall information and that, much to Taverner's chagrin, he was actually telling the truth.

'I'd say about three, maybe four. Look, she was genuinely upset, I spoke to her, she explained she had a boyfriend and that was that.'

'How exactly did you test the water?' Wildblood prompted.

Lynch looked shamefaced. 'I asked if she wanted to meet for a meal one time, probably put my hand on her knee, touched her arm, that sort of thing, asked her if she wanted to meet up somewhere more private. She was nice about it, bless her. She said she hadn't wanted to give me the wrong idea and that she had no desire for anything else and there were no hard feelings.'

'And you just left things like that?'

'Of course, Inspector. What do you take me for? I had obviously misread the signals, I apologised and left it at that.'

'Has there been other students that you've taken a fancy to?'

143

Lynch looked uncomfortable. 'A couple. I did have an affair with a student once, but it ended when she met someone else.' He noticed the look on Taverner's face. 'I can assure you it was consensual, and she was a mature student, so quite capable of making her own mind up and I did inform my Head of Department.'

Taverner looked at Lynch contemplatively. He was right that once eighteen, even though he was in a position of trust, unless the girl was vulnerable, they would struggle to get any sort of prosecution. To his way of thinking, Lynch was in a position of trust and students would look up to him, therefore, they were strictly off limits.

'You know it would have helped us a lot if you had told us this earlier.'

Lynch shook his curls mournfully. 'I know, I know. I suppose I thought I might become a suspect. But I can assure you, I felt stupid and embarrassed but nothing more. Emily was a lovely girl and she told me she was fine with it. I apologised and we agreed not to speak about it again.'

Taverner mellowed just a little. It must be very hard to have a wife with a dreadful illness that had such an impact on both their lives.

'Is there anything else you need to tell us about your relationship with Emily Morgan?'

Lynch shook his head. 'No, that is absolutely everything. She was a very gifted student and a lovely young woman, so I just hope that you find the murderer. The students are very worried too.'

'Well, in that case you're free to go. Just be grateful we haven't done you for perverting the course of justice.'

Lynch shuffled to his feet and left.

Cullen looked up as soon as they went back to the office.

144

'Hey, I was just about to come down. Not one of the staff recognised Lynch in the city centre pubs but I do have something. The HR files from the University state that Niall Lynch was having an affair with a student three years ago. Apparently, he disclosed this to his Head of Department, so he has form and could well be our guy if he was seeing Emily.'

Taverner and Wildblood looked at each other. So, Lynch had been telling the truth.

'We know, he told us all about it.'

Cullen looked disappointed. 'So, he wasn't having an affair with Emily?'

'He claims that she sought his advice, he took her for a drink, he tried it on, but she rejected him and that was that.'

'And you believe him?'

Taverner nodded. 'Yes, he was embarrassed, his body language was congruent with everything he was saying, so he was telling the truth. It's back to the drawing board, I'm afraid.'

Wildblood nodded. Haworth mouthed 'congruent' to his fellow officers and wiggled his eyebrows, with a puzzled expression on his face. Ballantyne widened his eyes and mouthed something in return. Haworth had been calling the boss something unflattering, she suspected. He was still struggling to live down his Earl Grey tea and falafel lunch. Idiots. Wildblood gave them a withering look and decided she would deal with them later.

Patel rose to speak. 'Well, I do have some good news actually. I've just been on to Forensics. They believe they have recovered the murder weapon from the River Ouse. Ives has stated that he is confident about the find too. It's a large wrench of sufficient size and the right shape to have inflicted the fatal wound. There are blood spatters on it and the lab will know if the blood belongs to Emily, but the likelihood is that there will be a match.'

Wildblood wanted to hug Patel but felt it would be unseemly.

'Great, that is really amazing.'

Patel stood there grinning, his eyes shining. 'And there's more, it might just be possible to get some latent fingerprints off it, so that's even better news.'

'Great work. It's time we had a breakthrough.' Taverner beamed at his officers. 'Let's keep it going and I'll see you all in the Golden Fleece at 8. The drinks are on me.'

'Cheers,' said DC Cullen. 'Listen, I've got Maggie Malone here. She wants to touch a belonging of Emily's, to see if that will help tell her anything…'

Taverner suppressed an eye roll, but in his present good mood he was prepared to be generous. Then a thought struck him.

'She doesn't expect to be paid, does she?'

DC Cullen looked taken aback. 'God no, she's just trying to help.'

'OK then. Find me something of Emily's that won't be needed for forensics.'

Which was how he came to be sitting opposite Maggie while she closed her eyes and touched Emily's roller ball pen and lip gloss. Psychometry, Maggie had explained.

'It's a way of finding out about the owner. Sometimes people leave vibrations and energy on objects that they regularly touch or use.

146

You can find out a lot about them from touching their things, you know.'

What utter bollocks, thought Taverner and as he watched Maggie work he was equally sceptical. As he sat, he tried to make notes on his pad about the next steps, his mind focused on what the breakthrough of finding the murder weapon might bring. Idly he doodled as he glanced at his phone. She was fingering Emily's pen, concentrating and seemed almost to be in a trance. He found her quite compelling, but it was hard to know why. He was so focused on his doodling that he dropped his phone and simultaneously Maggie opened her eyes. The phone had fallen near her seat and she deftly leaned down and picked it up.

'Anything?' asked Taverner, eager to get rid of her and talk to Patel about how long the lab thought it would take for the fingerprints from the wrench to be analysed, if there were any, that was.

Maggie gazed at him with her unnerving green, cat like eyes. 'I'm not sure. I think she was a good person and happy. No sign of depression. I'd say she was well balanced, but she was worried about something, or someone.'

Great thought Taverner, talk about stating the bleeding obvious again, they'd found out that much so far at least. In fact, Emily had seemed to be, by all accounts, a level-headed, thoughtful and kind girl.

'Great. Well, thank you.'

Maggie smiled and passed his phone to him. It was an old iPhone Georgia had bought him that had served him well. He hadn't yet got round to changing it for a more up to date model. He hadn't had the time. Maggie looked at him sharply.

'Whilst you on the other hand are certainly searching for something or rather someone. It must have been hard being adopted. But I'm sure your adoptive mother won't mind you searching for your birth mother. In fact, she gives you her blessing.'

Maggie stood up to leave and Taverner stared back at her open mouthed.

'How did you...?'

Maggie picked up her handbag. 'Your energy is very strong and vital. When I picked up your phone, those thoughts rushed into my head. I see I'm right though.' She went to the door. 'Look, if you need me again, you only have to ask, DI Taverner. I'll see myself out.'

'Can you do other things?' blurted out Taverner before she left.

Maggie smiled. 'Maybe. I need to charge my crystal ball and then I'll tell you if I see anything useful in it.'

Taverner thought he must be going mad, finally losing it by having this sort of conversation with this unusual woman. Charge her crystal ball!

'I'll let you know,' he said stiffly wondering who had blabbed about the circumstances of his birth. It must be Wildblood, damn her! She must have told Cullen who passed it on. Unless of course, no, he wasn't even going to go there.

Wildblood had gone straight home, so he didn't even get to ask her about whether she had discussed his adoption with anyone. Never mind, it would wait. At the Golden Fleece Taverner passed his credit card over to the bar and set up a tab for the team. It was a narrow, quaint traditional pub and hotel. Taverner had read that it

148

dated back to the fourteenth century and was supposed to be one of the most haunted buildings in York. There had been various sightings of different spirits; one eyed Jack who wore a sixteenth century red coat and carried a pistol, the landlord who hung himself and a Victorian boy who was trampled to death by the drayman's horse. Thankfully, none were in evidence that evening, but there was a skeleton at the bar which added to the spooky atmosphere. Haworth, Ballantyne and Patel were already there, and he waved them over so that they could order.

The mood was still upbeat.

'Reckon we'll get the results of the fingerprints and bloods tomorrow, guv,' said Patel, smiling as he ordered a pint of bitter.

'Pulled some strings?'

Patel blushed. 'Well, I said you'd be on the warpath, Sykes too...'

Taverner smiled. He didn't mind in the least being portrayed as a bit of a stickler. Sometimes it could be useful.

'Be grand if we find summat on t'wrench. Be a feather in yer cap, if the case is solved quick. Must be strange coming up North. What brought yer here?' asked Haworth.

'My mother was originally from York, that's why I came here actually.' He found he was getting used to the accent and actually managed to understand Haworth now. Taverner didn't explain the adoption, that was too sensitive an admission. Besides, his mother actually was from York.

Haworth was amazed. 'What? Why didn't tha' say? There's us thinking you're nowt but a southern softie when all the time you're one of us! Hey, listen, boss's mother is from York, lads!' This earned several positive comments.

'Och, that's good. We thought you'd nae last two minutes with your love of fancy foods and tea like cat piss,' Ballantyne added. 'But you'll be made of sterner stuff, bound to be.'

'Hey up, good on yer,' added Cullen who had joined them and was disconcertingly drinking a pint. 'Why do you speak posh then?'

'My father was originally from Kent. We lived in London then moved back there. That's how they speak there. We also like cat piss tea and falafel.'

'That's what those two call yer. Cat piss,' said Cullen nodding at Haworth and Ballantyne who looked rather embarrassed, as well they might.

Taverner frowned and looked at them, unsure whether to laugh or cry.

'Really?'

'Anyway, what made yer join the force?' asked Cullen, trying to move the conversation on. 'Yer don't seem like the usual type, if yer don't mind me saying.'

Taverner felt relaxed and positive enough to share some personal information. 'Well, I was apprenticed to Chelsea in my teens, but did my cruciate ligament then studied psychology with bits of criminology and that got me into the police.'

'Hold up, guv. Did you say you were apprenticed to Chelsea as a kid? Do yer mean the football team?'

'That's right. I was picked up by them at 10 and was lucky enough to get spotted but tore my cruciate ligament when I was sixteen, had surgery but lost half a yard or so in speed, so that was that. I left, did my A levels and decided on Uni.'

'Hey, did yer hear that? Our guv' was almost a pro footballer. Who was in charge like when you was there?'

'Mourinho, of course, not that we saw him much.'

'Yer poor wee lad, getting injured like that. You must have been gutted,' added Ballantyne.

Taverner nodded. 'Then I ended up being shot in the thigh at the Met by a drug dealer I was trying to arrest, so all in all I'm only fit for a Sunday League team now.'

Haworth gasped. 'Christ, guv. Who was it? I hope he were sent down for a good while.'

Taverner thought back to the incident and the thoroughly vicious drug dealer and low life he had put away. It had made the papers at the time and he had been presented with an award. But his failing football career was much more of a blow to him. He found it was actually quite good to get this stuff off his chest. He hadn't spoken about it for so long. Talking to Lawson's son had made him think about it and how the promise of a glorious future had been snatched away from him in a split second after a particularly bad tackle.

'Yes, it was. I would have loved to have been a footballer first and foremost though.'

'Bet it were a real disappointment,' added Cullen kindly.

'It certainly was, but life goes on and it worked out well. Uni was pretty good. At least I could drink and enjoy myself after all those years of tough training sessions. But things could have been so different.'

Haworth shook his head and patted Taverner's arm. 'I feel proper bad about it, n'er mind you.' He looked at Taverner with new respect. 'There was I thinking yer were a southern softie and find you're one of us and well into your footy too, even if it is Chelsea! And yer a hero too getting shot an' all. Fancy that!' They all laughed at his admission. 'But you're alright, I reckon.'

That was praise indeed. Taverner realised it was a momentous, watershed moment and had no idea what to say to that, so he was glad when Ballantyne changed the subject.

'Any info from Maggie?'

Taverner shrugged. 'Not really. It was the usual stuff, impressions she had of Emily I think, but nothing really. Has she helped on other cases?'

'Not her. A chap used to come in but she's a new one on me,' added Ballantyne.

'Me mum knows her and reckons she's the real deal 'cos she went to school with Magpie, says she's a proper Romany,' continued Cullen. 'So, I wouldn't dismiss her.'

Taverner took this in. 'No, I won't.'

They left before closing, nicely relaxed and on much better terms. Taverner realised that he had made a huge breakthrough, like a barrier had been lifted. Cat piss! The cheeky bastards. He had realised his team were puzzled by him. There was his move from the Met, and he'd noticed the nudges and funny looks from the team when he asked for Earl Grey tea and turned his nose up at their favourite Yorkshire brand. He had expected some raised eyebrows but calling him cat piss! He remembered Haworth's face when he asked for falafel. The funny thing was that York did sell exotic foods, and there were loads

152

of specialist shops, of course, it was just that the likes of Paul Haworth favoured plain, old fashioned fare, he supposed. His mood sky rocketed. He realised that although he had yet to meet his birth mother, at least she, by virtue of her origins, had provided him with some much needed credibility in his team and for that he was extremely grateful. His blighted football career had cemented it further. Who would have thought it?

Chapter 14

Wildblood missed the visit to the pub as it was Rob's meal out with John Armitage and his wife, so she needed to care for the twins. She was in good spirits when she arrived home. Like all the team, the new development of finding the murder weapon had buoyed her mood and meant that they could have some forensic leads provided the Gods smiled upon them. Anna had a feeling that they would.

It was teatime and Rob was just giving Jasper and Archie their dinner. As 3 year olds, they loved most foods but made a total mess of highchairs and their faces as they struggled to feed themselves. Jasper was enjoying a pasta dish whilst Archie chewed on a breadstick and had more sauce on his face than in his stomach. They beamed as soon as they saw their mother, Archie pointing and Jasper mouthing 'Mumma.' Anna dropped a kiss on their heads taking care to miss the orange smears of their dinner. Rob was still in his work clothes and looked rather flustered.

'Here, I'll take over, you go and get ready. Where are you going?'

'Oh, some fancy restaurant or other. I feel like crying off, but we need a big account like Armitage's. For all we're a progressive firm of accountants, we do have to bring in the money.' He shrugged. 'It's the way of the world nowadays. We're all being monitored regarding the amount of new business we have brought in, and it would really help my cause. Are you sure you don't mind?'

'God no. You go off and have a lovely time whilst I carry on feeding these two. Come on, enough of the main course, let's see what we have for pudding? Bananas and custard or chocolate pudding?' She was met with a goofy grin from Jasper and a cry of 'choc choc' or something similar. Archie wailed as she took his dish away. Rob grinned and set off upstairs.

About an hour later, he emerged looking very suave in a smart shirt and a pair of black trousers. Anna caught the delicious smell of his woody, citrus aftershave. Her heart lurched at the sight of him.

After their bath, she was reading the boys their bedtime stories, but Archie's eyelids were drooping alarmingly.

'Hey, I'll pop him in his cot and then you can carry on with Jasper.'

'Fab.'

Rob reappeared minus a sleeping Archie and kissed her lightly on the cheek.

'Right, I'll be off then. Don't wait up.'

'Fine, have fun. I'll see you later.'

Anna spent a happy evening, soothing Jasper, tidying up and finally settling down to a glass of wine and a slice of pizza as she watched a crime thriller on TV. Funny how it always seemed so much more glamorous than it actually was. Nevertheless, she found herself immersed in the programme, willing the good guys on and before she knew it, it was eleven. She checked on the boys and drank some red wine as she turned on her kindle, then switched off the light, exhausted by midnight. She woke up at 4 ish, stretching her hand over to the other side of the bed expecting to feel Rob's warm body, but the sheets were cold. She woke, suddenly alert and checked her phone. There was a text from him sent at about 2am.

Staying at John's as had too much to drink. Be back early to help with the twins. xxx

OK, it was the sensible thing to do, but she couldn't help but feel annoyed. Why didn't he get a taxi? Then she realised that taxis out to their rural village from wherever the Armitages lived, would be very few and far between, not to mention extortionate. She fell into a fitful sleep, feeling uneasy without quite knowing why. Eventually she was awoken by the boys at 6 am and began getting them ready. Archie was in a foul mood and refused to let her dress him, Jasper ate his breakfast and was sodden and dirty having ripped off his bib at least five times. Wearily she found him a clean pair of dungarees and was just trying to cram in a slice of toast for herself when Rob strolled in the door at about 7 am. He looked tired, pale and smelt of beer and cheap cigarettes when he gave her a kiss on the cheek. She felt herself stiffen in tacit annoyance and resentment.

'Sorry, sweetheart. We had a meal and I had far too much to drink. We stayed up chatting and drinking and I realised I was probably well over the limit, so I stayed at theirs. They have a huge place with loads of spare rooms, so I thought why not? You know how you're always saying how easy it is to get done for drunk driving the morning after and I did text you.' He took in her expression. 'Look, don't give me a hard time about this, I think John is a really important client and he knows so many people, he could really help us.'

Anna bristled but managed to bite back a sharp retort. What precisely could John Armitage do for them? Rob was so ambitious and always ready to mix with 'the right people' these days. He was

156

impressed by money and success, far more than she was. Still, it wasn't the end of the world. She knew that rationally but couldn't help but feel annoyed. She swallowed down her irritation, glanced at her watch and gathered the boys up ready to take them to Marian's.

'I know, I know, it's just…' She took in Rob's intent expression. 'OK, we'll talk about it later. I've got to go…'

She made a mental note to make some subtle inquiries about John Armitage. He was a businessman, had a large haulage company and fingers in lots of moneymaking pies. The question was whether or not these were entirely legal? A skilled accountant like Rob, could really help someone unscrupulous avoid taxes and launder money by turning a blind eye. Then she dismissed her concerns. She knew that Rob would never get involved in anything like that, but still once the thought was out there, it was hard to erase it entirely. It's just the job, she decided, as she drove to work. As a police officer, she had seen the worst of human nature and tended to expect appalling, self-serving behaviour, that was all, she told herself. She should stop being so cynical.

Chapter 15

'Did you tell anyone about me being adopted?' barked
Taverner the next morning as soon as Wildblood came to speak to
him.

'Good morning to you too, guv,' Wildblood shook her head
sorrowfully. 'As if I would divulge anything as sensitive as that!'

Taverner felt himself flush. 'Sorry. It's just that Maggie
Malone, that witchy woman who came in, knew about it. How?'

Wildblood raised an eyebrow. 'Maybe she really does have
special powers? It wouldn't be the first time psychics have helped out
with police cases would it?'

Taverner was about to point out that in the case of the
Yorkshire Ripper, a psychic may have positively hindered the case,
when the desk sergeant poked his head around the door.

'Sir, there's someone to see you. Says she's a friend of the
dead girl and thinks she has some info. She's just found out about her
death.'

Taverner's eyes met Wildblood's. 'Right, come on Anna, let's
see what she has to say, shall we?'

The visitor was a short, stocky girl who had long dark hair
and had obviously been crying. Wildblood handed her some tissues.

'Cuppa? I'll sort some out while you get started, sir.'

When the girl stayed silent Taverner said in a soft voice. 'I'm DI Taverner, that was DS Wildblood. Now take your time. What was it you wanted to tell us?'

The young woman smiled, eyes welling up and Taverner was glad when Wildblood returned with two cups of station coffee and one Earl Grey tea, on a small tray. Cradling the cup and taking a few sips, the girl seemed to revive somewhat and coaxed by Wildblood began to speak.

'I'm Rosie, Rosie Jones. I was at school with Emily, I've only just got back from holiday in Ibiza else I would have come in sooner. My mum told me about her murder and that you wanted any information that might be helpful. It's just that, it may be nothing...'

Wildblood wore what Taverner recognised as her sympathetic face. 'We're interested in anything you have to tell us; it may be relevant to the case however small or insignificant it may seem,' she added.

Rosie nodded. 'Well, Emily said she was looking into something, it was big, that was at the end of the summer. But then when I saw her before I went on holiday, she seemed less sure, I'd say she was stressed, almost conflicted. She was upset and preoccupied. You know she wanted to be a journalist? I think she was investigating something, there was something she was on to. I also think she might be involved with someone, romantically, I mean.'

'Did she say what she was looking into or who she was seeing?'

Rosie shook her head. 'No, but she became secretive, started being weird. I think she thought she was going to break a big story and didn't want anyone else to get there first. She had started a blog about news stuff, you know.' She shrugged. 'And as for the bloke, she seemed excited, sort of lit up, so I assumed she was seeing someone. I thought he was likely to be married as she never spoke openly about him.'

Taverner's mind was racing. 'Right. We certainly need to look at the blog. Do you think that there would be clues on it? What was it called?'

'Newshound or something like that. She got really into it.'

'Maybe she was going to blackmail someone?' added Wildblood.

'No, I can't see that. She was obsessed with the truth, smashing hypocrisy, that sort of thing. She is the most moral person I know.' A shadow passed over Rosie's face as realisation hit her. 'Knew, I mean. Oh shit, sorry.' This set off a paroxysm of weeping once more.

'Is there anyone that she may have told, do you think? How about the mystery boyfriend?' continued Taverner. After all, it was stressful, knowing something that no one else knew, and at Emily's age, it would've been hard to keep that to herself.

Rosie thought about this for a bit. 'No, I think that was what made it so hard for her, the fact that whatever it was, it was so explosive.'

Taverner exchanged a look with Wildblood. Emily, the truth teller, the possessor of secrets, just added a whole new dimension to the case. He was determined to go through her blog and see if there were any clues as to what she may have uncovered.

On their way back upstairs to join the team, Taverner glanced across at Wildblood. She had been moody all morning and when he thought about it, she did look pale and less well groomed than usual. He started to feel guilty about accusing her of talking to everyone about his adoption. He decided that a more conciliatory approach was required.

'Everything OK, Anna?'

'Yeah, no.' She ran her fingers through her hair. 'I'm just tired that's all.'

Taverner was sceptical. 'Come on now. You're always tired with two boys at home. I don't know how you do it actually. But this is more than that.'

Wildblood managed a weak smile. 'It's just that Rob didn't come home last night. I mean he came home this morning, but he went out with John Armitage and stayed there overnight as he said he'd had too much to drink. He did text me but I'm a bit peed off wi' him to be honest.'

Taverner noticed that her eyes looked bloodshot from lack of sleep or had she been crying? He stopped and put a hand on her arm.

'Look, Anna, I'm sure that's true and he did the sensible thing which was to stay over. You know how many people drive drunk the morning after.'

Wildblood looked mutinous. 'I know, I know. It's not really that, I just bloody hate that sodding Armitage. He tried to buy me by giving me tickets for a holiday in Paris and he's really flashy and probably a bad influence on Rob. Supposing he's trying to get Rob to do something illegal? I mean accountants can hide all sorts of stuff, can't they?'

161

Taverner's mind turned over the facts like a weathervane in a storm but he couldn't add anything certain or too reassuring. Rob sounded like a decent bloke, but he hadn't actually met him, so he had to be measured in any advice he gave.

'Listen, has Rob ever lied to you?'

Wildblood considered this. 'No never. Well, not important things. Just small things like when I've put on weight and he says he hasn't noticed or he likes my hair when it's horrible, you know when you've had the haircut from hell...'

Taverner laughed and rolled his eyes. 'Well, I can see why you're upset. It must be awful having such a supportive and sensitive partner.'

Wildblood grinned. 'Nah guv. You're right. It something and nothing. It will be alreight. It's just my mind going into overdrive.'

'It certainly is. Maybe you should try trusting him?'

'Yeah, don't mind me. Anyway, sir what did that psychic woman say to you?'

'Maggie wanted to do something called psychometry. She said some rubbish about Emily but then I dropped my phone and she picked it up. She almost went into a trance and then told me that my adopted mum wouldn't mind me searching for my birth mother ....'

Wildblood grinned. 'Maybe she intuited it off your aura or picked up vibes from your phone? Or perhaps it was just a lucky guess?' The thought seemed to have temporarily cheered her up anyway.

Taverner shrugged and they resumed their task of reviewing the evidence. But Taverner was worried. He needed his DS to be even sharper than usual with her mind fully on the job if she was going to help him and the team solve this one. And with this new information about Emily, the case had just got a whole lot more complicated.

Chapter 16

Wildblood could tell that Patel had news as soon as she entered the incident room, he had an air of suppressed excitement, a buzz about him, like fizzy champagne. Maybe I'm bloody psychic too, she thought.

'Guv, the blood matches our victim's so, as we thought, it **definitely** is the murder weapon. and guess what, we've got partial prints. We're running them through the computers now to see if we have a match, not sure it will be conclusive though.'

There was a sharp intake of breath across the team. This was very good news and if the prints were of sufficiently good quality, then it could be a game changer.

'Great. Good work, Patel. Right if I can have all your attention please.'

Bit by bit Taverner went through all the evidence and lines of enquiry. Anna's mind began to wander a little. Taverner talked about Rosie and her suspicions about Emily being involved with a married man and about the news blog. She turned over the new information in her mind, wondering if they had completely misjudged Emily, imagining a blameless, idealistic girl when she was really a calculating young woman who sought to get ahead, possibly by blackmail. Her friend thought she was interested in truth, but maybe she was not what she seemed and keen to gain money by any means possible? Clearly the team were thinking along the same lines.

'So, guv, the halo's slipped a bit, hasn't it?' concluded Ballantyne. 'Married man I bet, they are bound to be a suspect. Perhaps, the chap was paying her Uni fees?'

'Doesn't justify murder though does it?' added Cullen.

Taverner rolled his eyes. 'No, it certainly doesn't. Anyway, I still think Emily was essentially naive. She could be interested in truth and justice, but she was also short of money and her family could not really help with finances so maybe she saw it as a means to an end. But someone must have info, they just don't know it yet. Anyway, I want her student friends interviewed again and this time ask about anything she was actively working on and whether she'd mentioned any relationships to them. Patel, can you find her blog and search for any clues? Wildblood and I will go over her room again.'

Sykes who'd been listening at the door walked in and turned to face the team.

'Good news about finding the weapon. Look, I've talked to the parents just now and they are willing for us to do a reconstruction. Any thoughts?'

Wildblood always thought of that approach as being a last resort when they'd exhausted all other lines of inquiry. Besides, the murder happened at night and the likelihood of the general public being able to assist was much lower in that case.

'Maybe sir,' said Taverner his face grave. 'I wouldn't want to put them through it yet. And who knows there may even be a match on the prints? Let us follow up the lead about the story Emily was supposedly writing.'

'Mmm, OK, I'll leave it for a day or two. But I don't need to tell you the press are baying for news. An attractive young student murdered, who was studying at our prestigious University. It has captured their imagination. Even that Angie Curtis has talked about how her death is the result of cuts to police budgets in the area.'

Wildblood frowned. Bloody typical of the local journalists to get hold of the story and milk it. He had heard that Angie Curtis had a reputation of being like a dog with a bone when she got her teeth into something and it was not good that she was writing about Emily. On the other hand, maybe the publicity would flush out something useful to the investigation?

Patel showed Taverner and Wildblood the information gleaned from Emily's laptop. He went through the printout of information from her blog.

'The stories are pretty standard as you can see. There are articles about York as a University city, student haunts, University clubs which features the literacy group she joined, articles on careers advice and others on gigs and favourite restaurants. All pretty innocuous stuff.' Patel shuffled through his papers. 'But she had some draft articles saved in her documents but not published. Look,' Patel pointed at the paper. 'She was clearly thinking of publishing an article on The Geisha Club. Here's what she had written so far.'

Taverner and Wildblood craned their necks to read what Patel was pointing at.

The Geisha Club

For many of us, The Geisha Club is an atmospheric bar often frequented by students and with some great deals. But lurking upstairs in plain sight is the Gentlemen's Club which is to all intents and purposes a strip joint, where men can browse the scantily clad beauties and drink. To many feminists, this is bad enough as it endorses the role of women as sex objects. But there have been persistent rumours over the years that the place is a front for drug dealing, prostitution and even more sinister, people trafficking. Several employees have been coy about the exact goings on, but a source has confirmed that our worst imaginings are indeed true. It is up to us students to take action. Is it time to boycott The Geisha Club and rid the city of the evil men who live off the misery of prostitution and trafficking?

Taverner responded first. 'Christ, she makes some serious allegations here. If the owner was tipped off that she was going to publish this then that would be a motive for murder, wouldn't you think?'

Wildblood looked slightly sick. 'Oh yes, it certainly would. I wonder who the 'source' close to her is? Lola/Lauren?'

Patel nodded. 'Or have you thought that maybe Emily was the source? Maybe she knew so much about the place because she actually was employed there?'

Taverner looked grim faced. 'Can you get me everything you have about The Geisha Club and its license and owners.'

They worked late poring over the documents that Patel had unearthed. It seemed that the licence for The Geisha Club had recently been renewed and all the checks had come back clear, and it was obvious the officers tasked with making inquiries about the legitimacy of the place, had been extremely thorough, leaving no stone unturned.

Patel and Wildblood went through any crimes that had been reported which mentioned the club and Ballantyne, Cullen and Haworth cross referenced information on the registered owner. Eventually, Taverner yawned and told them all to pack up. He studied Wildblood.

'You look like death warmed up,' he agreed, 'go and get an early night. Let's hope you're not going down with something.' She drove home deep in thought, hoping that maybe the boys would still be up, and she could lose herself in her parenting tasks.

In the event the boys were both bathed and in their pj's when she arrived. Rob had also cooked her dinner. He had laid the table and a risotto was bubbling away on the stove. He was clearly pulling out all the stops and she wondered why.

'You look bushed love, you put them to bed and I'll just finish off here.'

Wildblood carried Archie while Jasper bounced upstairs after her. As she settled them down to read some stories, she could not help wondering what Rob was feeling guilty about and the thought terrified her. She had half heartedly searched for information about Armitage but could find nothing of concern, in fact, quite the opposite. There were several gushing articles about his philanthropy towards various local projects and eye watering estimations of his personal wealth. But what was more worrying was the article that they had found in draft on Emily's computer. She had bitter knowledge about previous investigations into The Geisha Club but knew that frustratingly nothing tangible had ever been found to pursue any sort of criminal conviction. She knew all too well how girls were groomed by giving them drugs as freebies, drawing them in subtly and then once they were hooked, asking them to do 'favours' in return for the payments they owed. Was this what Armitage was doing? She couldn't overlook his initial comment when he met her about hoping she wouldn't need to lock him up, and his attempts to ingratiate himself with them by buying her the main prize at the auction of promises. Suddenly Rob had stayed overnight when he went out with him, something he had never done before. None of it added up. What the hell was Armitage up to?

Chapter 17

Taverner found the psychic waiting for him when he arrived at the station next morning. DC Cullen was sitting with her.

'Maggie has some new leads, guv.' She looked meaningfully, urging him to take the psychic seriously. So, grimacing slightly he nodded for them to follow him. If he was quick the rest of the team may never need to know that she'd been in.

Today Maggie looked different, alert and excited. It was obvious to Taverner that she had news to impart. He may as well get it over with. He remembered what Cullen had said about the woman's skills.

'OK, what can you tell me?'

Maggie pulled out a notebook. 'I used my crystal ball. You remember I had to charge it during the full moon?'

'Ye-es.' What was she on about charging a crystal ball? Christ, just get on with it.

'I asked about Emily and I got a result...'Maggie's face took on a faraway smile. 'I saw a parasol and a dragon.'

'Right...'

Maggie gave him a penetrating look. 'Trust me, they have something to do with Emily's death...'

OK, so Emily was hit by a parasol and killed by the fire from a roaring dragon, all here in York by the River Ouse, Taverner thought, which was clearly ridiculous. Fortunately, he didn't say this out loud, although he was tempted.

Maggie stood up and gathered up her things. She appeared unaware of Taverner's scepticism, in fact, she seemed quite buoyed up by her recent insights.

'You know I don't always have success using the crystal ball, sometimes I look in it and see absolutely nothing. But this time the images were crystal clear, literally. And another thing the hierophant keeps coming up in my tarot readings…' She stared at Taverner with the zeal of a new convert. 'I'm really convinced this will help you, be sure to ask if you need any more assistance.'

Taverner did not know how to answer this and grunted in a non-committal manner. Dear God, he'd need to be desperate to use anything that this woman said. Sodding tarot cards? He gave himself a shake as if to rid himself of such ridiculous ideas. How the hell could the appearance of a card called the hierophant help them?

His mood was not improved when the results from forensics came in. The information that the prints from the wrench were incomplete and therefore useless, was bitterly disappointing and the murder weapon had no distinguishing characteristics either.

'It's just a common all-garden wrench, guv, nothing unusual about it. Sold in a set from all sorts of outlets like B and Q, that sort of place. They sold thousands in the last year, I checked.' Ballantyne shrugged.

'And the partial prints are not of sufficient quality to be any use. Looks like a ruddy dead end,' added Haworth to this gloomy assessment.

Taverner frowned. 'Any luck on the Mulberry bag and Tiffany bracelet, Cullen?'

DC Cullen looked down at her feet. 'She had the Tiffany bracelet as a Christmas present and the bag was a gift for doing well in her 'A' levels. The FLO, PC Lambert, asked Emily's parents and their bank accounts confirm this, so they're verified. They probably look new because Emily looked after all her stuff very well, so they were from a few years ago but look like they were bought yesterday.'

'OK. Well, there's still the draft story we found on Emily's laptop and the older man or possible lover info from Emily's friend.'

Ballantyne's hand shot up. 'Lynch might still be our man. Students often admire their tutors, I reckon.'

Taverner paused. He thought that the guy had been quite honest, even revealing his previous form in this area. He didn't like the man, but he thought he was telling the truth. Maybe that was just because he realised he'd be found out anyway? But perhaps it was worth some more probing. There were precious few other leads anyway.

'OK, talk to him again and his wife separately. Anything else?'

Patel cleared his throat. 'Boss, there's a Facebook page which has been put up, a tribute to Emily. I think you should take a look, there's some weird comments…'

The team crowded around his computer screen.

Patel made a few clicks. 'See here, 'You got what you deserve…' and here later, 'What goes around comes around.''

'Mmm, not the usual outpourings of sadness and grief, are they?' said Wildblood.

172

'Sounds like she had some enemies, doesn't it? Rivals? Someone who knew she was onto something. Can you tell where it was posted? The time?'

'York Library guv, 16.04 hours yesterday.'

'Right, you and Haworth get down there, check the CCTV and speak to the librarians about what they saw too.'

'OK, will do.'

'We're still doing some digging on The Geisha Club, but we have to tread carefully as they have recently been awarded a further license for the Gentlemen's Club and inquiries carried out at the time, checked out.'

Taverner had hoped to find some anomalies to allow them to go in with a search warrant, hard evidence about trafficking or prostitution would be good, but if not, they could still have a good look at the place. Hopefully they would also find out about the love interest. He would certainly be a prime suspect, especially if he was married and had a lot to lose. If Dan Charlton knew about this relationship, then it would be worth having another look at him too. Despite the disappointment about the fingerprints, he felt a surge of optimism. Their luck was bound to change. Things would finally come together, like the last leg of some interminable journey, he was sure of it.

Chapter 18

Ballantyne and Cullen spent the day trawling through information about The Geisha Club but turned up nothing new.

'Perhaps, we should try contacting Lola again. She may be the key if she's working there?'

Taverner nodded. 'Good idea. Anna, can you get on to it?'

Wildblood rang the CSE team, but it seemed that Lola had been very evasive and there was nothing new to report. It was just a question of building up a relationship with her, her keyworker had told Anna, adding that this could take months. Unfortunately, they didn't have months, Anna realised, damping down her irritation. The worker promised to get back in touch with any relevant information, but she was sceptical that any would be forthcoming.

She relayed this to Taverner. 'So, it's a no go there. I hope the others have had better luck with the nasty comments on Emily's tribute page.'

They hadn't actually. Patel and Haworth came back to the station within an hour.

'Bloody CCTV was down and the email address of the 'Concerned Citizen' is mickeymouse22@gmail.com. We'll send it to the tech guys but I'm not sure they'll be able to find anything.' Haworth shook his head. 'Any intel on The Geisha Club?'

Cullen and Ballantyne looked up. 'Nothing so far, but we'll keep looking.'

It was now past 7 pm and the mood of the team had dipped considerably. Maybe they all needed a break?

'Fancy a pint?' suggested Taverner, who felt that they needed cheering up.

Haworth and Patel grinned. 'Now you're talking.'

Anna decided to go along too, just to have a quick glass of wine with her colleagues in The Old White Swan in Goodramgate, a favourite of Haworth and Ballantyne's because of the real ale. The pub dated back to the 16th Century and was reported to be haunted by papists who used the place for meetings to plot their escape to France. The haunting was supposed to take the form of muffled footsteps and fires being relit with no explanation. Anna took no notice of this as she settled by the fire and listened to Haworth and Ballantyne extol the virtues of real ale. As usual, she was keen to get back to Rob and the boys, but it was just so tempting to offload about the case.

'So, are we still looking for a lover?' asked Haworth as he sipped his beer and made light work of a packet of dry roasted peanuts.

'God knows. Maybe Emily was in a relationship with a married man. If she threatened to tell his wife, then that would be a good motive for murder,' muttered Wildblood.

'I wonder what she knew about The Geisha Club. She must have had concrete evidence surely, otherwise why write the story?' added Cullen.

'But she didn't publish it so perhaps she was in the process of verifying the information?' suggested Patel.

175

'Her family might know, or her friends or boyfriend. Surely, if she was worried enough to draft the story, she would have spoken to a friend or to Dan? It's hard keeping information to yourself, don't you think?' suggested Wildblood.

Taverner frowned. 'Hmm. Maybe. Her friend said she thought she was worried about something, preoccupied, but we could talk to her again, I suppose. Sometimes witnesses don't know they have vital information.'

Anna glanced at her watch, downed her wine and put her coat on. 'Right, if I set off now, I might just make it in time for the boys' bedtime stories. There's one they can't get enough of. It's a story about Police Officer Olivia at the moment, they love it.'

Haworth raised his glass to her. 'That's right, no harm starting 'em off as you mean to go on. If they're half as good a copper as their mum, then they'll be alreight.'

'Here, here,' added Ballantyne.

Anna grinned awkwardly. She did not feel like she was doing a good job at the moment, not even close, but it was meant kindly, she knew. Haworth was a good sort, despite the 'dad' jokes, they all were.

'OK, 'bye then, I'll see you all tomorrow.'

They said their goodbyes and Anna drove home her head full of Emily. Dead people always left clues about how and why they died, it was just a question of finding them. Despite what Haworth had said, she felt she wasn't pulling her weight. She had lost Lola when she tracked her and she had an uncomfortable feeling that she wasn't doing very well at anything, her job or her parenting. Then there was her relationship with Rob. The children undeniably caused stress, it was really hard working full time and delegating a lot of the parenting to Rob and Marian. She was sometimes so tired; it was all she could do just to put one foot in front of the other. But she had the horrible feeling that things between her and Rob were spiraling out of control. All this stuff about John Armitage was coming between them and she didn't know how to address it. Things were still awkward with overly polite conversations, both fencing around the difficult issues. They hadn't really talked about his night out. She hated any sort of confrontation with Rob and went through his explanations in her head. It was the first time since their marriage seven years ago, that he had stayed out all night. She had quizzed him gently, but he had replied that being married to a police officer, he was only too well aware of the consequences of driving over the limit. He simply said that he and John had stayed up drinking and before he knew it, it was 2 in the morning and he hadn't wanted to wake her up drunk. Anna had accepted his explanation, sort of, but it didn't mean that she was happy with things. She just didn't like the influence John appeared to have on Rob. She was too tired to even think and was not about to have an almighty row, so they would just hedge round each other, she supposed. Her mood was not improved when she realised that Rob had already put the boys to bed when she arrived home

'They were exhausted after a trip to the park, wore themselves out, Mum said.'

Anna bit back her disappointment. 'Never mind.'

Rob hugged her. 'How was your day?' He popped her dinner in the microwave. 'It's fish pie.'

177

'Oh brilliant. Well, let's just say that we are progressing slowly, too slowly for my liking.'

Rob donned his oven gloves and when the microwave pinged, placed the plate on the table in front of her.

'Oh, I nearly forgot. I've got a bottle of white wine to try, it will go beautifully with the fish. John gave it to me. He has an excellent wine cellar and is something of a connoisseur. I left it in the car.'

Bully for bloody John Armitage, thought Anna, biting back a retort. Still she could do with a glass. With that he disappeared outside.

Anna breathed in the delicious scent of haddock in parsley sauce topped with mashed potato sprinkled with grated mature cheddar. Delicious. She was just about the take a bite when her phone rang out. She hunted around for it and finding it in her bag realised that it was Rob's phone that was ringing. She traced the sound back to his coat pocket, which was placed on the back of the kitchen chair. John's name flashed up. Anna placed Rob's phone on the table, intending to tell Rob when he came back in. As she did so, a wallet sized card fluttered onto the floor. She picked it up, as she heard the front door closing. The card looked vaguely familiar, she had definitely seen the pink and white striped design before. There was an outline of a Japanese woman, her hair in a bun, her expression meek, with a parasol. She turned over the card and read *The Geisha Club-Bar, dancing, entertainment and so much more* and gasped. She was still staring at it when Rob came into the room.

'Your phone was ringing, so I pulled it out of your pocket.'

'Right.' Rob nodded put the bottle of wine down and scooped up his phone. 'Oh, it's John Armitage. I'll ring him back later.' He looked at the card Anna was holding. 'Oh, John said they were looking for an accountant. It's owned by someone called Mark Fenchurch apparently. Have you heard of him?'

Anna took a deep breath. 'I certainly have, I would steer well clear if I were you.'

Rob's face fell. 'Really? Why's that?'

'Have you ever been there?'

Rob looked blank. 'No, I've seen it and walked past sometimes but I've never been inside.'

'So, you didn't go there with John Armitage after the meal the other night?'

Rob looked genuinely shocked. 'No, I didn't. Anyway, would it have been so bad if I had? It's just another student bar, isn't it?'

Anna sighed. 'Well, on the face of it, but upstairs there is a private club where there is pole dancing and strippers and rumours of so much more…'

Rob studied her. 'Oh, OK. Are you saying it's a knocking shop?'

Anna nodded. 'Possibly, could be all sorts really. They could have trafficked girls there. Not that we've managed to pin anything on Mr Fenchurch, but it's worth knowing.'

Rob poured out the wine and handed her a glass, stooping to plant a kiss on her head.

'Well, that's settled then. That's one account I won't be picking up then. Thanks for telling me.'

Anna sipped her wine. She couldn't help but feel rather irritated with John Armitage with his dodgy friends and posh wine, though she had to admit it did taste rather good. She could not help persisting. 'Does John know him well?'

Rob shook his head. 'No, they are just business acquaintances, I think.'

'Good.' If Rob was going to be working with John Armitage, then she certainly hoped he steered clear of the likes of Mark Fenchurch. She remembered Armitage's opening remark to her at the auction, about not doing anything she'd have to arrest him for and wondered again why he had said such a thing. The trouble was that Rob seemed to be in awe of him and it might affect his judgment. She fervently prayed that he wouldn't be led astray because she was afraid that John Armitage was up to no good and he might involve Rob in something illegal.

Chapter 19

Taverner faced his team who were all looking at the links board frowning with concentration as if waiting for him to perform a magic trick where the real culprit would be revealed. If only detection was that simple. The images of Emily were central on the board surrounded by photos of the suspects, Daniel Charlton, Ross McAllister and Niall Lynch.

'So, Daniel Charlton appears to have been in Hull on the evening of Emily's murder, Ross McAllister also had an alibi and claims not to have left the nightclub he went to and certainly was seen on CCTV helping his friend home. Next, Niall Lynch has been seen in a pub near the University with Emily but states that he tried it on with her, was rejected and left it at that. He justifies it by saying he had an ill wife, and she is vouching for him on the evening in question. We have Emily being involved in a literacy group where Laura/ Lola was involved and she seems to have stayed to talk to this girl, who we have spoken to. She claims she did know Emily but that their conversation wasn't anything concerning and she has no idea why she was murdered. We have referred her to the relevant authorities to safeguard her.'

Ballantyne shook his head. 'I know but it doesn't feel right to not follow up on Lauren Jackson, young wee lassie like that, we can't just leave it.'

Taverner sighed. He sympathised with Ballantyne's view but on the other hand they couldn't get too distracted from their aim, to find Emily's murderer and it wasn't as though they had done nothing.

'I know what you mean. Lauren also has a social worker who will be checking out where she is living and with whom. We have no hard evidence of any concerns. And besides social services are the experts in this field.'

'Aye, but underage drinking and God knows what else. She's fourteen and was last seen in a pub!' muttered Ballantyne.

'We don't even know that. She could have been drinking coca cola for goodness sake...'

Ballantyne shrugged. It was unlike him to be so vehement, but then he had daughters of a similar age and no doubt had them in mind.

'So, any further information from the tech guy on Emily's laptop?'

Patel nodded. 'She was researching journalist roles and journalism jobs so perhaps she was intending to go into that area after her degree and there is her blog and the article she had done in draft. So, nothing other than The Geisha Club story.'

'What's it like, this club?' asked Taverner.

Haworth shrugged. 'The bar downstairs is popular with students, but it's t'private club upstairs that has the pole dancing, and what not,' he added. 'The owner is Mark Fenchurch and we've had a really good look at the place in previous investigations, but he's Teflon, alreight. To all intents and purposes, it's a late bar with dancing...' He shrugged. 'But there are rumours of much worse, drug dealing and prostitution. Usually there are objections from some of the other businesses in t'street every time the license comes up for

182

renewal. Every objection were checked out and they found nothing iffy, everything seems to be above board, and it's not for lack of trying.'

Taverner nodded. 'Well, we'll just have to go and have a look without a search warrant. Wildblood and I will do some sniffing about there. We can take photos of Emily and Lola and ask their clientele. That should put the wind up them. Anything else?'

Patel leafed through some papers. 'I'm still checking ANPR's for signs that Lynch and Charlton were in York city centre on the evening Emily was murdered. McAllister's alibi checks out, but it is still possible that he disappeared from Izzy's night club and went back to pick up his friend Mick later. The murder site is only twenty minutes or so walk away and the cameras peter out as you reach the river. Cullen and I are still checking the city centre CCTV.'

'What about Lynch's wife?' persisted Taverner. 'Did we check out Lynch's alibi?'

'His wife was at the hospital when I called but we are chasing her up,' added Cullen.

Taverner sighed. It was just so frustrating; everything was coming to a dead end. He had really hoped to be able to find some solid evidence regarding The Geisha Club and go in there with a search warrant and all guns blazing. They would have the element of surprise and might be able to unearth something relevant. It was like all their lines of inquiry were disappearing fast, like New Year's resolutions by February.

'Right. Haworth, can you help Cullen and Patel? Come on everyone, the tide will change, and the murderer's luck will run out, it's bound to, law of averages.'

183

Wildblood was frowning and staring at the links board.

'Right, you ready?'

Wildblood agreed, but there was a marked lack of enthusiasm from his Sergeant. The mood of the entire team had plummeted, but he really needed Wildblood on board so she could motivate the other officers. She seemed to be struggling with her work/ home life balance but then again, she had been different ever since they'd talked about The Geisha Club. Perhaps it was something to do with that? Then he had a brainwave.

'Shall we call into Ma Baker's for a bacon sarnie on the way?'

Wildblood, he knew, could never resist the lure of a bacon sandwich. She had told him that she had been a vegetarian for a year before succumbing when her boyfriend, now husband, made her a cooked breakfast. It was the smell of bacon that did it, apparently. She grinned and it was like the sun peeping from behind a cloud.

'Now you're talking, guv.'

Taverner hoped to get Wildblood to open up. They chatted en route in a desultory way about inconsequential things. Taverner really hoped his Sergeant would open up about what was bothering her as it seemed to be linked to discussions about The Geisha Club.

Chapter 20

'So, what's the story?' Taverner bit into his sandwich under the bright lights of the local greasy spoon, Ma Baker's, with its gingham plastic tablecloths and artificial forlorn looking flowers and watched his colleague.

Wildblood chewed her sandwich and then sipped her coffee. 'I don't know what you mean.'

Taverner raised an eyebrow. 'Well, you've been moody and a bit strange ever since we've been looking more closely at The Geisha Club. You've obviously had a lot of dealings with the place from what Haworth said. Is there something you're not telling me?'

Wildblood shook her head. She could have sworn that she had kept a poker face, but obviously not. She took a deep breath. She'd had some cases that she still felt bad about, when the police tried to do the right thing but for various reasons the legal case collapsed. It was a part of the job, she supposed, but this case had really got to her, because a dangerous and manipulative criminal had walked free, despite her best efforts.

'OK. I worked on a domestic violence case, where we suspected that the girl was being controlled by her boyfriend who was more like a pimp. He was Fenchurch's right-hand man, a chap called Wayne Davison. He had previous for drug dealing and was suspected

185

of living off immoral earnings running a range of girls who worked at the Geisha Club, but Fenchurch was the brains behind the operation.'

'And…?'

'It didn't end well. Mandy was going to be a witness in Wayne's trial, but in the end was too scared and did a runner, so Davison got off scot free. We offered her witness protection, of course…'

Taverner sipped his Earl Grey tea and studied her.

'Hmm, anything else.' There was a long pause as Anna wondered how much to tell him. She still felt uneasy about Rob and what happened on his night out with John Armitage, but it might help her to talk about it. Taverner was watching her, he invited confidences somehow and the need to unburden herself was irresistible.

'Rob was asked to be Fenchurch's accountant. When he met John Armitage and stayed out all night, I found a Geisha Club card in his pocket and that's when he told me.'

'Has he been there?'

Wildblood shrugged. 'He said not, and I believe him. I did warn him off Fenchurch without going into too much detail, so that's it, I suppose.' She realised as soon as she had articulated the words that she did believe Rob, of course she did. But it was hard when her work and private life collided.

Taverner drained his cup and studied her. 'Look, we can't save the world in this job, you know that. You just have to chip away and be happy with the cases we can prosecute. I'm sure you did everything that you could for Mandy, Anna.'

Anna shrugged. That was the thing, she didn't feel she had. The woman had confided in her about all sorts of shit, the manipulation, the alcohol and drugs, Davison had used to get her hooked and then how he had used the debt to force her to work for him. Mandy had been worried about witness protection and she felt that she should have pushed it much harder. She often wondered what had happened to Mandy and suspected that she was probably still working for Davison in order to get her heroin fix. Davison had clearly terrified the woman and likely threatened serious harm to her and her family if she testified. She shook her head and tried to rid herself of her gloomy thoughts.

'If there is a link between Emily and the Geisha Club then that really won't be any comfort at all.'

'Do you think there is?'

Anna shook her head. 'I'm not sure, but it is possible.'

Taverner stood up ready to leave. 'Well, we're never going to find out anything out sitting here, are we? I would have liked to have steamed in there with a search warrant but it's not going to happen. So, why don't we go there? How about I do the talking, you have a nose round and talk to the staff and the dancers and see what's what.'

He made it sound so easy that Wildblood found herself nodding.

'I'll deal with Davison if he's there, if that's what you're worried about.'

It was, sort of, combined with the deep and abiding sense of failure she always felt when she knew one of the bad guys had got away. Wayne was clearly one of those, he was just so thoroughly obnoxious and had taken great delight in rubbing in the fact that the prosecution's chief witness had disappeared. Eventually, he had to trip up, so it was worth another try, surely?

Wildblood drained her cup and set it down on its saucer. 'OK, let's do it.'

The Geisha Club was situated on Mickelgate and was a four storey, old, whitewashed building nestled next to pubs, bars and restaurants. The students frequented this part of town and toured pubs in the Mickelgate run, a well-known student circuit. The club was built on the site of an old convent, which contrasted starkly with the hedonistic practices that were rumoured to take place in there now. The ground floor was a normal bar, pleasantly decorated with wooden floors, a stone fireplace, and a bar boasting thirty different types of gin, the usual draught beers and saki. There was a life size model of a geisha girl wearing a pale pink kimono decorated with dark red flowers, her hair was knotted up into a bun, her face painted white. Wildblood was struck by the fact that it was very similar to Maggie Malone's description. The model had a pale straw parasol which she held over one shoulder. There was melodic Japanese music tinkling in the background. The decor looked inviting and fresh. It also looked expensive. Business was booming, she noted sourly. The place had a few people in, sipping drinks and reading the lunch menu. There was a young girl with her dark hair in a high ponytail behind the bar who smiled as Taverner approached. She changed her expression and swallowed nervously when Taverner got his warrant card out.

'DI Taverner and DS Wildblood to see Mr Fenchurch please.'

'He's upstairs, I'll just go and get him.' The girl scurried off.

Wildblood had photos of Emily and Lauren Jackson in her bag ready to produce them to customers, once Fenchurch agreed. Of course, detectives had already been to the bar but this time, Taverner

188

had wanted to get a feel for the place himself and whilst they were there, it would do no harm to ask about Lauren.

Mark Fenchurch was smartly dressed in a navy suit, brown shoes, neatly cut blond hair and impeccable manners. Wildblood was curious to see him again. The case with Mandy was some three years ago, but he was wearing well and looked little changed since their last encounter. Who said crime didn't pay?

'DI Taverner, DC Wildblood, what can I do for you?'

Anna straightened her shoulders and took a little satisfaction in stating.

'It's Detective *Sergeant* Wildblood now.'

Fenchurch merely smiled. 'Can I get either of you a drink?' They both shook their heads. 'What can I do for you? I presume it's about the murder of that poor girl. I have already given a statement to your officers.'

Taverner nodded. 'Yes, you have, but we still have some questions. Would you mind if my Sergeant showed some photos of Emily and another girl we are interested in, Lauren Jackson, round to you and your customers?'

Fenchurch gave a slight nod.

Wildblood spread the photos on the bar. Fenchurch looked at them closely.

'Do you know either of these girls?'

His face gave nothing away. 'No, I can't say I do. 'He pointed at Lauren's photo which was one of her in her school shirt wearing minimal makeup. She looked heartbreakingly young. 'That girl is certainly not old enough to be in licensed premises and as you very

189

well know, we ID everyone and have very strict policies, no exceptions. But please, feel free to ask away.'

Wildblood spotted a group of people drinking coffee near the windows and went over to talk to them, whilst Taverner went through Fenchurch's statement. She had noticed that the boss had a memory like an elephant which would really help in these situations. She showed the girls her warrant card.

'Mind if I ask you some questions? We are investigating some serious crimes.' She placed the photo of Emily on the table. 'Were any of you here on the night of 6th November and if so, did you see this girl on that date?'

The girls looked closely. A blonde girl with heavy eyebrows and not nearly enough clothes for the weather nudged her friends. 'Hey, that's the girl what was murdered, isn't it? Found in the river, wasn't she?'

They waited until Wildblood had explained that the photo was indeed of the dead girl before the blonde girl added that they were day trippers shopping for clothes for their friend's wedding. They had travelled from nearby Wetherby. It was near enough for them to have heard about Emily, she supposed, but she was irritated that they hadn't said that from the outset. Wildblood nodded and didn't even bother to get Lauren's photo out of the envelope. After she had gone through the same routine four more times and drawn a blank, she turned back to Taverner who took his cue from her disconsolate expression.

'Is it OK if me and DS Wildblood go upstairs to talk to staff and clients in the Gentlemen's Club?'

For a second a flash of irritation transformed Fenchurch's face, then he smiled.

'Of course, I'll show you around myself though there'll just be cleaners up there at this hour.'

Taverner met Wildblood's eye and they followed through a locked door at the rear of the property and up a staircase into The Geisha Club proper.

Again, Wildblood noticed that the decor had been updated and was of a very high quality. There was delicate sprigged wallpaper on the walls, luxurious flooring, a very realistic looking cherry tree, complete with blossom and a further Geisha model by the door, similar to the one downstairs, welcoming customers with an uncertain smile. Business was clearly booming. Upstairs there was a large room with subdued lighting, a dance floor complete with poles and cages and seating arrangements. There was a large mural of a dragon painted on one wall. It was red and gold, fiery and very intricate. At the side of the room was a large bar.

'The girls take centre stage and dance here as you can see. There is a dressing room for them over there. We take good care of our dancers and have strict policies about no touching, of course.'

Taverner nodded. 'Do you have an employee list available?'

'Of course, I can get you that. Our girls are all checked in terms of age and have to bring in their birth certificates to verify they are all over eighteen. We do run a tight ship here and their welfare is paramount.'

Wildblood very much doubted this and resisted the urge to say more.

191

'Can we look in the dressing rooms?' she asked.

'Of course.' Fenchurch led them to two rooms with large mirrors and dressing tables. There were baskets of makeup piled high, hairpieces and underwear, in straw baskets.

Opposite the two doors there was a row of small stalls with curtains covering each entrance. There were a couple of chairs, a table and a mirror in each stall.

'What are these?' asked Taverner.

'Individual changing cubicles. We sometimes have dancers who change outfits very quickly so they can use these.' Wildblood noticed that there were locked cupboards in the rear of each compartment.

'Can we have a look in those cupboards?' she asked.

Fenchurch shook his head. 'Each girl has their own key. They store their own costumes and props in them. You'll have to come back when we're open if you want to look inside. It's all harmless stuff, of course.'

Wildblood found this very hard to believe. She could think of lots of uses the cubicles could be put to, including entertaining clients who wanted more than just dancing.

Taverner had a good look round. 'There are four floors to the building, what's upstairs?'

Fenchurch smiled. 'There's the flat for my manager, Mr Davison.'

'It must be very large,' added Taverner amiably enough.

'Oh, yes. He has plenty of space.'

'And the floor above that?' persisted Wildblood.

192

'Storage, no one goes up there,' added Fenchurch smoothly. 'Now. I'll get you that employee list from the office downstairs.'

He spread out his arms, as if herding them out of the way. Wildblood wondered if Taverner had been going to insist on seeing upstairs, but in the end he turned back. A few minutes later, Fenchurch had handed them a typed employee list, and wished them success in their investigations.

'Bloody bastard,' muttered Wildblood as they walked out into the cool November afternoon. 'All that guff about employee welfare. What a load of bollocks!' She nodded at the list Taverner was still holding. 'Bet that's a load of crap too.'

Taverner sighed. 'I know, I know but we have nothing to justify a more in-depth search of the property and no link to Emily apart from the fact that she drank there as a student. Yet she clearly knew something about what was going on here.'

Wildblood knew he was right, but it was just so frustrating. The whole investigation was stalling, all their carefully followed up leads had headed to no man's land.

Taverner was looking exasperated at the lack of progress and peered at the shops in the street particularly the one either side of the Geisha Club. These were a coffee shop to one side and a gift shop on the other.

He sighed. 'Shall we just pop into the shops either side and see if they know the girls?'

Wildblood shrugged. She didn't see the point but was prepared to try to salvage something from their abortive day.

'OK, why not.'

The gift shop staff sold a large range of items, mugs, glassware, jewellery, paintings and mini replicas of the Minster along with 'I love York' items. There was even Yorkshire tea, tea towels and phrase books translating typical Yorkshire sayings. Strange because the staff were Eastern European and spoke broken English.

'We are the police. Can I ask if you have seen either of these girls?' said Wildblood.

The blonde haired woman behind the counter frowned and studied the photos. She shrugged theatrically. 'I not know them,' she added in a heavy accent.

'Is there anyone else who works here?'

The woman held up her finger. 'One only, she start today.'

'OK, thanks. We'll leave you to it then.'

So much for that. They made their way to the building at the other side of The Geisha Club, without much expectation.

'We may as well pop in whilst we're here,' added Taverner.

The coffee shop was pleasantly decorated and served a vast array of teas and coffees and the huge range of cakes including iced Yorkshire puddings of all things. The young woman behind the counter beamed at Taverner, frowning with concern when she saw the warrant card. She was in her mid-twenties and had sharp eyes that took everything in. She studied the photos carefully.

'That's the girl who was murdered, isn't it?'

'Yes, we're just wondering if you have seen her or this girl in the area over the last few weeks,' continued Taverner.

194

The girl studied the photo of Lauren carefully. 'OK. No, I haven't seen either of them around here. I only know Emily from the news.'

'Do you get any hassle from next door?' asked Wildblood conversationally.

The girl laughed. 'Not really, we close at seven most evenings, so they don't bother us. That is the least of our worries.'

'What do you mean?'

The girl leaned forward conspiratorially, clearly delighted to have someone to talk to.

'Well, the place is haunted, you see.' She took in the sceptical expressions of the faces in front of her. 'No, really, it is.'

Taverner nodded, deciding to go along with the conversation. 'So, what form does the haunting take?'

The girl suddenly became very animated. 'Oh, I think it's a poltergeist, it moves things, bangs about upstairs and generally makes a nuisance of itself. We've had a vicar out to do an exorcism a couple of times, but it didn't do any good. The boss even got this psychic person in. She was dead cool, said the spirits were just restless. It doesn't really bother me though, I don't feel scared, it's just annoying.'

Taverner raised an eyebrow. 'Maggie Malone by any chance?' He was rewarded with a nod. 'Thought so. I would imagine it might be hard to recruit staff because of it. I mean other people might not be as brave as you are.'

The girl beamed. 'Yes, that's true. I'm very interested in the paranormal and stuff like that and it's quite good for trade, though. We do get all sorts in wanting to see the ghost. It's believed to be the

195

spirit of a man called Black Jack who was murdered by a thief and had his throat cut in the sixteenth century.'

'Really?' Taverner's lips were twitching. 'Right. Well, thanks for your time anyway,' he paused. 'Can we have a couple of coffees?'

They waited at a table for their coffees to be brought over. Wildblood's back was rigid with fury. 'Bloody hell. What a waste of time. No leads on Emily or Lauren, but we find the ghost of a murdered man instead! Black Jack! Christ almighty! Whatever next? I felt sure we'd get somewhere next door too!'

Taverner guffawed. 'Well, you've got to admit it's quite funny. I suppose York is full of ghosts and ghouls. I might go on one of the ghost walks, they look really interesting.' He absently picked up a leaflet of local tourist attractions and looked through them.

Wildblood gave him a tight smile 'OK. You win, I suppose it is funny. But seriously though, we're getting nowhere fast. Let's have this coffee and go back to the office.'

Wildblood disconsolately put the photos back into the envelope she had placed them in. By mistake she had also put in a photo of Niall Lynch. The girl bought their coffees over and saw the photo of Niall just as Wildblood was shoving it back into the envelope.

'Now, him I do know.'

'Really?' Wildblood was stunned.

'Yeah. I studied English at Uni and he was one of the lecturers.'

Taverner smiled politely and took a sip of coffee. York was quite a small place, so it was no real surprise that she had studied at the University. Wildblood wondered at her working in a coffee shop afterwards. Degrees didn't seem to be worth anything these days it seemed.

'I'm doing a Masters now, so I'm here less,' the girl explained. 'But I have seen him a lot. He probably doesn't remember me, but he comes in for a coffee at least once a week before going next door.'

'Oh, so he's a regular at The Geisha Club, is he?'

The girl laughed. 'Yes, I think he goes upstairs to the Gentlemen's Club, though I'm sure it's just a strip place, actually.'

Taverner looked at Wildblood. Now this was much more interesting. He looked around the place. It was a quiet afternoon business wise so there was no one to overhear.

'Let me buy you a drink and you can sit down and tell us all about it,' said Taverner pulling out a chair.

Ten minutes later, the girl, Rachel, had served them all a drink and they were sitting at a table by the window.

'Oh, yer see all sorts in here,' explained Rachel, after introducing herself. 'If yer keep your eyes and ears open, yer make all sorts of connections.'

'What sort of connections?' asked Taverner.

'Well, I worked out that Dr Lynch likes strip joints and God knows what else. He waits here, desperate for the place to open. He were a bit of a letch at Uni, but strip joints and prostitutes, I never thought he'd be into all that and he's not the only one. Lots of fellas come in here waiting for the place to open.'

'Is there anyone else you have noticed coming in here a lot? Perhaps, you could describe them?'

197

'Oh, it's mainly sad old gits whose wives don't understand them.' Rachel rolled her eyes. 'Apart from that well-known businessman, what's his name, you know. He does a lot of charity stuff too. I were surprised to see 'im! He's often waiting for a girl and he sometimes comes in here with her. I haven't seen him go in there, but she works there, I'm sure.'

Taverner and Wildblood looked at each other. Wildblood had a sinking feeling and pulled out her phone and tapped away on it. A photo came up and she showed it to the girl.

Rachel nodded. 'That's him, dirty old sod.'

Wildblood paled and showed the photo to Taverner. He frowned.

'Who is it?'

'Armitage, it's John Armitage.'

Wildblood brooded as she negotiated the traffic back to the station.

'So, if Emily was onto Lynch's little secret, that wouldn't go down well with his wife, would it?'

'No, probably not.' She couldn't get the image of the Geisha Club card she had found in Rob's pocket out of her head and the thought of John Armitage. His friendship with Rob was a major concern, more especially if he was into strip clubs. Jesus!

'And John Armitage? You'd have thought he'd have had more sense, someone in his position. What does he do again?'

'He's a haulier but has lots of other businesses. Property mainly and is involved with charities. Rob does some of his accounts and he hopes he will get him more business. They're quite matey.'

'Oh, yes. Rob stayed at his house, didn't he?'

Wildblood scowled. 'Yes, and he's the one who gave us the Paris tickets and wants us to go out with them. He even suggested Rob work for Fenchurch, but I warned him off.'

Taverner studied her carefully. 'Well, maybe he uses the place as a sort of corporate hospitality venue.'

Wildblood frowned at the thought. 'Yes, you're probably right.'

'But we've been through the Mark Fenchurch files and they're as clean as a whistle and the club has recently got another license through. As you know the licensing folks have been over the application minutely.'

Taverner picked up on Wildblood's mood. 'Look, if you're so bothered about Armitage and his influence on Rob then sometimes it's best to face things head on. Armitage might let slip something about the place to Rob, or better still if you go to their place, you might have a snoop around. Sometimes, it's best to confront the enemy. Even if you don't find anything, you could warn Armitage off and let him know that you know what he's up to. That should dissuade him from trying to befriend Rob for his own ends.'

'Hmm.' Actually, that wasn't such a bad idea, thought Wildblood though she wasn't going to tell him that. It was interesting how Taverner picked up on nuances really well. She hadn't described Armitage's actions like that, but that was exactly how it felt. Perhaps, she ought to take the Armitages up on their next invitation?

'OK. I'll think about it, but none of this is going to help us with Emily's case. Let's get back to the station and find out what's what.'

Chapter 21

Back at the office, the first thing Taverner noticed was the odd atmosphere in the place. It was quiet too, eerily so. Ballantyne, seated at his desk working on the laptop, gave a barely perceptible half nod towards Taverner's office. The DI glanced inside and could see the bulk of Sykes through the glass window of the door. His stomach clenched. Trouble was afoot, he sensed it.

'Now Taverner, you seen this? Sykes' jowls shook as his fat finger prodded a folded copy of the local newspaper. Taverner sat down and scanned the headline, 'Spate of student drownings have police stumped!' The byline made him wince. 'Investigation stalls and parents demand action.' The piece was written by someone called Angie Curtis.

Taverner shook his head. 'I , I …' he stammered, ' It makes it sound like she's spoken to us, this Angie person but she hasn't…'

Sykes glared. 'No, but she's bloody well spoken to the parents and has started stirring. So, what have you got for me? How far off an arrest are we?'

Taverner felt the force of the man in front of him like a charging bull, his determination to do something, anything to get a conviction, but not necessarily the right one.

Before Taverner could reply Sykes frowned. 'I spoke to Ballantyne and tried to make sense of your ruddy links board and what do I bloody well find? You've got not one, not two but at least four bloody suspects.'

Taverner sighed. 'We're pursuing several lines of enquiry... I always think it's important to be flexible and look at all the evidence rationally.'

'Save it for the press. What I want to know is who's clearly in the frame? Surely, it has to be Charlton or Lynch. I want you to bring them in and bloody well have another go at them. Don't go off on some wild bloody goose chase about girls who are not even missing.' Clearly Ballantyne had told Sykes where they had been.

'Well, sir, we did find out that Lynch frequents the Geisha bar. I know Fenchurch has just got a new license for the place but we found a draft story Emily was working on for her new blog, suggesting that The Geisha Club was involved in the prostitution and trafficking of girls...'

Sykes looked momentarily interested. The force had been trying to get something on Fenchurch for years. 'Well, you can pass that on but it's Emily Morgan's death you're investigating. The Geisha Club is worthy of interest, but it needs a longer term strategy. We've had our fingers burnt there before. I have personally been through all the papers before their last license was granted and no matter how hard we looked, they were squeaky clean. Concentrate on Emily. Look, trust me on this Taverner, look at the men closest to her, especially the boyfriend, that's your starting place, believe me.'

'Sir, I'm not sure that Charlton is our man...'

'Lynch then, he's got form, he's got to be involved. And I want another appeal. Possibly a reconstruction. We need to do something, shake things up, right!'

Wildblood poked her head around the door. 'Sir, there's a journalist here. Angela Curtis.'

Sykes rolled his eyes. 'That is all we bloody well need! You deal with her, OK? And follow the protocol, don't mess it up!'

He charged out of the office in a filthy mood.

Taverner quickly filled Wildblood in and passed her the article. 'Anyway, what exactly does she want?'

Wildblood shrugged. 'Shall I come and talk to her with you? I've met her a time or two. Her bark is much worse than her bite actually.'

Taverner nodded in relief.

Angie reminded Taverner of one of those gothic girls you saw at Uni, the type who several years on, still wore the same black clothes and striking makeup. Angie was a bit like Georgia, his ex. Less fine boned but with neat features and a similar style. Her dark hair was cut in a blunt bob with a long fringe almost in her eyes and she wore a black skirt suit with a nipped in waist and red Mary Jane shoes with black heels. She stuck out a hand as Taverner introduced himself and smiled, showing sharp white teeth, rather like a shark.

'So, what can I do for you, Ms Curtis?'

Angie fixed him with an appraising stare. 'I can help you, contribute to the investigation, Inspector.' Her accent was rather refined.

'How do you mean?' asked Wildblood.

202

Angie wrestled a small pink cardboard folder from her bag and put it on the table in front of the detectives. She opened it and flicking through said, 'Five deaths by drowning, all students from York in the last couple of years. Mostly the students were too drunk to walk in straight lines, but there's one death that I think might be connected to Emily Morgan's.'

Taverner had read the files of the students recently, but only cursorily.

'In each case, the cause of death was ruled as misadventure, so unless you have new information, there's no case to answer.'

Wildblood studied the journalist thoughtfully.

'Which is the one you're not sure about?' asked Wildblood.

'Caitlyn Fear.'

Wildblood did not look surprised.

Angie watched them closely. 'I can see that the name means something to you. The fact it that DCI Sykes wouldn't recognise a murder unless he'd seen it with his own eyes. But what if I told you the parents have re-read Caitlyn's diary and feel like there was something funny going on with Caitlyn, something which might have led to her death ...'

'Then they should pass it on to us as new evidence.' Taverner sounded pompous even to his own ears.

'They have precisely zero faith in the police and will only talk to you if I'm present and also if you reopen the investigation, that's the deal...'

Taverner glared at her. Just who did this upstart journalist think she bloody well was?

'There is no case. As I said the verdict on Caitlyn's case was misadventure, so the case is closed. Now, if there's nothing else me and my DS have an investigation to run.'

Angie shrugged and dropped a small piece of card onto the table. 'That's my number for when you change your mind, and I'm sure you will. Ciao.' She gave a little wave and stalked off.

Taverner watched her leave and waited for Wildblood to comment.

'Guv, she has a point you know. Sykes was the investigating officer when Caitlyn was found three years ago. We never found anyone, and the inquest ruled misadventure. When I looked up those deaths, I noticed that her case was handled very poorly, the investigation left lots of stones unturned. It might be worth another look, you know…'

'OK, get onto the team and pass me the file.' He was kicking himself that he hadn't read every single detail on the drowning cases and has skipped to the conclusions without reading all aspects of the investigation, so he was not in a position to argue.

Patel appeared at this point, his expression animated. 'Sir, I have rechecked the ANPR information on the night in question. As you know we had no trace of Daniel Charlton's car being spotted on the route from Hull to York, but I have looked again, and we do have a record of his father's car being on the A63 at about 7 on that evening, but nothing further was seen after that. We are looking at York Park and Ride to see if he parked there and then came into the city on the bus.'

Taverner was suddenly alert, brain neurones firing. Supposing Daniel had borrowed his father's car to drive to York, gone to the Park and Ride and into the city centre? He knew that the Park and Ride buses ran until quite late. He and Emily could have had an argument, Daniel could have followed her, struck her with a wrench and dragged her into the river. This really was a game changer. Why would Daniel lie about coming to York unless he had something to hide? Their visit to The Geisha Club now seemed very naive, like a huge vanity project, chasing around after Lynch. Maybe he was losing it? He suddenly felt exhausted, as it meant that probably Sykes was right about Charlton after all

Chapter 22

Anna practically dragged her limbs over her front door, almost staggering with fatigue. She was looking forward to a quiet night in and some much needed rest and relaxation. She had stayed late whilst the team planned their strategy for interviewing Daniel Charlton. All her instincts screamed at her that he wasn't their man, but she knew where instincts sometimes led you, up a blind alley, that was where. She knew they had to follow the evidence first and foremost. Taverner said as much often enough but then a lot of police work was about ruling people out of their inquiries and focusing on who was left.

Rob handed her a cup of strong Yorkshire tea and busied himself with doling out the macaroni cheese and tomatoes.

'Boys both fine, they went out like a light. Mum said they'd had a busy morning at playgroup. Jasper was dying to get there early, he wanted to bag the policeman's uniform from the dressing up box, bless. Chip off the old block, right?'

Anna smiled but then her mind wandered off, thinking it should be her who dropped them off at the playgroup, her who knew which dressing up outfits they were looking forward to playing with. Still, when the case was over, she'd take some leave, take them to playgroup, meet the other mums, to stop herself from feeling like a total social pariah and inadequate mother. She scooped up the cheesy mixture that Rob removed from the oven and breathed in the warm, inviting aroma. Christ, she was bloody starving as well as shattered.

'So, how's the case going?'

Anna sighed and explained about Sykes' bollocking, Taverner's moods and the journalist's article.

'I'm going through the files just in case we missed something the first time. I'll just have a quick look at this.'

Rob shook his head. 'What you need is a holiday and I have just the thing. Do you know John has told me we can use his apartment in the Algarve anytime? You, me and the boys can jet off just as soon as you've sorted this case out. What do you think, love?'

Anna eyed her husband and seeing his hopeful expression decided to be kind. She really didn't want an argument about this now. 'Fab, brill, can't wait.'

But she knew somehow that it mustn't happen. The police didn't take favours off people, whoever they were. It compromised them and made them look vulnerable and subject to bribery. What was it the Mafia called it, compremat? Compromising material, that was it. Accepting a holiday from John Armitage, a rich and influential man, could easily look like that. Armed with another rich brew and somewhat revived, Anna flipped through the file on the investigation of the death of Caitlyn Fear. These days the force was largely paperless, with files and evidence scanned on to computers which could be accessed on an iPad, but this had happened fairly recently and there was a backlog. Caitlyn's file had only just been scanned. Anna took a sip of strong tea and flicked through the documents, eyes roaming up and down the pages trying to locate vital information. She was, she knew, so used to skim reading that these days she barely read a book from cover to cover. Sometimes she even read the end and then flicked through trying to work out what various twists and turns the author had thrown in. So, Caitlyn had been a student too. Anna's eyes danced over the pages. The case had been before she moved to the York station, when she'd been a DC. She scanned a statement and blinked. Christ, how had they missed this? Caitlyn had been studying English and her tutor was none other than Niall Lynch. Taverner needed to see this. She was also concerned about who had looked through the files and missed such an obvious clue. Anna recalled it had been DC Cullen. She made a note to tell him tomorrow, it was too late today. And to go through the online files for the other student deaths just in case Cullen had missed anything else. If she wanted something doing properly, she reasoned, she might as well do it herself.

She discussed holidays with Rob and looked through some options on the laptop. God they were expensive! She had tried searching for offers, even self-catering was not that cheap. Since they had moved into the barn a huge percentage of their money went on their mortgage. They couldn't possibly a justify the expense. Still, it would be nice to go somewhere abroad, a combination of sightseeing and sun, but she knew though, that the boys would be just as happy in Skegness as anywhere else. She googled cottages in the UK and was surprised about the price of those too. Rob looked over at the laptop.

'We could always take John up on his offer.'

'Well, if we did, we'd have to pay for the apartment and even then, it just doesn't feel right.'

Rob studied her. 'I don't really see why you've got a problem with it. He is just trying to help a friend. John wants us to go around for a meal. He seems very keen to meet you properly.'

Remembering what Taverner had said, she fought the urge to reject the offer. This might be the opportunity she needed.

'Might be nice to go out for an evening actually. Take my mind off the job, at least. And we can talk about renting the apartment.'

Rob grinned. 'If you can manage it, then brilliant. I'll text Mum to see if she'll babysit, as long as it's not on a Friday.'

Immediately he was on his phone making arrangements.

It was on the tip of her tongue to change her mind, but if Armitage was dodgy, she could hint that she knew what he'd been up to with his covert visits to The Geisha Club and hopefully stop him in his tracks.

A minute or two later, Rob's phone beeped.

'Fantastic. John said come around tomorrow and Mum can look after the boys too, so it's a date.'

'Great. I can't wait.'

Anna joined Rob watching Gogglebox on TV. Weird how a show about people watching telly itself could make quite an interesting show in its own right, was her last thought before she dozed off. Work, TV and bed was all that she was good for these days, it seemed, though tomorrow would be different. She felt almost excited at the prospect of a night out, but she would need her eyes and ears open to make the most of her visit.

Next morning at the station Wildblood caught Taverner at his desk. He had a take-away coffee on the go and looked as if he'd been there for several hours already. Despite the early hour he was neat and well groomed but she could spot the dark violet rings of exhaustion under his eyes and the swarthy five o' clock shadow. It actually suited him.

'Mmm, you sure you even went home, guv?'

'Course. Couldn't sleep though. Something's been chasing around in my head. We've got Dan Charlton and his dad coming in at 10. I want to find out more about the alibi he gave Dan. When it was run through HOLMES there were a few inconsistencies, I'm afraid. I think old man Charlton might have been economical with the truth.'

'Listen guv, there's something else. I looked through Caitlyn Fear's file.'

He noticed her tone of voice and looked up, intent on what she might have to say. 'And what did you find?'

'Caitlyn was studying English at York Uni, and guess who her tutor was?'

'Niall bloody Lynch?'

'It provides a link doesn't it?'

Taverner sighed. 'Wasn't it Cullen's job to look through those old student drownings?' He looked angry, exasperated even.

'To be fair boss, I think she may have missed this one. It was waiting to be scanned online and this had only just happened. I believe there's a bit of a backlog…'

Wildblood had no idea why she was excusing Cullen, except she was young and somehow vulnerable. She reminded Anna of her little sister Lizzie. She had a bit of attitude that she suspected masked a lot of insecurities.

Taverner shrugged. 'So, what do you think the link is? Lynch tried it on with her, gave her extra tutorials? Maybe he had a fling with her and then got cold feet when she threatened to tell his wife, so he hurt her and made it look like a pissed student's accident, same as Emily?'

'Maybe. We'll have to speak to him again, though won't we?'

'Yes. Straight after the Charltons' interviews. I thought you and I could start off and then get Ballantyne to come in with more information and see how he reacts. If he's guilty and lied for his son, there will be tells won't there. Of course, he could have driven to York for some perfectly legitimate reason. I want you to swap with Ballantyne and watch his body language as we wave the photos around. Haworth and Patel can interview Dan again. Sound OK to you?'

Wildblood's mind was racing. 'What time was Charlton Senior's car seen coming into York, guv? Does it fit in?'

Taverner grinned. 'Well sort of. Patel's running off the times from the ANPR as we speak. Trouble is the CCTV at the park and ride was on the blink, so we have no way of knowing if Dan or his father actually came into York city centre. We have Charlton Senior's car spotted as far as fourteen miles away from the city by about 7 on the evening of Emily's death, so he could have been going there. Patel is trying to establish what time the car was driven back to East Riding, if it was. Haworth's been looking into the wrench situation.'

Wildblood recalled that the murder weapon was a large wrench, possibly from a set.

211

'He's going to check Charlton's set. Hey, it may even be in his car if we're lucky. Cullen's checking through all the recent sales from the local B and Q, checking who bought them. We've had something of a breakthrough in that it appears to be from a particular set and it's not that common a size and therefore unlikely to have been sold separately.'

Wildblood sighed. 'I bought Rob a set of those for his birthday…'

'Well, we'll see how good she is, if she spots the purchase. Christ, these young recruits, not sure how they're trained these days, are you?'

'She's a good enough cop, guv, she just needs time, she's just wet behind the ears.'

Taverner merely nodded and she went off to grab a cup of station coffee, checking first if Taverner needed another cup of Earl Grey. The others had mostly arrived by now. Haworth was regaling Ballantyne with the action from a boxing fight last night and Cullen was sitting at her monitor, looking efficient and rather frosty. Anna returned to Taverner's office, hoping to talk through the interview technique again. Her boss was on his phone and one look at his ashen face told her that the news from the other end of the line was serious.

He put down the phone and made his way into the main office, his expression grave.

'Listen, something awful has happened. Lauren Jackson has been found in an alleyway in York. Looks like she was stabbed. She's in hospital and hanging on, just…'

'What?' Anna sat down, her legs shaky and her breathing shallow. She suddenly felt sick and clammy. Christ, how terrible! She couldn't help but feel responsible because of their failure to identify Emily's murderer. Nausea threatened when she remembered how she had lost Lauren when she was supposed to be tailing her. She prayed that the girl would pull through.

Chapter 23

Taverner contacted the hospital about Lauren Jackson's condition and the circumstances around the stabbing. She had been found in an alleyway, off Stonegate in York City centre. The knife had punctured Lauren's lung and she had lost a lot of blood. She'd had surgery and was still in intensive care. Cullen and Haworth had been dispatched to the hospital and a uniformed officer had been drafted in to keep watch outside Lauren's hospital room, in case whoever had hurt her might come back and finish the job.

Taverner looked thoughtful. 'We'll get down there after we've interviewed Charlton and his father. Patel and Ballantyne are looking at CCTV footage. It could be a coincidence or perhaps someone was really trying to silence her?'

Wildblood frowned. 'God, it's sickening. I know one theory about stabbings in other cities is that it is a gang initiation so it could be random, but we haven't had many stabbings in York to date, so I reckon it could be to do with Emily. God, fancy someone stabbing a young, defenceless girl like that! What is the world coming to? Just hope she pulls through…'

'Hmm. Maybe she does know something and threatened to reveal all. Anyway, I suppose we'd better concentrate on the Charltons for now.'

Wildblood nodded, but realised that it was easier said than done.

They saw Daniel Charlton first but had Mr Charlton Senior waiting in another interview room on the other side of the station so that father and son could not confer.

Wildblood kicked off. 'Now then, Daniel. We just wanted to clear up some points from your original interview and ask you a few more questions.'

Daniel scowled at them. 'About what?'

Taverner leafed through Daniel's statement. 'You said that you went to the football match on Saturday, 6th November, and then went out for a drink and were back home by half past ten…'

'Yes. I've already told you. Why aren't you looking for the man that murdered Emily? My fucking girlfriend is dead and what are you doing? I thought I was here so you could fill me in on where the investigation was going, tell me about suspects, but instead all you're doing is going round and round with the same crap. Jesus Christ!'

Taverner gave him a stern look. 'Just answer the questions, Daniel.'

Daniel shook his head, irritated. 'Well, like I said, I went to the match and out with friends in Hull for a few drinks and came home for about half ten. That's it.'

'So, you didn't see Emily on that evening?'

Daniel gasped. 'No, of course not. I was in Hull, she was in York, I saw her the previous week. I've already told you.'

Taverner paused. 'And you drive a Citroen C1, registration DY10 DAN?'

215

'Yes.'

'Your father drives a Vauxhall Astra and your mother a Fiat Panda.'

'Yes, that's right. What of it?'

'Do you ever drive their cars?'

'Occasionally, I do. Why?'

'Did you drive either of those cars on the evening in question?'

'No, of course not.' He shook his head as anger bubbled. 'I've heard it all now.'

'Are you sure you didn't use one of the cars to drive to York?'

'I've just told you, no.'

'Then why was your father's Vauxhall Astra spotted at 19.10 driving along the A63 to York?'

Daniel shook his head. 'I have no idea. I certainly wasn't driving it and I don't care for the inference that I was. Anyway, I think you're making it up for your own amusement.'

Taverner glared at him. 'I can assure you we're not in the habit of making information up. So, what was your father's car doing heading towards York at that time in the evening?'

Daniel shrugged. 'Search me.'

Taverner had studied Daniel pretty closely. When he'd mentioned his father's car, he had momentarily appeared shocked. Did he know his father had gone out that evening? Was he hiding something? Quite possibly.

Mr Charlton Senior was well dressed and had an aura of confidence. He explained that he had been working in York, so it was easy enough to come into the station.

'So, how is the investigation going?' he asked. 'We are desperate to find out why Emily died. Daniel has been through hell and back and I can't imagine what Emily's parents are going through.'

'Well, we are pursuing various lines of inquiry at present. We are in the process of checking and rechecking statements and just wanted to clarify some things with you,' asked Taverner.

'OK.' Mr Charlton nodded warily.

'Can I just check with you what time Daniel arrived home after his night out on the evening in question.'

'Elevenish give or take a few minutes.'

Wildblood leaned forward. 'Are you sure, only you said 10.30 in your initial statement?'

Mr Charlton sighed. 'I think it was more elevenish. My wife and I never usually sleep until he comes in though we do go to bed. I stayed up later and remember looking at the clock when he came in and it was just about eleven, as I recall.'

Taverner nodded. 'Does Daniel ever drive your car?'

Mr Charlton looked confused. 'Very rarely but he has done sometimes. Why?'

'Did he use it on the evening of the 6th November?'

'No. Why would he?'

Wildblood took a deep breath. 'Because we have had a positive sighting of your vehicle on the A63 towards York on that evening. At 19.10 to be precise.'

217

Mr Charlton looked from one to the other. Eventually he answered.

'Well, that's easily explained. I went to visit a friend, a colleague from work, just popped in to give her a 'Get well' card. She's been off sick, you see. She lives just outside Pocklington, near York and as her line manager, I do have a duty of care to the staff I supervise.' He looked from one to the other. 'She has recently had a diagnosis of cancer, you see. We all had a bit of a whip round and I volunteered to take the card and gifts, that's all.'

Wildblood looked at Taverner. 'So, what is the name of this person and their address?'

'It's Karen Ellis and she lives off Main Street in Pocklington, 32 Scaife Garth. Ask her.'

Taverner rocked back on his chair in exasperation. 'We will, Mr Charlton. What I find very strange is that you never once mentioned this when officers went out to see you and when myself and DS Wildblood went through your statements. In fact, your wife said, 'we had a quiet night in watching Strictly and The X Factor.'

Mr Charlton straightened up. 'You asked my wife, but no one asked me, otherwise I would have told you. It's the wife that likes those bloody programmes and she told you that, not me.'

'So, your wife forgot that you went out?'

Charlton shrugged. 'She must have, there's nothing sinister behind it. You can check with Karen, like I said.'

Taverner felt fury surging through his veins, more especially since there was probably some truth in what he said about them not checking what both husband and wife said.

218

'Can I remind you that this is a murder investigation and you could be facing a charge of perjury by giving false information. Do I make myself clear?'

Mr Charlton stood up, unabashed. 'Perfectly and as it is a murder investigation then I suggest you get on and find out the real perpetrator instead of pulling holes in the statements of those who loved Emily best.'

In the car on the way to the crime scene where Lauren has been stabbed, they talked the case through.

'So, what did you make of Mr Charlton?'

'Hmm. He has something to hide. He could be covering for Daniel, but I wonder if there's more to his relationship with this Karen. It could be an oversight, or it may be that they didn't have time to get their act together. If Daniel killed Emily then I reckon his father knows something about it, but we need more evidence.'

'Daniel could have taken his dad's car without him knowing. Pocklington is not a million miles away from York, is it?'

Taverner pulled up at Stonegate to where the police cordon was situated.

'Daniel could have borrowed his dad's car and used the B roads from Pocklington to get to York, which would explain the lack of ANPR sightings after that. We need to go through the CCTV again to see if there's any sign of him following Emily on foot.' He nodded at the alley where SOCO staff were scouring the place. 'Come on. We'd best look lively.'

'Do you think the same person who killed Emily, attacked Lauren?' asked Wildblood as they stepped out into the cold November air.

'Could be.' Taverner found it hard to admit that he really had no idea. The case was floundering badly. There were plenty of suspects, he had no shortage of theories but little in the way of hard facts. Nothing concrete. He just prayed that if they kept digging, kept going, all would be revealed. All inquiries had their low spots, he knew from bitter experience. Their luck had to change, it just had to.

SOCO were all over the alleyway off Stonegate where Lauren had been found. The alley was dark, dank with a row of large bins to one corner and a couple of metal staircases that presumably led to flats above the shops on Stonegate. Blue and white police tape fluttered in the breeze. About three SOCO staff wearing white suits were combing through the area, gathering any evidence that they could find, searching for fingerprints and DNA. Taverner noticed a dark blood stain in the middle of the cordon and shivered. He flashed his warrant card at the uniformed police officer who was guarding the scene. Wildblood handed Taverner coveralls and they put them on.

'We're involved in a murder inquiry in which the victim was interviewed, so this could be a related attack. Is there anything of interest?'

The officer nodded towards several evidence bags in a box. Wildblood sifted through them. Taverner made a note of the contents; a cigarette butt, several discarded sweet packets, cans of coke, a condom which was filthy and looked like it had been there for several months, and a clean looking pink and white card with the familiar lettering. A Geisha Club card. Funny how The Geisha Club kept popping up at every touch and turn, yet they still couldn't pin anything on them.

At that point Taverner's phone rang.

'Great. We'll call in tomorrow to interview her.'

He turned to Wildblood to relay what he had been told. 'Lauren has been moved from intensive care and is now stable. She may be up to being interviewed tomorrow.'

'Brilliant, that's really good.'

Taverner sighed. 'I just hope she remembers what happened.'

His phone buzzed. It was a text message. He frowned as he read it.

'And Matt Lawson, the vicar, called into the office. He has remembered something about Emily and thinks it might be important.'

'Interesting. I wonder what?'

Taverner's mood lifted. Perhaps, all was not lost after all.

Chapter 24

Anna Wildblood wanted to scoff about ten doughnuts in one
go. She was absolutely starving and craving carbohydrates. She
always felt like this when she was tired and stressed. What the hell
was wrong with her? At this rate she would put on all the baby weight
that she'd lost during her maternity leave. It didn't help that
Ballantyne and Haworth were always eating. Cullen too, had brought
in a homemade carrot cake, it was brownies last week and a lovely
date and walnut the week before. It looked gorgeous, with a moist
texture and creamy icing on top. Anna wanted to stuff several pieces
in her mouth at once. Eating all her Weight Watchers points in one go,
was not the way to go. Damn. They had the meal arranged with the
Armitages tonight, so she didn't want to eat too much. Funny how
what seemed such a good idea last night now filled her with dread.
What was she thinking of?

Cullen frowned. 'Ballantyne said I owed a cake fine, so I
thought carrot cake is vaguely healthy. Well, it's got carrots in it. And
it's Ballantyne's favourite.'

Wildblood realised that she hadn't spoken to Cullen much,
tearing around as she usually was with Taverner. She tried to make
amends now whilst turning her back on the offending cake.

'So, how are you finding things here, OK?'

Cullen looked down. 'Yep mostly, I've been looking through CCTV with Raj.'

Wildblood remembered that that was Patel's first name.

'He's been really helpful…' Cullen blushed, and Anna was reminded how young she was, early twenties tops. So that's how it was, she thought. Cullen's interest in the boss had now shifted to her fellow officer. It wasn't Taverner she was trying to impress, but Patel. He was a good looking man but he was engaged too, as far as she knew. Some girl from India, if she remembered rightly. Was it an arranged marriage? Who knew but she made a mental note to keep an eye on the situation. Office romances were usually a very bad idea and the cultural and religious contexts potentially at play here made it a worrying development. Still, they were both adults, so she had better leave well alone, it was just that at times, she felt like everyone's bloody mother.

She sighed and went to make a cup of tea for Taverner before they went to speak to Matt Lawson who was waiting in one of the interview rooms for them.

Matt stood up as they entered.

'I'm pleased that you were offered a drink,' said Taverner. He was always almost ridiculously polite. 'Thanks for waiting. So, what is it you want to tell us?'

Wildblood sat down and watched as Lawson got out a pad. He consulted it, rather like a policeman reading from his notebook. She stifled those thoughts when she saw how serious Lawson was.

'I've been racking my brains trying to think what I could tell you that might shed any light at all on Emily's death.' His voice

223

wavered. 'I feel responsible, you see, and it has been playing on my mind. Then I remembered.'

Wildblood tried and failed to remember whether he was so upset when they'd first interviewed him. He hadn't been. But then of course he would have been in shock, now maybe they were seeing a more natural emotion but one which made her realise how close Lawson had felt to Emily Morgan. She must have mattered to him, else he wouldn't be here.

Taverner nodded. 'Oh good, so what have you got for us?'

Lawson sighed and went on, his voice thick with feeling. 'I think I told you that I work as a tour guide at the Minster. Well, a week before she died, I remember that Emily came into the Minster with a young man, presumably her boyfriend. I saw her said 'hello' and I just couldn't help but notice the way the man was with her. Emily looked utterly miserable, so different from her usual vibrant self. Then the next time I saw her, just a day or so later, I noticed that she had bruising to her left upper arm. I asked her what she had done, and she just said she'd hurt herself playing squash, but it looked very much like fingertip bruising to me.' He paused and looked from one to the other. 'I know it doesn't sound much but I remembered the incident and thought you ought to know.'

'When was this exactly?'

Matthew flicked through his diary. 'About four weeks ago now,' he showed them the page. 'Look, I made a note to speak to her about it.'

'And did you?'

'I did and like I said she insisted everything was fine.'

Taverner opened a folder and pulled out some photos, one of Daniel Charlton, another of Ross McAllister and finally one of Niall Lynch.

'I wonder if you could identify the man from these photos?'

Lawson nodded and instantly pointed at the photo of Daniel.

'That's him, I don't know that young man,' he added nodding at the photo of Ross McAllister, 'but that is Dr Lynch, of course. He also comes to the groups to talk about University and arrange tours for the kids. He liked to visit midway to sort of review the group and also at the end.'

Taverner felt Wildblood stiffen beside him.

Lawson hung his head. 'I wish I'd done more to intervene, I mean you hear about domestic violence, coercive control and all that. I wish to God I'd probed more, not accepted her answer, of course I do, it might have saved her…' A look of pure anguish crossed his face.

'Look, I don't really see what else you could have done in the circumstances,' Wildblood added kindly.

Lawson sighed and it was full of regret. 'It's nice of you to say so, but I should have done more now I think about it. I just presumed that they had had a row, but it could be an indication of much worse…'

Taverner stood up. 'Well, thank you so much for coming in. We'll bear in mind what you have said.'

'So, what did you think?' Wildblood asked, when Matthew had left.

225

'Interesting. He seemed sincere enough. It means that Dan could have a temper and could be capable of controlling behaviour, I suppose. But what was more interesting was Lynch's involvement with the group. He never mentioned he was actively involved or had visited at all.'

Wildblood nodded. 'My thoughts exactly. Why not mention it, unless of course, he has something to hide.' Her eyes widened and she suddenly thought of something. 'Maybe his sexual interests extend to much younger girls, perhaps even Lauren herself?'

An hour later Wildblood followed Taverner down the hospital corridor. They passed the Cheerful Sparrows ward where her gran had been when she fought and ultimately lost her final battle with cancer. It gave Wildblood icy shudders as she read the sign directing them to the cancer ward and marched on, head down, hands in pockets, reflecting that she bloody hated hospitals. The linoleum reeked of lemons mingled with bleach, it was boiling despite the cold weather outside and everyone looked stressed, anxious and depressed.

Lauren was in a small side ward. In bed she looked tiny and vulnerable. A uniformed nurse, her face drawn with exhaustion, had showed them into the room and now took vital measurements from the dials and machines attached to the slight, recumbent figure.

'Don't tire her, will you? 5 minutes maximum, OK? She's had a busy day what with her parents and that.'

Taverner eyed her and then smiled. '10? This is vital you know; we may be able to stop further attacks or even murders...'

His charm worked Wildblood noticed, as the nurse smiled and gave him a

226

slight nod. 'OK. I'll let you get on then.'

Wildblood sat down in the chair. She noticed Lauren's eyes open.

'Hello love, how are you doing?'

Lauren whispered, 'OK'.

'We just want to ask you a few questions, did you see who attacked you?' Taverner leaned over the bed.

Lauren shook her head, a tiny but definite movement.

Wildblood took the young woman's pale hand in hers. 'Any clue about gender, race, did they say anything? Anything you can tell us, anything at all...'

Lauren's pale blue eyes looked entreatingly into Wildblood's. 'I think I knew his voice, but I can't remember who it was...' Her eyes filled with tears which flowed sideways onto the white, hospital sheet. 'Every time I try to remember, I realise I just can't...'

'Now look what you've done,' said the nurse, who must have been hovering nearby. 'Can't have you upsetting my patient. Come back tomorrow or even after the weekend.'

Taverner reluctantly rose and Wildblood found herself power walking to keep up as he left, striding down the corridors.

'Hey up, guv, wait on...'

Taverner ran his fingers through his hair, his expression bleak. 'This investigation is a bloody nightmare, Anna. I feel totally stuck. Supposing we've missed something, and Lauren was stabbed as a result. I'll never forgive myself if someone else gets hurt.'

Wildblood touched his arm briefly. 'Look guv, get some proper rest, talk to Sykes, take a day or two off, it'll all keep. I think things might look different after a short break.'

227

'Hmm,' Taverner sounded dejected. 'Maybe you're right. Might pop down to see my old man.' He smiled. 'Sorry, I'm just feeling frustrated, that's all. Listen, you go off and have a nice weekend. Any plans?'

'Well, we're off to the Armitages actually, like you suggested. See, I do listen.'

He squeezed her arm. 'Great, keep your wits about you and enjoy yourself.'

'I will.'

The Armitages lived in an expensive area of York in a manor house set in several acres of garden with a long gravelled drive. It was early evening, but the house was lit up by lights which were situated at regular intervals along the driveway and the front door had carriage lamps on either side. The house was stone built, dated from the 17th century in parts and was built with delightful mullioned windows.

'Christ, look at the place. It's amazing. How the other half live, hey.'

Rob squeezed her hand. 'Hey, don't worry. John and Liz are really down to earth so it'll be grand.' He took in her sceptical expression. 'No, honestly, they are lovely.'

Anna wanted to tell him about what the girl in the cafe next to The Geisha Club had said but bit her lip. Anyone using the sexual services of vulnerable, possibly underage, possibly trafficked children, was not as 'lovely' as they appeared in her book.

'They said it will be a simple supper, nothing fancy. Is that OK?'

'Yes, absolutely.' Anna was exhausted from her day and managed to stifle a yawn. As Taverner had said, she needed to keep her wits about her. She had dressed in a pair of smart black trousers, had a cotton patterned top and heeled boots. She had added a squirt of La Vie Est Belle and worn her hair down and naturally curly. Her makeup was subtle and was designed to look like she hadn't tried too hard, except now having seen the house, she wondered if she should have made more effort.

'You look great, by the way,' added Rob. He always knew just what to say and her mood lifted. She could do this.

The door was opened by John Armitage who beamed at them.

'Come in, come in, come in.' He turned to Anna. 'I'm so glad you were able to come. It must be hard getting babysitters for your twins.'

'Rob's mum came to the rescue.' Anna looked appreciatively around her. 'You have a lovely home.'

'Thanks.' John was more casually dressed in cream chinos and a polo shirt and looked less well groomed than she remembered but younger and much more relaxed.

Anna had thought that the house was likely to be decorated in a tasteless and 'more money than sense' style, but she saw as he led them into a vast hallway with a huge staircase at the centre, that the house had been sympathetically renovated and the improvements were very much in keeping with the age of the place. The hall had wood panelling on the walls, stone flagged floors and vast rugs with dark oak furniture and even a full suit of armour standing in one corner. A

229

couple of greyhounds clattered lazily down the stone flagged hall to see the strangers, barking half heartedly.

'It's alright, Jupiter and Saturn, they're friends.'

The dogs sniffed at Rob and Anna and then reassured by their master, followed them. As they walked, Anna spotted a room with a slightly open door that looked like an office, with a downstairs toilet next door, as they made their way into the sitting room. It was large but homely with a huge inglenook fireplace, flagstone floor, red leather chesterfields and a baby grand piano at one end. The surface of the piano was covered in photographs and to the rear were French doors that led into the garden. There was a huge display of sweet scented, white lilies. Liz Armitage rose and smiled warmly at them.

'Come and sit down. It's great that you could come, Anna. We really didn't get to speak at the fundraiser. I've made a light supper which will be ready in about half an hour but before we eat, would you like a drink?'

Rob chose coke as he was driving, and Anna had red wine. Liz was dressed in elegant grey trousers and an asymmetric grey woollen jumper which set off her blonde bob and blue eyes beautifully. She also drank red wine and sat down next to Anna. Close up, it was clear that she was several years younger than her husband. John and Rob began talking about politics which left the two women on their own.

'So, tell me about your little boys? It must be hard having twins, double trouble. Are they identical?' asked Liz.

'No, they are non-identical but quite similar to look at, different in personality though.' The boys were Anna's favourite

230

subject, so she talked at length about them, their likes, dislikes and development.

Liz smiled. 'They sound adorable, they really do, though hard work I'm sure.' Something about her tone sounded rather wistful.

'Do you have any children?'

A shadow crossed over Liz's face. 'I am stepmother to John's son and daughter from his first marriage. His first wife died of cancer, so it's been very hard for the kids, well I say kids, Seb is at University now and Izzy is finding herself at present. John is a very good father though.' Liz smiled, another shadow passing over her face. Anna realised that everything was not as rosy as it may seem, there was a story here somewhere. Perhaps the children resented Liz as the wicked stepmother or Liz was keen to have children of her own. She estimated her to be a similar age to her, about mid thirties, so there was still time for her to have a family.

'And you're a police officer, how wonderful,' continued Liz. 'I don't know how you do it rushing around catching criminals and raising two small boys. Amazing. Are you working on any interesting cases at present?' There was a hush as John stopped to listen, his bright blue eyes watching Anna closely. 'Are you working on that murder case, the case where the student was found in the river?'

Anna nodded. 'I am actually, but obviously I can't say much, for operational reasons, you understand.'

'Of course,' replied Liz, her head inclined. 'I just hope you find the murderer, that poor girl. Dreadful.' Anna turned to find John still studying her.

'We are making progress,' she added, 'good progress.'

Liz smiled. 'I'm sure you are. I work at the University as a student counsellor and the students have been very upset and worried about the whole thing actually.'

'Oh, right. How long have you worked there?'

'Several years. I moved there from working for the NHS. That's how I met John actually through counselling the children.' She flashed her husband a smile. 'I didn't know Emily personally from my work there though''

Anna was quite taken aback. She hadn't realised that Liz had a job, an admirable one at that. Quite wrongly she'd assumed that Liz would spend her time on committees or something, dispensing largesse and being a lady of leisure. How wrong she was.

'Course there are lots of investigations going on in York at present. We deal with all sorts, drugs, organised crime, prostitution…' Anna couldn't help but add for John's benefit. 'Anyone preying on vulnerable young women or girls need to watch their backs.'

'I'm glad to hear it,' Liz replied.

Rob frowned. 'You'll have to excuse my wife. She's very passionate about her job.'

'Excellent,' said Liz smiling. John smiled, but Anna noticed that it was a smile that didn't quite reach his eyes.

'Another drink?' John asked. 'I don't know about you darling, but I'm feeling rather peckish. Anyone else?'

Liz smoothed down her hair. 'Of course. I'll pop into the kitchen.'

'Would you like a hand?' asked Anna.

'No, no. You stay and talk to the men. I won't be long.'

'So, I was talking to Rob about our apartment in the Algarve. You really must go there free of charge, of course.' John waved his hand away airily. 'It's absolutely beautiful near Praia de Rocha but a little off the beaten track, I'm sure your boys would love it.'

Anna smiled. 'That's very kind of you. It would have to be when I can get time off work and of course, I would insist that we pay the going rate.'

John raised his eyebrows in surprise. 'Really, there would be absolutely no need. It would be our pleasure, honestly.'

Anna was about to launch into an explanation about corruption in the police and how she had to be very careful, when she saw Rob looking rather uncomfortable. It might be easier to play along with John for now. Discretion was the better part of valour, after all.

She gave him what she thought was a winning smile. 'Thanks. That is very kind of you.'

They dined in the huge kitchen which had a red Aga, vast pine table and chairs. The walls had modern shaker style kitchen cabinets. There were two sets of French windows that looked out onto the garden, which was lit in parts with fairy lights and looked large and well cultivated. Anna peered out into the garden.

'Are you a gardener, Anna?' asked Liz.

'I'm learning. We didn't have much space in our old house, but we have a larger one now so we're getting into it.'

'I have a herb garden and a few rare roses but John grows loads of vegetables.'

'It is rather relaxing and very grounding,' added John.

'You'll have to teach Rob. He tried to grow potatoes and carrots in our last house.'

'Try being the operative word,' Rob said wryly. 'It was a total disaster. We ended up with four dwarf carrots and a handful of tiny potatoes. We'd have starved if we relied on that meagre offering.'

They tucked into steak in a pepper sauce, new potatoes and salad, served with crusty bread and lots of red wine. The food was absolutely delicious and all homemade, even the bread.

'It's really easy to make actually, you just have to get the proving right,' added Liz. 'I'll give you the recipe.'

Was there anything that this woman couldn't do? And she had a worthy job too. It made John's betrayal by his visits to the Geisha club all the more awful. What on earth was he thinking?

When they had eaten lemon meringue pie, delicious, of course, Anna made her move, as soon as John had topped up her wine glass, she took a sip and clumsily tipped some down her top.

'Oh, damn. I must have missed my mouth. I'm so clumsy.' She clambered to her feet. 'Just point me in the direction of your loo and I'll clean up. I'm so sorry.'

'Down the hall, second on the left,' replied Liz.

Anna staggered about a bit, as though more tipsy than she was and dived down the corridor to the bathroom, quickly dabbed at her top and removed the worst of the wine stain, came out stealthily and entered the next door on the right. She turned on her phone's torch and shone it around. She felt momentarily triumphant as she realised that she had been right, this was an office. There was an old oak desk to one side, several metal filing cabinets, an armchair, bizarrely another suit of armour and a large cast iron fireplace. She quickly pulled out her plastic gloves and began to have a root about, starting with the desk. She found a large desk diary with various appointments written in what she presumed was John's angular handwriting, several invoices for household items, letters to Max and Josie, friends she presumed, several gold envelopes still containing their prizes from the Domus fundraiser, birthday and Father's Day cards from Sebastian and Izzy, going way back from when they were tiny, signed with hesitant and barely formed letters, and bank statements for the personal account of Mr J and E Armitage. The account had the best part of fifty thousand pounds in it. On the top of the desk were silver framed photos of a stunning young woman, who judging by the dated clothing and hair, was the first Mrs Armitage, and several more of the same woman flanked by two young children, the boy with a toothy grin wearing a football kit and a girl, blonde and angelic, who looked just like her mother. There were more showing the two children in various developmental stages, the son as a teenager with the beginnings of acne and a shy smile, the daughter blooming into a beautiful young woman, pictured laughing with friends looking self consciously chic in a strapless red dress and high heels. Anna felt a spasm of guilt about her own actions, then remembered that John had links to The Geisha Club, so she was right to be suspicious of him. She quickly resumed her search through the contents of the desk drawers. Suddenly she heard the clatter of dog claws on the flagstones and the muffled sound of someone shouting her. Her heart began to race as hastily she removed her gloves, smoothed down her hair and peered into the corridor. It was empty except for one of the greyhounds and as she exited the room, Liz came into view. Thank

God it was such a large house otherwise she would certainly have been discovered. She took a deep breath.

'Ah, there you are. Do you need a hand?' Liz nodded at the wet patch on Anna's top. 'I can always find you something to wear and pop it in the wash for you. We have a delicates cycle that works really well.'

Anna smiled. 'No, no, thank you, you're very kind, but I think it will be fine. I've removed the worst of the stain.'

Liz smiled. 'Well, as long as you're sure. We've moved onto coffee and liqueurs and we have a cheeseboard if you're still hungry.'

'Great, that would be wonderful.'

A few hours later when they had eaten more desserts and drank several liqueurs, they settled back down in the sitting room. Anna was starting to relax as she was sure that she had avoided detection. She still hadn't found anything untoward out about the Armitages and she was beginning to think that she wasn't going to. She relaxed and started to talk more openly to Liz.

'So, it must be hard being a stepmother? How did you find it?'

Liz nodded. 'It was, at first. There were a lot of challenges, there still are actually.'

'Oh, I'd have thought that things would have improved over time.'

Liz glanced at her husband and Anna had the distinct feeling that she was checking out with John how much to say. 'They did for a while…' John was talking about business rates with Rob but paused to listen to their conversation.

'I was just telling Anna about the kids…'

A strained look crossed John's face. 'Well, they're adults now. Seb's at Uni and having a whale of a time but doing well and Izzy, well, we're struggling with her.'

'How old are they?'

'Seb's twenty and Izzy is eighteen,' replied John.

'I suppose Izzy will go to Uni too,' suggested Rob. 'Has she done her 'A' levels? I bet she's undecided about what subject to take. It's always hard to make these decisions.'

John shook his head and grimaced. 'I wish. She spends a lot of time with her boyfriend and isn't even thinking about her career.'

His expression clearly said it all.

'You don't approve of her boyfriend?' asked Anna.

'That is an understatement and what is worse, I suspect he knocks her about…' He ran his fingers through his hair in an abstracted manner. 'She denies it, of course, but there are just too many injuries.'

Anna had worked with victims of domestic violence many times and knew how hard it was for victims to stand back and gain some perspective on what was happening. The effects were so subtle to start with that it was easy to get drawn in. She was also aware that the greatest risk to the victim was when they had decided to leave the perpetrator.

'You could always report your concerns to the police. We have specialist staff who can support her.'

237

Anna fished out a pen from her handbag and a post-it note. She scribbled the name and phone number of the Domestic Violence Team on the back of it and handed it to John.

'Trust me, they can really help.'

John took the paper and put it in his pocket. He swallowed hard, a look of pure anguish on his face.

'But that's not all, her boyfriend is involved in that bar, The Geisha Club. I know Mark Fenchurch slightly. He seemed OK at first. I even suggested Rob work for him but the more I've looked into the place, the more rumours come to the fore.'

Anna nodded, anticipating what was coming and felt incredibly guilty.

'I'm her father, for God's sake, and yet she is an adult and I can't do anything to protect her.' His face flushed with anger. 'God, it was all that time building the business and being away from home when she was little, letting their mother, Livvy, deal with it all. I keep trying to talk to her now but it's no good. It's no wonder she took up with such a low life…'

A horrible sense of foreboding gripped Anna. 'Does this man have a name?'

John looked at her. 'It's Wayne, Wayne Davison.'

Anna struggled to compose her face into a neutral expression like an actor at an awards ceremony hearing that they had just lost out on an accolade. It was a name she knew only too well. Suddenly John's presence at The Geisha Club made perfect sense. He was simply trying to contact his daughter who was in great danger. Shame oozed over her. She had got things so badly wrong.

'Do you know him?' John asked.

She didn't trust herself to answer.

'You need to ring the team as soon as possible and tell them you've told me. Promise me you'll do it tomorrow.'

John looked alarmed. 'I will, I definitely will.'

Chapter 25

Taverner turned on the kettle and once boiled mashed the tea bags, Earl Grey for them both. They had been introduced to the delicately flavoured tea by Taverner's mother, Helen, who had loved the stuff. He poured in the milk, a mere splash and handed a mug to his father, Lawrence. Taverner had come down to visit his father for the weekend, a visit he longed for and dreaded in equal measure. Home was a detached large thirties house, in a leafy, affluent street in Deal, a quiet coastal town in Kent where the family had moved after Taverner was released from Chelsea which coincided with his father retiring. The house was little changed, his father had tried to spruce the place up with a lick of paint and the long garden was still full of plants. The place smelt vaguely of polish but seemed strangely flat, his father greyer and more lined than when he had last seen him, and he appeared to have shrunk. Even their Springer Spaniel, Charlie, was quieter and less exuberant than he used to be. His mother, Helen, had died just over two years ago now from cancer and it seemed the lifeblood had ebbed out of the place. It had been a horrible time for them both, heartbreaking to watch his mother's bubbly, extravagant character gradually dim, as the cancer ravaged her body. Initially she had showed signs of beating the bowel cancer which she eventually died from, and her determinedly cheerful attitude towards her illness, made her death all the more unbearable. Then, Taverner had separated from his fiancée and had work problems at the Met after he had been injured. They say that bad things come in threes and that was certainly true in his case as he had been stabbed at work. Then the job had come up in North Yorkshire and he had felt a fresh start was in order. His father had really encouraged him to go too, so he had, but it didn't stop him feeling guilty. His father was a retired banker and had adjusted after the crushing blow of the death of his wife of thirty years, had many friends locally and was a stalwart of the local tennis and cricket clubs, so seemed to be doing well. Taverner had to admit the move to North Yorkshire had appealed to him because he knew his birth mother was from York. Initially, it had felt more like a feeling of belonging that drew him to the area and then almost imperceptibly the feeling had grown into a desire to meet the woman who gave birth to him.

His father sipped his tea and studied his son closely.

'You look tired, Gabriel. I hope you're not working too hard.'

'Well, I'm working on a murder case and a stabbing that may be linked, so it will be nose to the grindstone until we get a result.'

His father nodded. 'Ah, the student that was murdered in the city. I read about that. Damned tragedy for all concerned. Who are your suspects?'

'Several men she knew. There's rather too many suspects actually, but we're struggling to get hold of anything concrete on any of them.'

'Well, just keep going. Remember what Churchill said, 'it's the darkest hour before the dawn.'' Lawrence took another sip of his drink. 'So, are you enjoying York?'

'Yes. It's a beautiful city and my team at work are good people. I've had some ribbing for being a Southerner, but things have been going well. They are actually a good bunch.' Taverner swallowed hard. He needed to get something off his chest. 'You know I spoke about getting in touch with my birth mother, well, I have heard from the Agency and I have asked them to seek her out with a view to meeting up, probably after we've made headway with the case. My head is too full of the investigation at the moment, but I'll let you know when it happens.'

His father appraised him. 'Good. You've always had our blessings to meet her and find out more. I always wondered what became of her…' His hands began to tremble with emotion. 'Helen would be pleased too, you know. You have nothing to feel guilty about. We were just so pleased to adopt you, but we always knew you'd want answers and there's only one person who can help with that.' His voice was quavery with emotion. 'I am just so proud of you and so was your mother. You have turned out to be a fine young man, and a wonderful son. I hope the meeting goes well and you find what you're looking for.'

Gabriel swallowed the lump in his throat. Like many fathers and sons, it was sometimes awkward to talk about emotional things, especially about how he felt about seeing his birth mother, someone who had given him up from birth and played no role in his upbringing. It was hard to explain his need to know about where he came from, to find someone that was actually related to him. Growing up all his friends looked like their parents, hair, eyes, height were all commented upon, but in his case, he was dark and had an athletic build whereas both his adoptive parents were smaller and slighter. He had always known he was adopted, had a different 'tummy mummy' as his adoptive parents had always told him. He had accepted it as a child, as children do, but it was only when he got older and understood the enormity of someone giving up a child that he had wondered about his birth mother and the circumstances of his birth. He winced when he thought about how surly and ungrateful, he had been in his teenage years, moaning that Helen and Lawrence were not his real parents and had no right to discipline him. He had gone to a top school and had done well. Lawrence much preferred cricket and rugby but had uncomplainingly taken him to endless training and then to matches when Chelsea signed him. The football had helped him channel his teenage angst until he got released then all hell broke loose and Taverner had been a right royal pain in the arse. He'd got into drunken teenage scrapes, some really bad. When he was released from Chelsea having ruptured his anterior cruciate ligament in his knee, he decided to make up for lost time after all those years of training and discipline. He had grown into a broad, well muscled and handsome lad, so much so, he was often in demand with the girls. He had lots of female interest, a lovely girl called Alice who he had treated appallingly. On one particular beach barbeque he had taken up with Jasmine, the girlfriend of his close friend, Ben Hardy. Ben was an unstable personality, charming but he enjoyed experimenting with drugs and was rumoured to be involved in some small time drug dealing. In that long, hot summer before 'A' level results, passions had run deep. He'd been unable to resist Jasmine's appeal despite Alice. He knew it was wrong, more especially since Ben was really keen on Jasmine. One thing led to another and before long they disappeared together on a secluded part of the beach, under the stars.

243

It was that evening that Ben disappeared, believed to have drowned as his clothes were found neatly folded on the beach. Gabriel had been overcome with self loathing and remorse as he had spoken to the devastated family and helped undertake a search with the local lifeboat crew. The search was unsuccessful and Gabriel had to face the grieving parents, wondering all the time whether or not Ben had spotted him and Jasmine together and was so devastated and distraught that he had ended his life. Not a soul knew about what had happened between him and Jasmine, he'd made out he had left the party early and Jasmine was too consumed with her own anguish to contradict him. He'd done well in his 'A' levels, enough to go to University but the rest of that summer he was grieving, unbearably rude to his parents and consumed with self loathing. Eventually, he had grown to accept the situation as the received wisdom was that Ben had got in with a bad crowd and been murdered because of a drug deal gone wrong. Gabriel grew to accept that story, but privately promised to lead a good life and seek to help people as a way of assuaging his guilt, hence his desire to join the police. Together with his parents' devotion, he was really lucky that they were so understandng, he'd come through, but he often wondered about Ben. No body had ever been found, not one single trace of Ben Hardy, no phone usage, nothing had been touched from his bank account, there was no evidence he had used his passport, it was as though he had never existed. Gabriel often wondered what had happened to him and was in a position to search the Mispers which he frequently did, without result. It was a complete mystery. None of his friends or family had heard from Ben ever again. Over time Gabriel accepted the situation and had felt marginally less guilty about what happened that night.

244

Was he inherently a bad man, or just a stupid confused youth? He opted for the latter view and thought that Ben must have had some sort of mental breakdown and had amnesia or had indeed been killed in a drug deal that had gone wrong.

This coupled with the mysteries of his own birth, was hugely puzzling. His visit to his old social worker had made him even more curious. Who was his father? Why couldn't his grandparents have helped his mother to care for him? How had his mother felt when she handed him over? How was she now and did she ever think about him? Round and round these questions went. He smiled at his adoptive father, who after all was the only father he had ever known. He was truly thankful for his understanding and for the life he had given him.

'Thanks, it means a lot, really.' He drained his cup. 'I know I wasn't always the easiest teenager…'

His father stood up and patted his arm absently. 'Nonsense, you just had questions and high spirits, of course you did. We never thought any the less of you, far from it. Right, I was thinking of lunch at The Admiral and a brisk walk with Charlie on the beach.'

Gabriel nodded, grateful for the change of subject. The Admiral served the best fish and chips for miles around. 'Now you're talking. Did I tell you that I'm going out for a drink with Hannah and Guy later?'

'Ah, great. What are they doing now?'

'Guy works in IT and Hannah is a Forensic Psychologist.'

'Marvellous. Perhaps, Hannah can give you some pointers about your case?'

Gabriel grinned. 'I must admit that thought had crossed my mind too.'

It was great to see his school friends, Hannah and Guy. They met in a trendy bar off the seafront. Over the years Deal had become much smarter due to a lot of investment and was now a thriving seaside town. Gabriel was relieved to note that the overall character of the place had not been changed in the process, which was something. Gabriel had been at sixth form with Guy and Hannah and they kept in touch regularly since.

'So, how's life working in IT?'

Guy ran his fingers through his sandy hair and grinned. He had filled out but was still hyperactive and twitchy.

'Oh, alright. I'm doing stuff in cybersecurity and it's all good.'

'Certainly pays well,' added Hannah dryly. 'Much better than my job.' Hannah tossed her dark hair and regarded them from under her heavily kohled eyes. She had to be one of the most glamorous forensic psychologists in the business. Hannah had been everyone's dream date when they were at college, but she had only had eyes for Jamie, their friend, who had married the daughter of a duke. Hannah had been devastated. She was not a girl who gave her affections lightly and he wondered how she was doing these days.

'Anyway, heard about you heading up that murder case in York. How's it going?'

Both friends sipped their drinks and studied Gabriel. It was lovely to be out of the office relaxing with friends, but a knot of anxiety tightened in his gut as he realised that the case was

246

floundering and that people, namely Emily and her family were relying on him to get a result.

'Hmm. We have a lot of suspects but nothing really concrete on any of them as yet. There is also a recent stabbing that may or may not be related.'

Hannah nodded. 'I bet all the suspects are males, all in potentially close relationships to the victim. Not sure about stabbings these days, there's an awful lot of gang initiations to do with county lines going on, so it may or may not be linked unless your victim knew something about the gangs…'

Gabriel nodded. He was impressed that Hannah had grasped the details of the case with such scant information.

'Yep, we had thought of that.'

Guy frowned. 'God, I do hope you two are not going to be talking shop all night…'

'No, we're really not. Anyway, how's the football going?' He remembered how when he was a sixth form, Guy had welcomed him into his local football team. He had been dismissive at first but had gone along and found he enjoyed playing at a less competitive level, although he still daydreamed. He sometimes wondered what it would have been like being a professional footballer. Stop it, you idiot, he told himself. He had gone onto University and used to come back to play for Deal Town Football Club, part of the Southern Counties East League before joining the police. He had loved every minute of it and adored the banter and camaraderie.

Guy grinned. 'Oh great, we're doing well in the Cup. You should come down if you get the chance.' Guy's face clouded. 'One of the lads had had a hard time in their youth teams actually. Turns out

247

one of the staff had been sexually abusing him, so they're in counselling now. God, I don't know how you do your job actually. All those filthy bastards, how do you cope?'

'Yes, how do you do it?' continued Hannah, her expression softening.

'Well, we do see the worst of humans, I suppose. The Family Protection Team mainly deal with historic sexual abuse inquiries of children, but the victims really need specialist care. Which team was it?'

'Oh, a youth team in Canterbury. The coach sounded like a real bastard. He had been telling the lads he could get them a trial at all sorts of clubs and that no one would believe them if they said anything.'

Gabriel nodded. 'It sounds all too familiar. I suppose the police are dealing with it?'

'Yep, I think so. It seems to be a problem in clubs, then he told me about a young player, seventeen, who had to be moved on for abusing girls. The team trained in a secondary school and he was making contact with the girls. Fourteen they were.'

'Well, surely the police dealt with that too?'

'Don't think so. The lad moved clubs and the whole thing was covered up. It's a few years ago now.'

Taverner tutted. 'Appalling. Which club was this?'

'I think it was somewhere in Manchester. He got taken on though as a pro, so there was no justice there.'

Taverner shook his head. 'Hope he got done in the end though. What was he called?'

Guy grinned. 'Of course, my friend wouldn't say.'

Hannah looked serious. 'If there's anything I can do to help you with your case, then I would be happy to do a consultation and profile your perpetrator.'

Guy shook his head. 'Maybe I could look at the IT or something. It's actually really exciting having a mate solving real life murder cases.'

Gabriel laughed. 'Sadly, it's not exactly glamorous, far from it, but I appreciate your offers of help.' He studied them. 'Things are not coming together as well as I'd like and there's nothing concrete for the suspects we have, all the evidence is circumstantial. Still, we just have to keep looking that's all.'

Hannah began playing with her cutlery. 'I saw Ben's sister the other day...'

Taverner gulped and his heart began to race. 'Oh, how is she?'

Guy and Hannah looked at each other. Guy took over. 'She's fine, doing well by all accounts. His parents have coped but as you know, there was never ever any trace of Ben, so there was never closure for them. Listen, she said you should call in. Moira and Dennis would love to see you...'

'Well maybe, if I've got more time...' Taverner tried to calm his racing heart. No matter what anyone said he always blamed himself. His friend had vanished without trace and all because of him. He listened as his friends continued with the usual speculation about what had happened to Ben. He feigned interest and tried to quell his anxiety.

'So, what do you think happened? Do you think it was a drugs deal gone wrong? You must see all this sort of stuff on a daily basis...' asked Guy.

249

Gabriel realised that they were both staring at him as he tried to frame a response. 'Could be, I suppose. Or maybe he was high and went for a swim and drowned, we all know what the tides are like off Deal coast, they can be treacherous.'

Hannah studied him. 'But Ben knew that too and besides he was a strong swimmer, and it doesn't explain why there wasn't a body? They always resurface at some point, don't they?'

Gabriel took a deep breath. 'Of course, the mortuary is full of people that no one can identify due to the state of the body. I do check with Mispers every now and again, of course I do, but nothing so far.'

Guy nodded. 'I'm sure you do. I guess we have to accept that we will never know. Now let's talk about something more uplifting like who's gonna win the league…'

Hannah laughed. Gabriel was glad of his friend's common sense. The rest of the evening passed enjoyably, and the friends exchanged phone numbers and invitations for visits. Gabriel was left with a nagging feeling of self doubt and guilt. Had his betrayal really caused his friend to kill himself? He vowed to be a better person, be less selfish and one way to do this was to direct his attention to finding out who murdered Emily.

Taverner sighed as he drove away from Deal and headed over towards the motorway with mixed feelings. It had been a relaxing visit. And he had plans to return for Christmas and had also invited his Dad and Charlie up to see York in all its pre-Christmas glory. As usual, the presence of the sea, the coastal light and the change of pace had done him good. His father seemed in good spirits too. They had made the usual pilgrimage down to the bench at the nature reserve where his mother's ashes were scattered and sipped coffee from the battered thermos his father always used.

'I come and talk to her every week you know son, just to tell her what's what. Even tell her about the World News, talk about the politics, news about you, all sorts really. Daft I know but it makes me feel better.'

Gabriel had smiled. 'I think that's great, Dad.'

'It's how I know she would like you to find your birth mum. When you have time, of course, when you've solved your case.'

'If we solve it, you mean.'

Dad laughed. 'Course you will. Just keep at it. I believe in you.'

Taverner smiled. If only he had faith in himself.

His mind went back to his conversation with Guy and Hannah. Of course it was good news that the family were doing OK, that they wanted to see Taverner. He had seen the family at the funeral and a few times since. Ben's mother, Moira, appeared to have aged ten years in a few days after Ben went missing but she was always so pleasant and interested in his life, oblivious to his guilt which made him feel even more like a murderer. He couldn't face seeing them now, but he made up his mind to contact the family when the case was over. And after that even the barmaid whose number he still had tucked away in his phone. As he drove he found himself thinking of Wildblood, thinking he should tell her about Ben and his potential role in his disappearance, he knew she'd understand and give him good advice, help him think of what to say to Ben's parents who he'd definitely visit when he went at Christmas, he promised himself. A good dose of Yorkshire common sense was what he needed. Taverner pressed the accelerator, he realised he was looking forward to returning and facing the challenges of the murder investigation.

Chapter 26

Anna took her own advice and spent a lovely day off taking the boys to the park. pushing them on swings and feeding the ducks. She was a little hung over from drinking more than she was used to at the Armitages, but after a coffee and a slice of toast, she felt fine. She also felt hugely relieved that Rob hadn't been hanging around with a man who frequented strip clubs, but this was tempered by compassion for the plight of the Armitage's daughter, Izzy. She had felt a cold chill when John had mentioned Wayne Davison's name and regretted that their previous attempt to prosecute him had failed. Rob commented on their night before they went out.

'It was a good evening, wasn't it?'

'Yes. I liked them both very much.'

She meant it. They were both so different from how she imagined that she was pleasantly surprised.

Rob nodded then suddenly looked serious. 'You knew the name of their daughter's boyfriend, though, didn't you?'

Anna nodded. 'John really needs to speak to the police. Can you remind him?'

'I will. Is she at risk?'

'Maybe, but there's a lot that can be done to help her.'

Rob nodded and squeezed her shoulder. He peered out of the window.

'It's not a bad day, anyway. Shall we go out?'

Anna had been about to say more about how she knew Wayne Davison but decided against it. She didn't want anything to tarnish her precious day.

The clouds dispersed as they walked. Rob pushed the empty pushchair. Both boys were at the stage where they walked fairly well but also needed the pushchair when they became tired. Anna and Rob pushed them on the swings after wiping the damp off the plastic seats first and then spent an hour or so feeding the ducks. Archie was the bolder of the two and shrieked with delight when the mallards came squawking towards him whilst Jasper ran off crying. Rob went to comfort him, scooped him up and soon had him laughing. It was the sort of winter's day where the sun was glinting from behind the clouds, it had melted the early frost, but the air was clear and bright. The playground was deserted, no one else being mad enough to come out in this weather and although she had been there hundreds of times, the place looked magical like a scene from a fairytale, under the clear sky.

Anna's spirits soared. 'It's so good to just do normal things with the kids.'

Rob grinned. He was so deliciously handsome, Anna still had to pinch herself that such a gorgeous, blond, giant of a man could ever have fallen in love with her. Anna thought that Rob could have done so much better, but she was just so glad that he had chosen her.

Rob tickled Jasper and put the empty bag of duck food in his pocket, as the birds clucked disconsolately and began to drift off.

'Duckies, back, back, come back,' yelled Archie and then held out his hands in a comical fashion. 'Mummee, ducks all gone…'

'All gone,' repeated Jasper as the ducks retreated. His face crumpled and he began to whimper as he watched them swim away.

'Never mind. How about an ice cream?'

Rob shook his head. 'In this weather? Are you mad?' But the children jumped up and down in crazed delight.

Anna gazed at them, her heart bursting with love. 'Quite possibly. Come on then, I'm buying.'

Rob grinned. 'You're on.'

Later, the boys were exhausted from all the fresh air and running around. Rob lit a fire in the wood stove burner, and they ate a curry and drank wine as they watched a schmaltzy, romantic comedy on TV. Anna cuddled up to Rob and thought she could get used to this. She hadn't thought about work or the horrors of human nature once.

On Monday, Taverner beckoned her over. He looked relaxed from his time off and animated somehow.

'So, did you have a good weekend? How was the meal with the Armitages? Did you find anything out?'

'Loads. I think we did him a disservice, actually. Well, I did, anyway.'

'How come?'

'Well, it seems that John's daughter has a dodgy boyfriend. I thought maybe he wasn't posh enough, or maybe didn't have good enough prospects for John but it's much worse than that. You remember I told you about that case of mine, Mandy and the man who abused her? Well, Armitage's daughter is involved with him! Wayne Davison!'

'Who?' Anna had forgotten that Taverner had only been in North Yorkshire a few months. It felt like it had been a lot longer. Wayne Davison was very well known amongst the local officers.

'You know, the man we tried to prosecute for pimping out girls including his girlfriend, getting them onto drugs and all sorts. He works for Fenchurch at the Geisha Club. Armitage has noticed bruising on her that she dismisses.'

'So, that's why he goes there…'

'Yes, he goes to try and see her and talk some sense into her.' Something else came to her. 'And if you think about it, the girl in the café never actually said he goes into the place, just that he waits next door hoping to catch this blonde girl, who we now know is his daughter.'

'I hope Armitage is going to report this?'

'Don't worry, I have insisted he does. Anyway, how was your weekend?'

Taverner looked pleased. 'Yep, good. It was nice to get away for a bit and my father is well, so it's all good.' He smiled. 'So, now it's back to work. Let's call everyone together and press on.'

'Right you are, guv.' At least Taverner seemed in a better mood and rejuvenated which was something.

Taverner started to wipe the links board down and began to move the pictures about. He certainly had his mojo back.

Chapter 27

As he closed the door of his cottage to set off for work, Taverner looked out for Pebbles, the tortoiseshell cat that regularly came to his door, wrapping herself around his legs and demanding food. He had not seen Pebbles for several days and wondered what on earth had happened to her. He looked in the hedgerows behind his cottage and the field which was another of her usual haunts. Taverner had moved to a village, Langdale outside York, nearer to the town of Walton, a place crammed full of racing yards. It had been idyllic when he came to view it a few months ago, but now he was questioning his decision as winter hit. He had to regularly scrape the ice off his windscreen before driving the forty minutes or so to York on narrow B roads. If it snowed, he would have to think about getting a 4x4 and more supplies of coal. He called for the cat and noticed further down the field a very unusual sight. He walked to the back fence to look closer. There were three modern caravans, a brilliantly coloured old gypsy caravan, three tethered piebald horses of varying sizes and several dogs ensconced a little way from the road. Gypsies. He thought it was likely that Pebbles had found some food there and despite the dogs was likely to be curled up in a warm place.

Taverner would like to bet that the farmer would not be happy about the gypsies moving in. He wondered how they had managed it and noticed that the chain on the gate had been cut straight through with bolt croppers, so the gate was placed next to the post but with the chain drooping forlornly. It occurred to him that this was a crime and perhaps he ought to deal with it, but he really didn't have time. He would suggest that the farmer contact the local bobbies if he needed any help to move the gypsies on, as he had a murder case to crack. As long as the gypsies didn't get in his way or cause him any bother then that was fine as far as he was concerned. As he drove off, he thought he saw the curtains in the nearest and smartest caravan flutter. His car engine must have woken one of the occupants from their sleep.

At the station, he called the team together to plan the rest of the day. The story on Emily's computer suggested that she had some knowledge about the goings on at The Geisha Club, but the team's inquiries had so far drawn a blank. They now knew that Niall Lynch frequented the place as did John Armitage, but Armitage's presence was now explained away by his concern for his daughter. Then there was the curve ball thrown in by Angie Curtis, the journalist who suggested that Caitlyn Fear's drowning was in fact murder. Of interest was that Caitlyn had also been an English student who also had Niall Lynch as her tutor. Had Lynch had an affair with Caitlyn and killed her when she threatened to tell his wife? They now knew from Matthew Lawson that Niall also visited the literacy groups and gave talks to the youngsters. Had he managed to groom Lauren too? The team were actively looking at possible links between Lauren and Niall, as the girl herself was not giving anything away. Maybe Emily had worked this out and confronted Lynch? Was this the reason she had been murdered?

Taverner ran through the latest updates and plans for the day.

258

'Patel. Any intel nationally about trafficking that could have links to York and to The Geisha Club in particular?'

Patel shook his head. 'No, nothing so far. There are lots of youngsters being trafficked and with the National Referral Mechanism, this has helped to identify victims, but whilst there are youngsters coming in and being moved to the major cities in the UK, there's nothing to link any of the gangs with York.'

OK. Well, thanks. Keep trying. Cullen, is there anything specifically that links any of the victims who drowned to this investigation?'

'Three of the six deaths, including Emily Morgan, were students who were studying at York University as opposed to other colleges and Universities in the City. Caitlyn Fear studied English and had Niall Lynch as her tutor, so that is a definite link. But as we're all aware, all the deaths were ruled misadventure as a result of drug and or alcohol consumption. Caitlyn Fear didn't appear to have made any complaints about Lynch, but I've tracked down a couple of her friends who might be able to shed some light on her relationship with her tutor.'

'Great. Good work.' Taverner studied his team who were all listening and taking notes. He had a feeling that they were not far off from a breakthrough. 'Ballantyne and Haworth, any information from Emily's friends?'

The pair had been tasked with re-interviewing Emily's friends and family.

Ballantyne shook his head. 'No, nothing of note. They are all telling us that Emily and Dan were a great couple, and they weren't aware of any tensions between the pair. As you're aware, Mr Charlton

Senior was found to have visited Pocklington near York on the evening of the murder but his alibi checks out, he was visiting a staff member who was off sick after a cancer diagnosis, and ANPR does back this up, as he arrived back in Hull by 9 which fits in with his version of events.'

'OK. Thank you. We also have some information from Matthew Lawson, the ex- vicar who ran the literacy group, that he saw Emily and Dan in the Minster where he volunteers, the weekend before the murder. He stated that there was definite tension between the pair and Dan practically dragged her out of the place by grabbing her arm, leaving red marks. If he can do that in front of people, imagine what could happen if they were alone? So, Ballantyne and Haworth, can you go and speak to him about this?'

Haworth nodded. 'Yes, guv.'

Taverner pursed his lips and looked at the links board, circling Niall Lynch's photo with a red marker pen. 'So, as you can see, Lynch is definitely the number one suspect now. Right, we definitely need to speak to Caitlyn Fear's friends, Anna and I will do that. Patel and Cullen, can you review all the forensic evidence and go through it once again with a fine toothcomb. Ask the tech guys if there are any other places you could hide sensitive information, whilst you're at it. Emily could have evidence to back up her story about The Geisha Club, but if so where did she hide it? And we need to keep at it to see if we can link Niall to Lauren or other girls at the literacy group. We really need to get all our ducks in a row before we arrest Lynch.'

'Right, sir,' replied Patel.

Ballantyne put up his hand. 'Suppose we don't manage to get all this done and there's another murder? Maybe Lynch had his claws into another wee lassie from the group?'

Taverner sighed. Trust Ballantyne to be gloomy but he had to admit it was a possibility.

'Let's hope not. Lynch is still our main suspect, but obviously I'll get the final say so from Sykes. He may be implicated in Caitlyn Fear's death. As you know, the coroner's finding was that her death was misadventure due to drowning after taking drugs and alcohol, but there is some debate about an injury noted on her body and whether this was significant and occurred prior to death. Ives was away at the time and it seems another pathologist was drafted in who has made some questionable calls. We are ordered to be very discreet in our inquiries until Ives has made his judgement, hence the decision not to speak to Caitlyn's parents at present.'

Haworth piped up. 'Good old Ivesey. It's not the sort of mistake he would ever make! Why don't you ask him to review the files?'

'That is exactly what we are going to do, but obviously this is informal at this stage. And it goes without saying, no one in the room says a word to anyone, right? The last thing we want is the press getting hold of anything and certainly not the parents at this stage.'

'Are you seeing the friends with the journalist, Angie Curtis, sir?'

Taverner sighed. 'No. Angie will not be sitting in on any interview or be a party to the contents, I have made that very clear.' He nodded at Ballantyne. 'We will of course keep an eye on Lauren Jackson's situation. She has a police presence in the hospital and the

261

local social services team are seeking to take her into care when she is ready for discharge as neither parent has appeared to care properly for the girl. We ought to alert Matthew Lawson to see if there are any other girls from the group who might be vulnerable, but at least Lauren will be safe.'

'Thank the Lord for that, at least,' muttered Ballantyne. 'Poor wee lassie.'

'Right everyone, we need to feed back by tomorrow at four. We are planning to arrest Lynch as soon as we can but we want as much on him as we can possibly get beforehand, because as you well know, as soon as he is arrested then the clock is ticking and we want to be in a position where he can be charged and locked up. We are in the final stages of the inquiry. I know how hard you have all worked but we need one last push, and we'll get the bastard.'

There were murmurs of approval and a heightened energy in the room as each officer drifted off with renewed purpose.

Wildblood touched Taverner's shoulder. 'Stirring stuff, sir. Listen, that bloody psychic woman is in reception again asking to see you. Shall I head her off?'

Taverner sighed and glanced at his watch. If he grabbed lunch on the way to see Caitlyn Fear's friend, he might just have time to see the psychic.

'No, I'll pop down now.'

The woman might well be crazy but imagine the furore if she did know something? After all she did seem to know about his adoption and possibly the parasol and dragon from The Geisha Club, though it was unclear where the club fitted in at present. The press would be utterly damning if he didn't talk to her and she was proved right, and so for that reason he took a quick mouthful of cold tea and swept through the doors to reception.

Mrs Malone looked up and smiled when Taverner walked through the doors. In spite of himself Taverner couldn't bring himself to be brusque or difficult. It was hard to analyse why he had agreed to see her at all. Was he just being polite or just covering all bases? Perhaps, she really did have psychic powers?

'I'm afraid I haven't got long, Mrs Malone, but I do have about five minutes if that's OK.'

'Fine. I just wondered how yer case was going, that's all?'

'Well, as you know I can't say too much, but we are making good progress.'

Mrs Malone nodded. Taverner noticed her dark brown eyes, set in a remarkably unlined face. Her expression was calm and knowing. Taverner wondered how old she was but it was very hard to gauge accurately. She could be anywhere from thirty to fifty. Her fingers were full of rings and her arms adorned with bracelets. She was wearing a long fitted, bottle green velvet dress, long black coat with a large felt flower attached and black leather boots. She looked every inch a paid up hippy.

'Well, that's as maybe but I had my tarot cards out and the card, the hierophant, came up again.' She showed him the card which showed a man in ceremonial clothing wearing an intricate gold headdress.

'Yes, yes you've told me this. Right, so what does that mean?'

'It points to spiritual authority, maybe a teacher, counsellor or wise man. You should seek advice from these quarters perhaps.'

Taverner took this in. Well, Lynch was definitely a teacher so that could fit. Then he told himself that it was probably just a lucky guess, Emily had been at University after all.

'Then there was the moon, as I said. That means you should follow your intuition, but it also warns of deception, things might not be as they appear. And finally, I got this one.' Maggie held up a card depicting a young man dressed like a medieval page and holding a sword. 'The page of swords. This card can be a message, it can suggest a real person, some young man who's not mastered power over himself. Possibly someone who's immature and detached about relationships maybe…'

'Well thanks, that's all very interesting.' Taverner wished the ruddy woman wouldn't talk in bloody riddles. He pulled out his notebook and made notes on what she said just to look like he was trying but honestly, she did go on. Tarot felt to him like horoscopes, card meanings so vague and general that they were bound to be right.

'But I reckon you'll get there, a man of your determination.'

Taverner sighed. This was really too much. 'Look, you don't know me at all.'

Mrs Malone smiled enigmatically. 'I know you better than you think.'

Taverner saw Wildblood hovering and glanced at his watch. 'I'm sorry, I do need to go now if you'll excuse me.'

Mrs Malone stood up and nodded. 'Your friend doesn't blame you, you know. The one that went missing,' she said as she left, giving him a knowing smile. With that she disappeared.

'What was that all about?'

Wildblood looked at Mrs Malone's retreating figure. Taverner felt immobilised by shock, like a powerful force was pushing him over. How could she possibly know anything about Ben Hardy? But then if she did why didn't she say something useful like what had happened to him? Probably she had used nothing more than the mysterious powers of Google to find out about Ben's disappearance. If she knew he'd come from Deal, it was certainly possible as there had been a lot of media speculation at the time, and there was plenty on the internet about the case, but still! He took a deep breath and tried to compose himself before answering Wildblood.

'Oh, nothing, she drew a few tarot cards, one of a wise man, the hierophant, or something, from her pack of cards.'

Anna shrugged. 'Wise? Can't be Sykes then...'

Taverner laughed to cover his shock but couldn't bring himself to tell her about the reference to his missing friend. Despite the rational explanation he had concocted, he was still deeply troubled. The woman knew so much, it could be a coincidence, but he didn't believe in those.

Chapter 28

Julie Sinclair was Caitlyn's best friend from her home town. She was dark haired, smiley and very chatty. She told them she'd had the afternoon off to see them and was quick to offer tea and cake.

'I just had to see you as soon as I could. Have you found anything out or are you reopening Caitlyn's case? I never thought she would have drowned just like that, you know. It just didn't feel right.'

Wildblood smiled and Taverner launched into a lengthy discussion about the reasons behind their visit. It was the sort of thing he was good at, soothing troubled people.

'We are not opening the case as such, just doing an overview about people who have drowned in York in similar circumstances. We also have a role in crime prevention, you see, but no, we don't have any new information as such.'

Julie's face fell. 'Well, in that case, I'm not sure what I can really say other than what I said at the time. You will have read my statement?'

They both nodded. Wildblood took a sip of the tea which was strong and more Typhoo than Earl Grey. She suspected Taverner would leave his untouched.

'You said that you were a close friend of Caitlyn's from home? Did you see her much when she went to University?'

'Yes, a fair amount. She was lonely at first. I went to visit her a few times when she first went. I didn't go to University, you see, but stayed at home and studied at the local college for a degree instead. So, it was great to visit her to get the whole Uni vibe.'

'When you saw her last, did she have any worries about anything at all?'

Julie frowned; her eyes sharp. 'No, nothing really. She had dyslexia but that didn't seem to stop her doing well. As I recall the University gave her some software for her laptop and that helped.' She put her head on one side. 'Do you think that the stress of study may have contributed to her death?'

Taverner put his hand out like he was in uniform and stopping traffic. 'No, I'm not saying that at all. But she may have confided in her friends about something that was worrying her, maybe relationships that sort of thing…?'

Julie considered this. 'No, nothing springs to mind. She found it hard to begin with, missed home, but seemed much more settled by the third term, in fact…'

Wildblood nodded. 'Yes?' She paused waiting for Julie to fill in the gaps. It was a technique that she had observed Taverner use to great effect. People always seemed to say more than they intended when someone actually listened to them.

'We grew apart to be honest. I was here, she was there, she seemed very bothered about going out, had new friends, new clothes, new ideas. I sometimes felt as though she thought she was better than me because she was studying there, so she seemed a bit shut off, if you like…' Julie dabbed at her eyes. 'I felt really guilty afterwards. I thought she was being a bit superior if you must know and then she drowned, and I felt terrible for thinking that…'

Taverner felt in his pocket for a tissue but couldn't find one. Anna rummaged in her bag and pulled out a plastic packet of tissues she always kept in her bag.

'You mustn't blame yourself,' continued Taverner. 'Tragedy sometimes strikes without warning and you weren't to know what was going to happen.'

Julie sniffed. 'I suppose so.'

Wildblood gave her a minute before asking. 'Did she ever talk about anyone at the University? A friend, boyfriend, lecturer?'

Julie sighed. 'No one apart from her friend Amanda, that was it. It was Amanda this, Amanda that. Nothing else. I think she had various boyfriends, no one special and liked the lecturers. If she had any problems, then she didn't tell me...'

That told them everything they needed to know. If Caitlyn had been propositioned by Lynch and she had grown apart from Julie, then she wasn't likely to have confided in her. Clearly, Julie felt pushed out and irritated.

'Are you going to have a word with Caitlyn's parents? Only I do still see them, and I don't want to put my foot in it.'

Taverner smiled. 'Quite right too. It's best not to say anything at this stage. I think they need to hear any updates from official channels and as I said, these inquiries have a wider remit about preventing further deaths.'

'Right. What are you going to do about the students drowning then?'

'Talk to the University, encourage some sort of campaign about avoiding walking by the river alone, especially after a night out, that sort of thing,' answered Taverner smoothly. 'We'll ask the local PCSO's to speak to students and publicise the concerns about drinking too much and walking home by the river alone.'

'Absolutely,' added Wildblood, impressed with Taverner's inventiveness. 'We'll liaise with the University and develop a strategy.'

'Now, we'd better press on, Ms Sinclair, but thank you very much for seeing us.'

As usual they debriefed on the drive back to the station.

'Well, that was a waste of time,' Taverner sighed. 'She was rather a bitter girl, didn't you think. I think she was a bit jealous of Caitlyn. Let's hope we have more joy with Amanda.'

'Yep, I hope so, otherwise it will be back to the drawing board.' He didn't like to admit it, but time was of the essence. The spectre of a third girl being harmed loomed large in his mind.

Taverner and Anna spent the rest of the day going through witness statements in his office. Patel popped his head around the door with a sheaf of papers in his arms.

'I'm going through Lynch's finances, guv. His wife is the one with the money, it seems. She inherited a large sum from her parents, so the finances are in a good state.'

He showed her the bank account details which showed several healthy bank balances and several savings accounts. They had in the region of £250,000 in total, just lying around in savings accounts doing nothing, never mind the posh house and car.

Anna suddenly remembered Emily's Mulberry bag and Tiffany jewellery, both expensive items for a student. If there was a link to Lynch, then that would help their case. Cullen had said that Emily's parents had bought her items from both retailers a couple of years ago, but she remembered that Emily's bag and bracelet looked very new. Her parents had said they had bought them as gifts for her and she had simply looked after them very well, but the bracelet in particular, had that shiny lustre to it that made her question this.

'Are there any payments to Mulberry or Tiffany within the last year?'

Patel shook his head. 'No, nothing so far, but I'll keep looking. There are several large cash withdrawals though, £2000 in March and £1500 in June. Unusual in this day and age.'

'Yes, it certainly is. Having a rich wife gives Lynch a clear motive. He wouldn't want Emily popping up and blowing his marriage apart and depriving him of his luxuries. Keep up the good work.'

However, it was not enough. They needed more to nail Lynch, so they would just have to keep on looking. Anna was home at a reasonable time for once, She scooped up her letters, kissed the boys and Rob and took great delight in presiding over the boys' bath time. When she came down, Rob had cooked steak in wine with a salad which smelled delightful. She chatted to Rob and was feeling quite buoyant until she opened her bank statements and a couple of credit card bills. Damn. She was overdrawn. The car insurance and tax had come out of her account, not to mention a hefty sum for electricity and gas. She paid the bills and Rob the mortgage, and if there was anything over then it went into their joint savings account, not that

270

there had been lately. She felt a black cloud descend upon her like she'd been dowsed in icy water. Sometimes, she felt like she was a hamster running round and round a wheel, always busy, always working but getting precisely nowhere.

'Are you OK,' asked Rob noticing her expression.

'Yeah, just more bloody bills, that's all. I'm just tired.' But it wasn't just that. She thought about Lynch's bank statements and shook her head. It struck her once again, that although they lived in their dream home, they were both at work all the time and hardly spent any time in it, never mind with her gorgeous twins. She dampened down her frustration and switched on the TV hoping to find something light and uplifting to take her mind off things.

Chapter 29

At home Taverner was relieved when Pebbles returned. He found her miaowing outside when he came home and bent down to stroke her. It was then that he noticed that one of the clay plant pots, which contained a small bay tree either side of the front door, had been moved slightly to the left leaving a telltale ring of soil. When he moved the plant pot back, he noticed that an envelope had been slipped under the pot. He picked it up, fumbled with his keys, ignoring Pebble's insistent miaowing and let himself in. When he had fed Pebbles, made himself a cup of Earl Grey tea and popped a ready meal into the microwave, he collapsed onto his sofa and opened the envelope. He gasped in surprise as he opened a sheet of paper and a lock of blond hair fell out. Shit! Whose hair was it? Was Emily's murderer toying with him? His other thought was that he wished he had donned plastic gloves when he had opened the damned thing. He was sure that whoever had put it there had done so today. He was generally pretty observant so he would have noticed it otherwise. He gathered the hair up onto a sheet of paper and popped the paper into a plastic freezer bag. At least forensics would be able to exclude his own prints which might help as they always kept officers' fingerprints precisely for this purpose. He was suddenly alert. Christ, this could mean that the murderer knew where he lived, and it also meant that there could be another victim. He remembered that the previous tenant had installed a camera, a type that was connected to a motion sensor. The camera was a wide angled one and should easily pick up whoever had placed the envelope under the plant pot. He fiddled with the camera, removed the SD card and after eating a chicken curry, popped it into his computer. After scrolling through images of foxes, cats, the postman, a young lad delivering what looked to be leaflets, he noticed a figure dressed in dark clothing in the dimming light approach, look about him, dip down by his front door, remove something indistinct from his jacket and lift the large plant pot, placing the envelope underneath. He rewound the images, trying to enhance the picture but it remained grainy and indistinct. Damn. The figure was average in every way, in height and weight, with no distinguishing features as far as he could see. He couldn't even tell if it was a man or a woman. It could be anyone. Frustrated, he removed the SD card, vowing to take it to the tech team along with the hair sample. He slept poorly, his imagination running wild, his rest interrupted by images of dead girls and the sense that a dark figure was laughing at him.

He was getting used to seeing the colourful scene of the gypsies and caravans as he left in the morning. The piebald horses looked up at him, not quite familiar enough with him to approach, the dogs stirred but it was usually so early he hadn't yet seen any adults. He wondered how long they were planning on staying but decided it didn't much matter. They seemed to be harmless. It was a charming scene and he decided he quite liked it, especially the old gypsy caravan, with its bright green and red paintwork. As he drove to work, his head was full of the interview that he was conducting with Lynch today and how it might play out. His fingers tightened on the

273

steering wheel as the green fields gave way to the urban sprawl of York. Today was going to be a good day, he could feel it. The net was tightening on Niall Lynch. The power of arrest, because of reasonable suspicion that a crime had been committed, also allowed them to search Lynch's house. An officer would talk to his wife whilst others could search for anything incriminating and he hoped beyond hope that they would find something. The other officers would work on other evidence and at last they might find enough to charge Lynch with one or maybe two murders. Then he thought about the envelope and the SD card and shivered. He'd take it to forensics and the tech guys first thing, and he'd need to speak to DCI Sykes.

DCI Sykes looked bemused by Taverner's news.

'Keep me in the loop once you have the information from Forensics. It might be some local nutter, I suppose, but we need to cross reference the hair sample with our Mispers to be on the safe side. Now we need to focus on today.' He had clearly been poring over the evidence carefully. 'Hmm. Well, let's hope you've got your man. Mind you, he's a University lecturer, bound to have a good solicitor, so we had better be sure of our ground.'

'Absolutely sir. As you know, we're reviewing the Caitlyn Fear case too. Dr Ives is looking at the post mortem results for Caitlyn. Interestingly enough, she was an English student and had Lynch as a tutor too. And Lynch also attended the literacy groups and gave talks so he could have groomed Lauren Jackson. We're looking into links between them.'

'And do we know where Lynch was on the night of Caitlyn Fear's murder?'

274

'Officers will be at the University as we speak, to see if there were any complaints about Lynch that weren't properly followed up, just to get a general feel of what the University knew about his relations with students.' Taverner sighed. 'We don't have anything to connect Lauren and Lynch as yet, we could visit her again, but suppose he groomed her and other girls from the group...'

Sykes frowned. 'Do you think there may be other girls who are at risk?'

Taverner took a deep breath. 'Possibly.' He didn't want to be alarmist and he would rather wait and get more solid evidence before arresting Lynch, but on the other hand if other girls were groomed, they would be at great risk if Lynch thought they would go to the authorities.

Sykes looked very serious. 'Then I think you should just get on wi' the arrest. You've enough wi' the links to both Emily and Caitlyn, so don't bugger about. Just bring 'im in. We can't afford to risk another murder.'

'Are you sure? Ives will be reporting in a couple of days, perhaps we should wait...'

'No, just get on wi' it. You've a lot to do. Make sure you update me.' He half smiled. 'Two murders for the price of one would be very good indeed, Taverner.'

Taverner nodded in agreement. It certainly would but only if it was the right culprit. No pressure then.

After the initial shock at being formally arrested and realising that there would be a search of his large house, Lynch's chief concern had been the welfare of his wife. When he was reassured that officers would talk to her but make sure she was sensitively dealt with, Lynch visibly relaxed. He looked positively chipper when his brief arrived, the experienced James Napier, a smooth, silver haired man, who was wearing a very well tailored grey suit and a supercilious smile.

'Now, my client has voluntarily given you statements about the unfortunate death of Emily Morgan, he has an alibi for the night in question so I'm beginning to think you are absolutely clutching at straws, Inspector.'

Taverner merely pressed ahead. 'Your wife, Mr Lynch, has made a further statement which casts doubt on your alibi. She cannot now recall with any certainty the time that you came in on Saturday, 6th November as she was asleep having taken a herbal sleeping remedy. As you recall in your statement, you said you were at home all evening with your wife, but she says you were in later and she cannot be certain when you arrived back.' Taverner watched Lynch's expression change for just a second. Thankfully, Cullen's insinuations about her husband's young, female students had had a positive effect on Mrs Lynch's memory.

'Well, I may have been mistaken. I probably popped into the pub on my way home but only for a couple of drinks with colleagues.' Lynch swept his thick greying hair off his forehead. 'When I said I was at home with my wife all evening, I meant after calling into the pub.'

'What were you doing in the University on a Saturday anyway?' asked Taverner.

'I was picking up some notes for a Departmental meeting on the Monday and stayed all afternoon to do some marking.'

Wildblood was sceptical. 'This is a murder inquiry, Mr Lynch. It is essential that you tell us the truth.'

'That is the truth,' insisted Lynch. 'It's in my original statement. University teaching is hard work, you know.'

Taverner sighed. 'So, what public house did you visit and what time did you, in fact, return home.'

'It was The Fox and Roman near the University.'

'And who were you there with?'

Taverner blinked. 'No one. I had heard a few colleagues were going but when I arrived, they had gone. As I recall I had a quick pint and went home for about half 8.'

'What time did you go there?' asked Taverner.

'Oh, about half 6 or 7, I should think.'

'Did you speak to anyone when you were there?'

Taverner shook his head. 'Not really, I don't recall. I may have had a word with the odd student. That's it.'

Taverner sighed. What's the betting that the students were female and rather attractive. The team were sorting through the CCTV footage of the pubs on the night of the 6th November, hoping to find some evidence that Lynch had been there.

'Does the name Caitlyn Fear mean anything to you?'

Niall gasped. 'She was the girl that drowned a few years ago.' Realisation flickered over his face. 'It was said to be a horrible accident, you can't think I had anything to do with it?'

'It's interesting how you tried it on with Emily and she winds up dead and we now think that Caitlyn died in similar circumstances. You were both students' tutor. Did you try it on with her too?'

Taverner had the satisfaction of seeing James Napier give his client a sharp look. He clearly didn't know about Lynch's admission regarding Emily.

'No, no you can't think I had anything to do with either of the girls' deaths…' Lynch ran his fingers through his hair in an abstracted fashion. 'There's no evidence…'

'Quite; any evidence you have is purely circumstantial, so I suggest you either charge my client or let him go, Inspector,' James Napier added smoothly.

Taverner ignored him, he really wanted to rattle Lynch. 'But you do like them young, don't you? We have evidence that you're a frequent visitor to The Geisha Bar in town.'

James Napier raised an eyebrow. 'As are half the population of York, Inspector. This doesn't prove anything.'

Wildblood continued the theme. 'You have often been seen in the café next door before going into the club at seven o'clock and we have reason to believe that you are a frequent visitor to the Gentlemen's club upstairs, which is a strip club amongst other things.'

Lynch flushed and swallowed hard. 'I have been to the bar a few times, I admit, and I have been to the strip club. There's no shame in that.'

Taverner continued to press hard. 'Well, that depends on whether the girls are over eighteen and work there voluntarily. We have reason to believe that some of the girls are certainly under age and could have been trafficked.'

Lynch looked horrified. 'You know what my situation is at home, I do love my wife, but she is so ill, this would crucify her. Can I have assurances that she won't find out?'

'That very much depends on whether you co-operate with us or not. Now tell us everything you know about The Geisha Club…'

At the end of the interview, they had several useful pieces of information about the club and some evidence that very young girls, mainly of Eastern European origin were working as strippers and possibly prostitutes. Some seemed 'very young' to Lynch and were 'possibly' underage. The information could form the basis of an inquiry into The Geisha Strip Club and suggested prostitution and possibly trafficking, but that was about it. Again, there was nothing concrete.

James Napier drew himself up in his seat.

'Now my client has been very co-operative, more than co-operative in fact but there is no evidence of any wrongdoing on his part and furthermore nothing to link him to the death of Emily Morgan. I insist that my client is either charged or released.'

Taverner nodded. Napier was right of course. He really hoped that his team would find something more substantial. He glanced at Wildblood and feigned confidence.

It was at that point that Ballantyne came in and passed Taverner a note. He read it twice with mounting excitement and passed it to Wildblood.

Taverner scrolled through the iPad and showed Lynch a photo of the wrench that had been found in the River Ouse which, from the size and shape of the wound to Emily's head and forensics, was deemed to be the murder weapon.

'So, can you tell me if you have ever owned a wrench like this? For the tape I am showing Mr Lynch a photograph of a ten-inch wrench.'

Lynch frowned. 'I don't know. I do have some tools, a wrench set with different sized wrenches, like most men.'

Taverner scrolled to another photo of the murder weapon which had the sizing clearly identified by a metal tape measure which was placed next to it.

'A search of your garage shows that you indeed own an old imperial set of spanners. The ten-inch wrench is missing from Mr Lynch's set as is the 6 inch wrench.'

Lynch shrugged. 'Why on earth are you looking in my garage, at my tools, so what?'

Taverner sat back on his chair and stared at him. 'The wrench shown in the photographs was recovered from the River Ouse and is a similar size to the one missing from your set. It has also been confirmed as the murder weapon for Emily Morgan.'

Lynch gaped, opening his mouth and closing it like a fish. Napier whispered in his ear.

'That's enough. My client will not answer any further questions, Inspector. Can I remind you that as you have said yourself, the wrench missing from my client's set is similar but not identical to the one you claim to be the murder weapon for Miss Morgan. I think you'll find that you will have to do better than that. Do you have any forensic evidence? I request a break so that I can brief my client thoroughly.'

Taverner caught Wildblood's eye and nodded, getting out of his seat. 'For the tape interview suspended at 14:29.' He reached over and switched off the tape.

'We'll leave you to it.'

Taverner's earlier optimism began to fade. After Lynch had spoken to his brief he would be locked up in a cell. Napier was right, they didn't have enough to charge Lynch. He hoped that the search and other work might give them something more. They could hold a suspect for twenty four hours, thirty six if an extension was granted, but if they didn't have enough to charge Lynch, then they would have to let him go. He was a man who liked young women, that much was clear, but they had no evidence that he had committed any offence. However, chemical tests would be rushed through to determine if the wrenches were actually from a similar set. Older sets with imperial sizes tended to be made of a higher quality metal and if they could find enough similarities between the two, then they could be in business. Unfortunately, the wrench did not have any DNA or sufficient quality fingerprints when it had been retrieved from the river, so again they needed more. Taverner certainly hoped that the search of the house and outbuildings might be useful, and his officers would find something incriminating. They really needed a big bloody breakthrough soon because although Lynch was currently locked up for now, the clock was ticking and hopes of a conviction were draining away like sand through his fingers. If they hadn't made any headway, they couldn't apply for an extension and Lynch would have to be released.

Chapter 30

Wildblood and Taverner were sitting with the team going through Mrs Lynch's statements and the items that had been found in the search of the property. Lynch's laptop and mobile phone had been seized, together with supervision notes and records of academic marks given to his students, Caitlyn Fear and Emily Morgan amongst them. Wildblood could sense a real purpose and feverish urgency about Taverner.

'Right, we have been through Caitlyn Fear's parents' old statements and there is no mention of any concerns about staff at the University. What other evidence did you find?'

There was precious little that would have any bearing on the investigation it seemed. The written supervision notes were in order and there was nothing else suspicious.

'What about Lynch's spending habits, anything unusual? Anything that might suggest he was buying girls expensive gifts?'

Patel shook his head. 'No sir, nothing else. He gave us an explanation for the two large cash withdrawals I mentioned earlier. One was for building work to his house, a barrow job to repair the roof of his conservatory and the other a cash payment for a diamond necklace for his wife. That also checks out.'

Taverner sighed. 'What about Lynch's laptop? Any compromising emails or anything of that nature?'

Patel shook his head. 'The tech guys have had a cursory look and will search for any deleted stuff, which they can recover, but nothing so far.'

'Right. You carry on and when forensics have analysed the wrenches, we'll hopefully get a match. Right now, get on with it.'

Wildblood had already been through the statements of Caitlyn Fear's friends with a fine-tooth comb.

'There was no mention of any concerns about Lynch, sir, but you never know. Perhaps the officers didn't ask the right questions?'

'Mmm. Well, we'll see, won't we?' Wildblood pulled outside the house of Caitlyn's best friend, Amanda Jameson, her friend from University. 'Let's see what Amanda has to say for herself. If anyone knows then Amanda will.'

Amanda Jameson was in her mid twenties, had bobbed blonde hair and blue eyes.

'I couldn't believe it when you said you wanted to talk to me about Caitlyn,' she sniffed. 'Have you reopened the case?'

Taverner sipped his tea and helped himself to a digestive. 'Well, not strictly speaking, you see the verdict regarding her death was misadventure, so there is no case to reopen, unless new evidence comes to light.' He repeated the story he had given Julie Sinclair.

Amanda looked from one to the other. 'Right. So, do you have any information?'

Wildblood shook her head. 'Not as such but we do have a role in crime prevention and another student recently died.'

Realisation dawned. 'Ah, the other student, Emily, who drowned?'

'Obviously we can't say too much, but we wondered if you would answer some questions for us,' added Wildblood.

Amanda eyed Taverner. 'OK, if I can help in any way…'

Bloody typical, thought Wildblood with resignation. She may as well not be there as Amanda only had eyes for him. Not for the first time, she wondered if her boss realised the impact he had on women and decided he was probably oblivious because he didn't seem remotely cocky which was very refreshing. So different to some of her previous bosses who thought they were the answer to a maiden's prayer.

'So, you were obviously close as you lived with Caitlyn at Uni, could you tell us how she was in the run up to the accident, did she have any worries or concerns at all?'

Amanda blinked back tears. 'Sorry, it just brings it all back. I just felt so guilty, you see.'

Wildblood had read about how Caitlyn had lagged behind her friends as they walked home, so much so, they had left her to it. Amanda was accompanied by a new man and obviously had other things on her mind, probably even wanting to give her friend the slip. She had been devastated the day after when she found out what had happened.

'What sort of things?'

'Well, problems with boyfriends, her course, anything really?'

'Well, she did struggle with dyslexia of course, but she had loads of help from her tutor, so it wasn't really a problem. She was actually good at English, just struggled sometimes with writing it. I think she had access to some software that helped, her marks were pretty good.'

Wildblood smiled. 'How did she get on with her tutor, Niall Lynch? Did she talk about him?'

Amanda looked baffled. 'Fine, I think he was pretty helpful.'

'So, she got on well with him?' continued Taverner.

'Yes, I think so, she never said anything different.'

'Did she have a boyfriend?' continued Wildblood.

Amanda smiled. 'Several actually, but nothing serious.' Amanda suddenly looked into the distance, her eyes tearing up. 'I still miss her, you know,' she choked. 'She was such a laugh, a great character. I just wasn't there for her when she needed me.'

Wildblood patted her arm. 'You weren't to know what was going to happen.'

Amanda smiled through her tears.

'Did Caitlyn seem different before she died?' continued Wildblood.

Amanda thought carefully. 'No, just her usual carefree self, we all were back then. We all thought everything would be fine, it would all turn out OK. I'm afraid there is nothing else I can tell you. Everything is in the statement. I haven't thought about it much, just wanted to put it out of my head, I suppose.'

Not for the first time, Wildblood reflected on how a death changes people, especially the death of a young person. It had certainly had a profound effect on Amanda. Scratch the surface and she was deeply troubled.

Taverner was on his feet. 'Well, thank you Amanda. Here is my card. If you think of anything, anything at all then give me a ring.'

He took in her strained face. 'And my Sergeant is right. You are not responsible for Caitlyn's death. We'll see ourselves out.'

Wildblood glanced at Taverner's impassive face. There hadn't been so much of a hint of impropriety in Caitlyn's relationship with Niall Lynch, so they had not moved forward a jot. She hoped her colleagues had had better luck.

They hadn't. Back at the station there was an air of gloom and despondency. They went back through the evidence before Taverner went to see Sykes to discuss the next steps. Cullen and Patel had consulted with the tech team and there was nothing of note deleted from the laptop. A thorough search had found nothing major except for some pornography and even that was pretty tame and certainly not illegal. The killer blow came from the analysis of the remaining wrenches from Lynch's set which did not match the composition of the murder weapon. Taverner raked his fingers through his hair. He looked absolutely exhausted and deflated like a popped balloon.

'I'll go and speak to Sykes and let Lynch go. Everyone can go home and get some rest and we'll come back fighting tomorrow.' He managed a smile, but Wildblood could sense the utter desolation behind the brave words.

Chapter 31

Gabriel felt completely depressed and frustrated. His conversation with DCI Sykes had not gone well either. Sykes was just as disheartened about the investigation into Niall Lynch floundering as he was, and was quick to point out that the papers were baying for blood at the perceived departmental failure. However, typically Sykes' annoyance had turned to belligerence. He had thrust a copy of the Yorkshire Post under his nose with the headline, '*Cops baffled by death of murdered student. University lecturer released after questioning.*'

He winced and noted that the journalist, Angela Curtis, of course, had been clear to peddle her own pet theory that a mass murderer was on the loose killing students, and had made veiled links with Caitlyn Fear's death several years before.

'At least we can rule that out,' Sykes had grumbled, passing Dr Ives's full report over the desk. 'Seems the girl fell down a staircase in a night club on her way home, so the injury could have been from that. CCTV evidence had been gathered, but that part of the tape had not been checked. The fall was quite nasty and she banged her head quite hard. Ives reckons she was concussed and could easily have fallen into the river walking back home as the effects of concussion can often be delayed. Combined with the alcohol she had drunk, she just keeled over. The previous pathologist missed it.' He glowered at Taverner. 'What's that Lauren lass saying? We definitely need to know if the stabbing is related to the murder.'

Sykes had a real skill for stating the bleeding obvious, Taverner noted. He took a deep breath before replying. 'Yes, sir. We have asked her, of course, but she's dazed and has not been in a fit state to answer in depth questions. We will go back. Me and Wildblood.'

Sykes scowled. 'Do we still need the police presence at the hospital?'

'Yes. Until we can rule out any link with Morgan's death then we have no alternative, sir. She could be at real risk.'

Sykes sighed heavily, no doubt weighing up the considerable costs to the force.

'And we're keeping a list of visitors?'

'Absolutely. She's only allowed to see her next of kin and anyone else has to have a good reason to see her and they have to show ID.'

Sykes pursed his lips. 'Well, go and see her again. She's had plenty of time to get over the shock to my way of thinking, so suggest getting rid of the officer. It might make her talk…' he added darkly. 'And we really need her to. She's the only one that might know what happened to Emily.'

Taverner seriously doubted such draconian action would work but promised to visit with Wildblood the next day. He began to despair. He didn't like the idea of frightening the girl to make a disclosure.

Sykes frowned. 'And the hair that you found at your place, any news on that?'

288

Taverner had come straight to see Sykes before he handed the sample to Forensics. 'I handled the hair and the envelope as little as possible but forensics have my fingerprints and DNA so they can rule out contamination from me. They did ask for a further sample of my biometrics, which I gave them yesterday and the tech guys are looking at the SD card from the camera, but no news so far.'

Sykes looked sick. 'I suppose they are just being thorough. So, assuming it's human hair, we might have another victim?'

'Well, that's the thing. There's no recent crimes of abduction, but it could always be from a historical crime, I suppose, maybe something that links to Emily. There's nothing from the Misper checks so far.'

'Good. Like I said, it's probably a bloody nutter. We certainly get plenty of those.'

Taverner nodded at the truth of it. After a police appeal, plenty of so called new evidence could be discounted and a lot of police time was wasted in sorting the facts from the fiction. Appeals seemed to bring out the worst in unstable people who would often fantasise about helping the police and gave spurious information that had to be taken seriously. Wildblood had said the same when he told her, explaining that people were sometimes so keen to help, they would do anything, even it seemed dream up events.

'How did they know where you live?' asked Sykes.

'I have no idea, sir. I can only presume I have been followed.'

Sykes studied him intently. 'Is there something you're not telling me?'

For a second Taverner thought about confiding in him about the trouble he'd had at the Met when he had encountered one of the nation's most vicious and vindictive criminals, the head of an organised crime group who dealt in drugs and guns. He had asked for armed response, but it had arrived too late and he had been shot in the leg. Sykes would have some knowledge of it from his files, but not the intimate details. He still suffered pain in his thigh as a result of a horrible encounter, but he had come off better than his adversary who was still languishing at Her Majesty's pleasure and would do so for several more years. It couldn't be anything to do with him, surely? No, it was most unlikely, he decided, closing down that line of thought almost immediately. The villain he knew was not exactly subtle and specialised in guns and other horrific forms of torture like chopping off fingers or hands, just to make a point. A lock of hair pushed under a plant pot was hardly his style, far too subtle and harmless.

'Well, you'd best watch your bloody back,' Sykes had added gruffly. 'I presume you have reasonable security at home?'

'Pretty good. I keep checking it.'

'Well, don't take any chances and get back to me as soon as you know anything.'

Taverner had wearily agreed to do so and made his way home, his heart heavy.

He had brought his iPad home with him and after feeding Pebbles, ate a quick omelette. He poured himself a double Macallans, put on his collection of Bowie's greatest hits and started to analyse the evidence. He pulled out a roll of drawing paper, dug out his felt tips and began. It was a strange process, investigating any crime, and he found it helpful to let the clues sort of marinade in his brain. Music helped him concentrate, the Macallans made him relax and the notes

290

helped structure his thoughts. It was easy to give too much weight to a small piece of information and end up making mental leaps that led down blind alleys, and on the other hand miss something seemingly inconsequential, which turned out to be of vital importance. It was a bit like getting a crossword clue wrong early on and having to go back and redo the whole thing. He had to go back to first principles. He wrote Emily's name in the centre of the page and wrote the names of the suspects around her. He wrote Dan Charlton, Ross MacAllister, Niall Lynch, and the evidence for and against each of them. As Golden Years was playing, he continued to work through the evidence. All the alibis added up and they had been checked and double checked. CCTV, ANPR and phone information had been used where possible to verify the information. The music continued, Suffragette City, Let's Dance, Sorrow, Rebel Rebel, The Jean Genie, Major Tom and through to Heroes when he realised they were missing something. There had to be another suspect, some other person who they may not yet know about, or someone who had been hitherto ignored. He pored over witness statements and forensic evidence, spending hours working through the documents that he felt were crucial to the investigation. He even factored in Maggie Malone's information. What was it she'd said? He remembered the tarot card with the man in the cloak, the hero or something. And she had mentioned a card to do with the moon and a page carrying a sword. Damn, he could not remember; it probably was nonsense anyway, certainly it did not appear to relate to Niall Lynch.

At the end of the evening he had sunk a few more Macallans had a conversation with his father who told him not to give up and felt slightly better, but only slightly. At the end of the evening, he was pleasantly tipsy, calm yet absolutely none the wiser. He had vague feelings of disquiet because of the lock of hair that had been placed under the plant pot. Was it some sort of prank or was it from the killer? He had no idea. He rinsed his glass and stared out at the kitchen window into the night sky. It was surprisingly light, and the moon was almost full as it shone brightly illuminating the field and hedgerows below in its magical glow. He had grown accustomed to seeing the bulky outline of the caravans, their exterior lanterns blinking into the dark but realised with a pang that they had gone. His eyes searched the area to see if they had moved position perhaps, set up in another part of the field, but he could see nothing, not even the jagged outline of the patches of the piebald ponies they'd had with them. He surprised himself by feeling almost bereft. At least the farmer would be pleased, and he could stop feeling guilty about not challenging them about the damage to the chain on the gate. He wondered briefly why they had come and then left just as suddenly. Probably it was just the traveller way, he concluded.

He stroked Pebbles and considered that it was now nearly December, three weeks since Emily's body had been found and now Christmas would soon be upon them and they were still no further on. He had read that the human brain was amazing, vastly superior to any computer that had been made to date. The contents of the conscious mind were said to be like car head lights illuminating the way ahead. The unconscious depths were the rest of the world in darkness, vast and very powerful, able to process information unprompted. He certainly needed some help from this area of the brain. He scrambled into bed and as he was falling asleep, hoped that his subconscious brain would work its magic. He thought about Maggie Malone with

292

her tarot cards, suddenly remembering the name of one of the cards. The, hierophant, that was it. He was rather drawn to the image of the man in the ceremonial robes for some reason that he couldn't fathom. Then the moon and the page. It was almost as though the characters reminded him of someone. And the moon she had said represented deception. Well, she was right in a way. Someone was bloody well lying. Maybe he should contact her and ask if she'd had any more insights. Then he dismissed the thought. God, he must be desperate was his last thought before he drifted off.

As promised, they made their way to the hospital and en route, Taverner updated Wildblood on his conversation with Sykes. He had told her about the incident with the envelope being left at his house but had asked her to keep it confidential for now. Wildblood had agreed that the hair might not even be human, so it was sensible to wait for it to be analysed.

'Any news on the hair found at your place?'

'No, nothing so far. I'll get back to Forensics.'

Wildblood tutted when he told her what Sykes had said about removing Lauren's guard and seeing if that might force the girl to talk.

'Typical, tight old bugger. Anyway, we could try it, I suppose.' She glanced at Taverner. 'I mean just mention it in passing and see what she says,' she added guardedly.

'No, I don't want her being scared into talking, if we can help it.'

She was relieved to hear Taverner explain that Ives had reached the conclusion that Caitlyn Fear had in fact died as a result of a head injury that hadn't been picked up. It had caused concussion and dizziness which could have resulted in her fall into the river.

Wildblood shook her head. 'Christ, how did Sykes miss that?'

Taverner shrugged. 'Not sure. Seems like he did, although he blamed the locum pathologist.'

'Typical and he got bloody well promoted after that. Probably to do with being one of the funny handshake brigade, because it has nothing to do with his detective skills, I can tell you.'

Taverner felt he had to correct his colleagues about her view of the Masons and their link to the police. 'That sort of thing doesn't happen, as you very well know.'

Wildblood raised an ironic eyebrow. 'I wouldn't know because as a woman I can't join, not that I'd want to. At least that should keep the press off our backs for a while.' She pulled into the hospital car park. 'OK, let's hope that our Lauren is in a more talkative mood today because we need all the help we can get.'

Taverner nodded in silent agreement.

Lauren lay in bed, pale and quiet amidst machinery that beeped rhythmically. She wore a silver necklace with a silver heart pendant that shone brightly and was obviously quite new, but apart from that, she looked unkempt and absurdly young. The hospital smelled of bleach overlain with polish, the atmosphere stuffy even though the temperature outside was nearer freezing. Lauren was flanked by an older man, her father apparently, dressed in jeans and a jumper and wearing a bleak expression. Lauren's mother appeared to have had other concerns, namely where her next dose of heroin was

294

coming from, so she hadn't kept a good eye on her daughter and hadn't queried where she was when her father had said she hadn't turned up there. Taverner recalled reading that Lauren's father had been upset and then furious about his daughter's assault, but also angry with himself.

'Do you know anything, have you got someone for the attack?' he asked when Taverner explained that they wanted to interview Lauren again.

He could hardly bear the hopeful expression that flitted across the man's face.

'No, but we are making progress…'

Mr Jackson got up to exit the room. 'If only we'd checked more. She told her mum she was at mine and told me she were there. All the time she were at her friend's getting up to God knows what. I'd like to ask his parents why they didn't ring us, I mean, can't you do them for harbouring a minor, or summat? I know this lad's a school friend and that, but it's not right, not telling us where she is.'

'Well, that's possible. Do you know who she was staying with?' asked Wildblood.

'Some lad in her class called Nat by all accounts,' he whispered. He glanced at his daughter, his expression tender. 'Not sure of his real name. Don't keep her too long, will yer? She's still very weak…'

'No, we won't…'

Lauren looked pale and scared.

'We just want to see if you've remembered anything, that's all. Whoever hurt you is still out there and could still be a danger to you or someone else. You're not in any trouble. So, anything you can remember would really be a help.' Wildblood smiled.

'Did you remember anything about the person who attacked you? Was there something familiar about them? You said you remembered the voice, was it male or female…' continued Taverner.

Lauren just looked blank, huge blue shadows under her eyes, shock and distress in her expression.

'Male, I think…'

'Anything else?'

She shook her head.

'What about the lad from school who you were staying with when you should have been at your parents? What's his surname?'

Lauren merely stared, her lip trembling slightly. She blinked back tears.

The questions continued but Lauren still refused to answer. Taverner gave her some time then made a decision. He tried to be gentle but decided to be honest.

'The thing is, Lauren, my boss is on at me about the cost of having around the clock protection for you. We might have to lose the officer outside your room, so it's important that you tell us if you're at risk. If you're afraid of someone or think that the perpetrator might come back, then now would be a good time to tell us.'

Wildblood looked at him in surprise. But it was no use, Lauren turned her head away and refused to speak. As they stood up to leave, Wildblood touched her shoulder.

'Bye, Lauren. We'll let you get some rest and if you remember anything at all then please ask one of the nurses to ring us and we'll come right round.'

'Yes, we just want to help. We are not the enemy,' added Taverner, quelling his irritation.

'What a waste of time,' grumbled Wildblood as they made to leave. 'You changed your bloody tune! So much for not threatening to take away the officer!'

Taverner grinned. 'I merely told it like it was. I won't let Sykes take the officer away, though. It's just that other girls might be at risk and we're getting precisely nowhere.'

He nodded at the officer standing outside the room. 'I'll just check the visitors' list. I won't be a moment.'

He wondered about Lauren's relationship with Nat. Perhaps the lad had put in an appearance at the hospital. He had noticed Lauren's shiny new necklace too, was that a present from an admirer?

The young PC looked flustered when addressed by his superior and handed over a clipboard with a list of names.

'It's been parents mainly, apart from a couple of others, sir.'

Taverner scanned down the list. The Jacksons dominated the list plus a few other names. No one called Nat though. His eyes were drawn to a particular name, Matthew Lawson.

He beckoned Wildblood over and pointed at the name written on the paper.

'Look, our friendly ex-vicar has visited.'

'Strange since he claimed not to know any of the young people in the group, don't you think?'

'Yes, he was very clear about that. Maybe he was just having an attack of conscience? I wonder why he retired early from the clergy. We never did find out…' continued Taverner.

'Perhaps he lost his faith when his wife died, he mentioned being depressed, didn't he?' added Wildblood.

'Yes, and he also mentioned that Niall Lynch used to go to the group, something Niall never told us. I wonder why?'

'He could have his own suspicions about Niall. The group could be a way for Lynch to meet young girls.'

Taverner frowned. 'The link could be the literacy group. Maybe it's a front for something else and Emily worked it out. He may not even know what is going on, but vulnerable groups of kids could be targeted for loads of reasons. I think we should have another look at Matthew Lawson, don't you? He must know more than he's letting on.'

Chapter 32

The house was quiet, and the twins were in bed by the time Anna arrived home. Rob was on the phone with his back to her, the low hum of the TV masking the sounds of her arrival, so she was able to catch his words.

'Yep. I'm glad you've done that. I'll pass it on to Anna, she'll be really pleased.'

Rob turned and looked momentarily alarmed before smiling. 'Hey. I didn't hear you come in. How are you? Good day?'

'Not bad. Things are coming together on the case.' She leaned in for a kiss. 'Who was that on the phone? What did you need to pass on to me?'

'Oh, it was John. He's had a long talk with the police domestic violence staff, and they are going to talk to Izzy.'

Anna smiled. 'Thank God for that.' That was really good news. She just hoped that Izzy would listen. In her experience, it was hard to get victims to see themselves as just that. It was almost as though they had been brainwashed into thinking they deserved to be knocked about. It made her very sad. She thought about Mandy from her previous investigation and wondered how her life had turned out. Not well, she suspected.

'Right, I've made a shepherd's pie. Do you want some? It's just in the oven.'

'It's fine, I'll dish it out.' Anna put on the oven gloves and removed the pie from the oven. It smelled delicious and she realised she was very hungry.

'John was asking about his apartment in the Algarve. How about a spring break? Early next year?'

'That could work actually. It would be something to look forward to.'

'I suppose your investigation will be over by then?'

Anna laughed. 'Christ, I certainly hope so.'

Matt grinned. 'Good. It will be really nice to get back to normal. I liked it when you investigated the usual stuff, the odd burglary, agricultural thefts, sheep stealing and the like...'

She shook her head. 'Sheep stealing, since when have I ever investigated anything like that?'

But he was right. She really needed a break. Trudging over remote hills searching for sheep for hours sounded blissfully easy after this murder inquiry.

She arrived in the office stocked up with bacon sandwiches and doughnuts from Ma Baker's, anticipating a long day as they scrutinised Matthew Lawson's details and the literacy group. Taverner looked alert and ready for action as he addressed his team.

'We are now seriously looking at the literacy group as it is the only thing that links Emily and Lauren, so we need to conduct checks on Matthew Lawson, the vicar who claimed to have set up the group. He also said that he did not know Lauren, yet he did visit her in hospital. If the literacy group is a front for criminal activity and Emily and Lauren found this out, then that would have given someone a very good motive to shut them up.' He tapped Niall's photo on the links board. 'And Niall used to do talks there so he could have targeted Lauren, and Emily may have realised what was going on and confronted him.'

'Hmm. Do you think Lawson knows something? Perhaps, he turned a blind eye?' suggested Patel..

Haworth shook his head. 'Wouldn't be the first time, though would it? Bloody clergymen!'

There was a general ripple of laughter.

'Maybe it's to do with drug smuggling like county lines and someone else is exploiting the kids in the group,' volunteered Cullen. 'Maybe even another young person? They are all vulnerable.'

'Good thinking,' replied Taverner. Cullen blushed bright crimson at the unexpected praise. 'You and Patel go through the list of the kids and see if there have ever been any concerns about any of them to do with drugs or criminal exploitation. Haworth and Patel speak to the schools too. Someone in Lauren's school is likely to know something and chances are it may well have come to the teachers' attention. We also need to know who Lauren's friend, Nat, is. She stayed at his quite often, so he's bound to know something, and she won't tell us his surname.' Taverner surveyed his team. 'I feel like we are making progress, I just need each and every one of you to pull out all the stops. I will brief DCI Sykes, and then Wildblood and I will follow up on Matthew Lawson. Now it goes without saying that I want to know the minute you think you have anything significant. Got it?'

There was a murmur of agreement and everyone shuffled off to do their bit. Wildblood sipped her coffee and went through Matthew Lawson's statement, reading the opening paragraph where he stated his previous occupation, clergyman, and which parish and church he had worked in last. Holy Trinity Church in Barrow-upon-Humber, forty odd miles away to the East. They needed to speak to the present incumbent and see what was known about Matthew Lawson. She was curious to know why he had left the clergy as it might be crucial to the investigation. Maybe he had lost his faith when his wife died? Strange though, because she'd have thought that religion would be a great comfort in a time of need, but she supposed everyone acted differently.

Taverner looked tense after his meeting with Sykes.

'I told him about Matthew Lawson, that he was the vicar at a church in Barrow-upon-Humber on the East coast before running the literacy group. I don't think he was convinced but he thought it was worth a look when I explained about his visit to the hospital. So, let's go.'

'I'll drive,' added Wildblood. She had not forgotten the last time he had driven her and how she had felt horribly sick at his speeding interrupted by heavy braking. Fortunately, Taverner did not complain.

'Fine.'

The drive out to Barrow on the East coast was unexpectedly picturesque, especially when they travelled south over the Humber Bridge. There was a light mist over the Humber which made the bridge look ethereal and atmospheric. Taverner looked at the structure as they drove.

'Wow. That's seriously impressive,' he commented.

Anna had driven over the bridge hundreds of times, so she was more used to it.

'I suppose. It spans about two miles, I think. Used to be the longest single span suspension bridge in the world. Still is the longest in the UK. A real feat of engineering. Anyway, what are we looking for?'

Taverner frowned. 'I'm not sure. I think it's really odd that he visited Lauren. Maybe he was trying to warn her off and the more I think about it, something didn't ring true about Lawson's last visit to us and all that stuff about seeing Emily and Dan arguing.'

'Mmm. I know what you mean, it could have been something and nothing. Maybe one of them wanted to go on a tour of the Minster and the other didn't?'

Barrow-upon-Humber was a quaint, rural village which was once home to the carpenter and inventor of the sea clock, John Harrison. Taverner seemed to know a lot about it. There was a pleasant market square where there was a bronze statue of John Harrison holding his clock and the local school was named after their famous resident with the motto, 'Success through effort'.'

'John Harrison certainly knew about that. It took him twenty years to win the Longitude Prize with his sea clock. Most amazing invention,' explained Taverner. 'In the seventeenth century there were loads of deaths at sea because the sailors could not navigate accurately. You need a constant, like time, to be able to work out something unknown and they didn't have that. If you think about it, clocks then relied on pendulums, which didn't work at sea. That put all the navigational calculations out, hence the huge number of shipwrecks and deaths. Harrison invented a clock they could use on a ship. It told the time reliably though it took him years. It saved loads of lives. He is a bit of a historical maritime hero of mine actually. I know about him from living by the sea in Deal.'

Wildblood laughed. Trust Taverner to know about such obscure things.

'Very interesting, but this isn't going to help us find Emily's murderer though, is it?'

'Sadly no. Look. That must be Holy Trinity Church, there.'

The church was situated upon a mound off the High Street. It was an impressive looking place and just opposite was a splendid Georgian vicarage complete with gravel driveway and a large garden. They pulled up and found the vicar's details on a noticeboard inside the porch way. The Reverend Edward Kane was the present incumbent.

'I think we're in the wrong job,' commented Taverner as they made their way to the back door of the Vicarage and rapped on the oak door with the large brass door knocker.

'Too bloody right,' replied Wildblood, taking in the size of the place. 'What a lovely house.'

The Reverend Edward Kane was younger than she expected, wore a black suit, dog collar and a wide, disarming smile. It was also clear that he had a brood of children if the lines of small brightly coloured wellingtons, bikes and scooters which were scattered about the boot room by the door, were anything to go by.

'Let's go into my study. I'm afraid it's organised chaos with three children under 5. My wife, Ruthie, will provide us with refreshments. Come this way.'

The study held two vast bookcases mainly filled with Ecclesiastical Books, but Wildblood also spotted a few Dick Francis novels and several by Jilly Cooper nestled amongst Dickens, which were certainly not what she expected. Diverse taste in literature then. The vicar had been writing at his desk and a notepad covered in black spidery handwriting with lots of crossings out, was visible. A large fire crackled in the grate.

'It's good of you to see us on spec,' began Taverner. 'We can see you're busy.'

'Not at all. I'm just writing my sermon for the beginning of Advent but I'm struggling as you can see. I'm trying to get across the value of relationships rather than material things which is always a hard one in the run up to Christmas.' She decided she was going to like Edward Kane. It felt as though she had gone back in time some hundred years or so. The decor in the drawing room was pale yellow, the cornicing was authentic, and the room had plenty of light from the large sash windows. There were two pale yellow sofas which were faded and comfortable. After tea and a plate of excellent scones provided by the plump but fresh faced Ruthie, Edward smoothed down his trousers and regarded them.

'Now, what can I help you with? It's not often I have police visiting me, so I'm intrigued. I'm guessing you are not seeking spiritual guidance, but if so I'm happy to give it.'

Taverner outlined the situation. 'We are investigating a murder and a violent assault and we have reason to believe that a literacy group run by the University of York and Matthew Lawson, previous vicar at Holy Trinity, may be connected in some way.' Anna noticed Kane's look of surprise. 'Although we don't yet know how, and we've decided to find out more about Matthew Lawson's background. Is there anything you can tell me about him?'

'Surely you don't suspect Matthew?'

Taverner was soothing. 'No, just the group he runs. It may be a front for something else, but we're not suggesting he knows about it. So, what can you tell us about Matthew? Isn't it unusual for someone to leave the clergy?'

Kane shook his head. 'Not as unusual as you might think. Believe it or not, we are a bit like social workers and fundraisers these days, overworked and underpaid, so it's hard going. I presume you have asked Matthew himself why he left?'

'Yes, but it's also useful to get information from other sources, to triangulate the findings,' Taverner explained.

Wildblood noticed Edward's hesitation, so decided to up the ante. 'It is a murder inquiry, of course.'

Edward Kane nodded. 'Right. I didn't meet Matthew personally, but parishioners do talk. He was the sporty vicar who ran a football team, whose son is a professional who plays for Sheffield?'

'Yes. That's the one.'

'I was told he left to help support his son's football career. He was very keen and had been a good footballer himself.'

Judging from Kane's slight flush, Wildblood thought there was more to tell.

'Did your parishioners say anything else?'

'Not really, but I got the impression that he lost his faith…' added Kane.

'Ah, after his wife's death, I presume?' Wildblood added.

Reverend Kane gasped. 'Death? Oh no, his wife is very much alive and well. In fact, she lives in the village.' He suddenly brightened. 'I can give you her address. Penny arranges the flowers in the Church, she's an absolute stalwart actually.' He scribbled something on a post-it note and handed it to Taverner. 'It's only round the corner.'

'Thanks. We'll call in,' added Taverner, getting up to leave. Wildblood reluctantly followed him. She felt that she could have stayed in the warmth and comfort all day.

'Sir, do you think this is a waste of time?' she asked as they walked the short distance to a cottage near the church. It was lovely wandering around this idyllic village drinking tea, but was it going to yield any results? She wondered if they should go back to the office and look again at Daniel Charlton and his father instead. Taverner strode on with his coat collar pulled up against the cold.

'Well, since we're here we may as well see Mrs Lawson. It will only take a few minutes.' He rubbed his hands. 'Besides it will keep us out of the cold.'

Taverner tapped on the door of the cottage but there was no response. Damn, it was disappointing. Taverner produced a card from his breast pocket and hastily wrote a note asking for her to contact him as soon as possible. Then they heard the sound of movement from inside and a smart looking woman with steel grey bobbed hair and an upright posture opened the door.

'Mrs Lawson?' Taverner proffered his warrant card. 'We're from North Yorkshire Police. Can we come in and talk to you?'

Seemingly satisfied with their ID, she beckoned them through the door with a smile.

'Come in.'

Mrs Lawson also produced cake, a piquant lemon drizzle and strong tea. Wildblood accepted a very small slice of the cake. It was delicious. She vowed to eat less tomorrow.

'Now, what can I help you with?'

'We'd just like to ask you some questions about your ex-husband, I presume Matthew is an ex now?'

'Oh yes, ex-husband and ex-vicar. We divorced a couple of years ago.' She sipped her tea. 'He wanted to support Nathaniel and I wanted to stay here. I hate football and became a football widow as soon as Nathaniel was taken on as an apprentice actually.'

'I can see how that would have been very annoying,' commented Wildblood. She couldn't see what all the fuss was about, grown men hoofing a ball about a field for ridiculous sums of money.

Taverner, she knew was a football fan but merely raised an eyebrow at this terrible heresy.

'So that coincided with your husband giving up his role in the Church too, I suppose. Couldn't he have found a parish near to Nathaniel's club in Sheffield?'

Mrs Lawson looked hesitant. 'I suppose so, but then there was that falling out with the Dean. It was all very unfortunate.'

Wildblood paused her note taking and looked at Taverner who was sitting very upright.

'Really? What was that about?'

Penny sighed. 'I never really got into the details, Matthew insisted that it was all a huge misunderstanding anyway...'

Taverner glanced at Wildblood who had her pen and pad at the ready.

'I know this is difficult for you, Penny, but it is important. What happened?'

She wiped her eyes and nodded.

'It started when Nathaniel was apprenticed to Lincoln and the apprentices used to train at a particular school and Nathaniel became friendly with a girl at there.' She looked at them, willing them to understand. 'The club were furious because the apprentices weren't supposed to associate with the pupils. There was a bit of a stink about it...'

'When you say became friendly, what do you mean?'

'They became friends. The club weren't pleased but when the Dean found out he insisted that Matthew do his Safeguarding training again.'

'Why would he do that?' asked Wildblood.

'Nathaniel was seventeen and the girl thirteen, I think. A social worker was involved but the girl didn't make any allegations. Matthew had a row with the Dean and sent him his resignation the next day. Matthew was so annoyed about the Dean's reaction that he decided to retire early. Nathaniel played football for Hull instead.' She suddenly looked up, tears in her eyes. 'It was about that time that we separated, and I stayed here in Barrow. You see, Matthew was just obsessed with Nathaniel's football career, that was all he was bothered about. It was just a misunderstanding, wasn't it?'

Taverner glanced at Wildblood and stood up. 'I really don't know is the honest answer, but we need to check it out.'

After they had said their goodbyes, Wildblood and Taverner debriefed.

'It's a bit of an overreaction from the Dean to Nathaniel being friends with a younger girl, wasn't it? Unless of course…Are you thinking what I'm thinking?'

'Mmm. It might be something and nothing. There would surely be a police record of a sexual assault but then if the girl didn't make a complaint, maybe not. Not sure how this fits in with the literacy group. Maybe Lynch and Nathaniel worked together to groom girls and Matthew was oblivious?'

'God, t'literacy group could have been a front to groom vulnerable girls.'

Taverner frowned. 'We really need to speak to Lauren again. I'll ring the guys to do some more checks.'

Wildblood screeched off en route to the station with Taverner frantically on the phone. He arranged for Cullen and Patel to look at the CCTV footage of the city centre coverage of Emily on the night she died and anything else that they could find that would link Lauren to Lynch or Nathaniel.

'Get back to me if you find anything urgently!' he barked into his phone.

Taverner sighed. 'The only problem with this is we need more. Lauren hasn't even identified him and we don't know that she even knows him. And he is a rising star, and we will be crucified if we get this wrong.'

Taverner ran his fingers through his hair and stretched out his legs.

'Do you think Matthew knew?'

'Hmm. My guess is that Matthew was fixated with Nathaniel's football career and had a blind spot about his behaviour.'

'I bloody well hope not!'

Just then Taverner's phone rang out.

'Taverner. Right, right.' He listened intently. 'Bloody good work, now go out and pick him up.'

Wildblood was stuck behind a lorry and struggling to overtake. She looked at him inquiringly.

'Listen, all the evidence is now pointing to Nathaniel. There's no Nat, Nathan or Nathaniel who would be friends with Lauren at the school and they can't find anything on the CCTV, but Cullen has spoken to social services and they have gone through their records extensively. Lauren did give a different address to a sexual health worker, probably assuming they wouldn't pass it on to her social worker. She refused to give the name of the person she was staying with but guess what? It's Nathaniel Lawson's address.' His eyes gleamed. 'The person Lauren has been staying with, Nat is Nathaniel. So now we do have a link. I'll feel so much better when he is locked up. Look, do you want me to drive?'

Wildblood began to speed up. 'No, it's fine.' She spotted a break in the oncoming traffic and steamed past the lorry. 'Listen, us getting back to the station won't get him arrested any quicker.'

311

'I know, I know, but if you could just hurry up…'

By the time they had come back to the office, from Barrow-upon-Humber, Nathaniel had been arrested on suspicion of child sexual abuse. They still had some work to do to establish that he murdered Emily. Sykes was waiting to brief Taverner on interviewing Nathaniel. Haworth and Cullen were out searching his property in a village just on the outskirts of York. The police also wanted to speak to Matthew Lawson, but he was nowhere to be found.

Sykes was bristling with tension. 'Bloody hope the search turns up something concrete because we have no actual allegation from that Lauren lass. Do you know who he is? The football club and Lawson will sue if you're wrong…'

Taverner noted the 'you're' which was typical of Sykes who would no doubt be happy to take all the plaudits if they were right. He chose to ignore it.

'I know, but the working theory is that Nathaniel somehow inveigled his way into the literacy group and groomed the young girls, Lauren included. Now we have her staying at his address, and concerns about Lawson's behaviour towards young girls, there's enough evidence to arrest him.'

'Well, I hope you're right because otherwise the press are going to have a field day. They don't take kindly to local football stars being arrested. He's a right good player, I saw him at Sheffield, bloody future international if you ask me.'

'Good player or not, he could have groomed Lauren with a view to harm her and if Emily suspected this, he has a motive to murder her.'

Right on cue Haworth and Cullen walked through the door with broad grins.

'Hey up, sir, put the kettle on. Looks like we got him,' said Haworth, holding evidence bags aloft. 'We found love letters from various girls including Lauren, receipts for some pieces of jewellery and used condoms in the bin. We have also seized his laptop and phone and what's the betting there is lots of interesting and illegal stuff on there.' He rubbed his hands together in glee.

'And it looks like he had relationships with other girls from the literacy group,' added Patel who wandered in with a sheaf of papers. 'We need to interview them. Look, here's the evidence.'

Anna took this in. 'So, is there a history of concerns around Nathaniel?'

Patel handed her a print out of the PNC check. 'There's a few allegations stacking up, same sort of thing, but there's never been enough to charge him.'

'What I don't get is how Nathaniel got access to the kids in the group? How did that happen?' asked Sykes.

'It seems as though Matthew invited him to some of the groups to act as an inspiration to other young people,' explained Haworth. 'The schools told us that and they thought nothing of it, and he was never fully vetted. His dad just did not want to admit that his son had a problem with underage girls.'

Taverner and Wildblood were preparing to interview Nathaniel and felt much more confident knowing they had hard evidence for the sexual offences but though this gave him a very strong motive for the murder of Emily, they needed more evidence.

Sykes directed the staff as Wildblood and Taverner went into the interview.

'Looks like he's our man,' Sykes commented, having done a complete about turn on the footballer.

'Yes, looks like it,' replied Taverner.

'Well done, lad,' replied Sykes.

Taverner grinned. 'Thanks.'

Chapter 33

Haworth was right. The evidence was completely damning. It was all rushed through to Forensics for DNA analysis. Taverner and Wildblood conducted the interview. Andrew Kirby, Nathaniel's solicitor, advised his client to state 'No comment' to all questions, but Lawson paled as the evidence was laid out in front of them.

'So, you claimed not to have met Lauren Jackson, yet we found five love letters from her to you in your house.' Taverner scrolled through the iPad and paused to read some of the text.

Can't wait to see you at the weekend. Told my mum I'm at Dad's and she won't check so I can stay over. Looking forward to showing you how much I care. Can't believe I'm gonna be a WAG! Love you loads,
Lauren xxxx

'And another one dated 7th July.'

Meet me after the group, usual place. Been missing you like crazy. Can't wait to show you how much. One day we'll be together and let the world know about our love.
Lauren xxxx

'And another dated 12th August.'

Sorry I've not been able to ring you. Mum grounded me when she found I wasn't at Michelle's. Hate her, just can't wait to see you. This is killing me.

Lauren xxxx

Nathaniel had turned grey.

Wildblood smiled. 'It's clear you were in a relationship with Lauren and we found letters from Chloe Fenton and photos of her and other girls, Olivia Jones and Kirsty Needham, who we believe were in the literacy group. We also found used condoms which are being analysed as we speak and what's the betting that we find both yours and Lauren's DNA on them. And don't get me started on what we're going to find on your laptop. It really would be a whole lot easier if you admit to being in a sexual relationship with Lauren, Chloe and Kirsty. You know the Judge will feel much more lenient towards you if you admit the sex offences and stop the girls having to give evidence.'

Nathaniel swallowed hard and tried not to cry. At this point Cullen walked in and handed him a sheet. The contents of Nathaniel's laptop proved very interesting. Hidden in one of the files were lots of indecent images of children.

Taverner waited for Nathaniel to compose himself.

'How well did you know Emily Morgan?'

'Like I said, I met her when I went to Dad's group to give a talk. He thought I would be a role model for the kids being a footballer and all that. It might give them something to aim for...'

Wildblood scowled at this. 'But Emily was no fool, was she? She was bright enough to be worried about your interaction with

Lauren and looked into your past. It's not the first time there have been concerns about your behaviour towards underage girls, is it?'

She scrolled through the iPad and came to a statement from the police who had investigated Nathaniel whilst he had been an apprentice.

'A PNC check has revealed that when you were seventeen and a football apprentice you were questioned about a relationship that you'd had with a thirteen year old girl who was a pupil at the school where you regularly trained. The girl's mother complained to the head about images and messages you had exchanged with her daughter whom you had met whilst training there, despite strict instructions from the club not to fraternise with pupils from the school. The girl, GH, denied this and would not speak to police but told other school friends about your relationship it seems. You were lucky to avoid being charged due to this, so the matter was not pursued. You went on to have several other sexual relationships with minors.' Nathaniel blinked. 'We have already found letters from other girls, together with the downloads. This is looking very serious.'

Nathaniel looked helplessly at his solicitor who was writing frantically and looking increasingly worried.

Taverner leant back in his chair. 'But that isn't the worst of it, is it Nathaniel? Because we believe that Emily Morgan knew about you and Lauren and spoke to others about your past, suspected you of involvement with other girls within the group and threatened to go to the authorities. This gives you a cast iron motive to murder her in order to shut her up, as you feared this coming out and ruining your football career. We also believe that you stabbed Lauren Jackson, the girl who you claimed to love, for fear that she would reveal your relationship. We are in the process of gathering evidence against you and believe me when I say it is only a question of time before we charge you for several counts of grooming and sexual activity with a minor, one count of attempted murder and another count of murder.'

Nathaniel's mouth gaped. 'No, no, no. I didn't murder Emily or do anything to Lauren. The girls just threw themselves at me, honestly any red-blooded male would have done the same...'

Taverner scowled. He hated this type of perverse argument which people like Nathaniel Lawson used to justify their behaviour. It absolutely sickened him.

'I doubt that. Now where were you on the evening of 6th November, the night that Emily Morgan was murdered?'

Nathaniel frowned, deep in thought. 'That's easy. We played Cardiff at home.'

'But you could still have got back to York in time to murder Emily Morgan.'

'No, no when I say at home, I meant their home and we had extra time, won 1-0 and went for a meal before coming back. I didn't get home until at least 2 am.'

Wildblood looked at Taverner. Christ, he must have had help.

'But you're injured, so how do we know you were even there?'

Nathaniel rolled his eyes. 'Because injured or not we still have to go to all the matches.'

Taverner thought back to what Daniel Charlton had said. 'But didn't Sheffield play Hull on that day?'

Nathaniel sighed. 'In case you hadn't noticed there are two football teams in Sheffield, and I play for the other one.'

318

Taverner looked at Wildblood and nodded at the door. It was time for a break.

'Thank you. That's it for now.'

Taverner checked the football matches for 6th November. He tapped at his phone.

'Damn, he's quite right, so if he was there, then he can't possibly have murdered Emily. So, someone else must have helped him. He thought for a minute as realisation dawned. Several pieces of information circled in his brain and settled into one terrible conclusion. The bloody bookcase and the weighty tomes about sexual deviance he had seen at Matthew's house! Suppose Matthew had tried to cure his son which meant he had most certainly known about his sexual predilections? Had he murdered to cover this up too? 'Christ, it's not Nathaniel, it was his father. We need to find Matthew Lawson as soon as possible.'

Wildblood looked confused. 'Do yer think he's involved?'

Taverner nodded. 'In his hallway he had some books on sexual deviance which I thought was strange at the time but I wondered if there were offenders in his parish, but supposing he knew about his son's preferences and was trying to help him?'

Wildblood gasped in horror.

Just then, Haworth popped his head round the door. 'Sir, the PC who's guarding Lauren Jackson in hospital has just rung. Apparently, she's gone.'

'Gone?'

'Yes. When he came back from the canteen, she'd left.'

'Why the hell wasn't he protecting her like he was paid to do?'

'He said that the Hospital Chaplain came to visit her, so he left them alone for a bit.'

Wildblood put her hand over her mouth. 'Suppose it was Matthew? Christ, he could have just put his dog collar on! What's he going to do to her? Oh God.'

Taverner fought the rising panic and tried to think straight.

'Right, we will need reinforcements to find Matthew and we also need a team to conduct a search of his home. Come on, we've no time to waste.'

Chapter 34

They drove to Matthew Lawson's house, a stylish three storey townhouse in a well heeled area. Officers had gone ahead and broken the door down, having found that Matthew wasn't there.

'At least we might get some clues as to where he has taken Laura.'

A white suited officer confirmed that Matthew's car keys and passport appeared to be missing, and it looked like he had packed some clothes.

'What's more, we have found a set of wrenches in his garage and the 10 inch one is missing, and we've also found a knife wrapped up in a cloth shoved in the downstairs toilet cistern. It looks like the one he used to stab Lauren. We might be able to get some prints and DNA off it.'

'Right.' Taverner sighed. It was something but where the hell was Matthew and more importantly Lauren?

Wildblood tugged at his sleeve. 'Sir, we just had an ANPR match of Matthew's car travelling on the A63 towards Hull. We've sent cars out to tail him.'

'Right, we need back up, armed response, helicopters the lot. Let's follow behind.'

'I'll drive,' replied Wildblood. 'I've done the advanced driving course.' She didn't want Taverner going all macho and roaring off nearly killing them.

'Fine, let's go.'

It was a cold night; the sky was inky black lit up with twinkling stars and a crescent moon shone brightly. The skies were different up north, Taverner realised, thoughts meandering in the unreality of the situation. He liked it, the city, the warmth of the people, even the flat vowels had grown on him too. The feeling had crept up on him but he realised that it felt like home. His reverie was interrupted by Wildblood putting on the blue lights and sweeping at high speed around a line of cars. She was a competent driver and she seemed to be enjoying the chase. The radio crackled into life as the driver up ahead contacted them, to give information on Lawson's position.

'Suspect has turned off the A63 and is heading towards Hessle.'

'We're about a mile from that junction but will follow.' Taverner signed off. 'Any idea why he could be going to Hessle?'

Wildblood shrugged. 'Unless, oh shit, the Humber Bridge turn off is that way.' Her eyes glinted in the darkness. They were filled with fear.

Taverner thought back to his one trip over to North Lincolnshire a few days ago. 'Are there footpaths over the bridge?'

'Sadly, yes. It's something of a suicide hotspot.'

'Oh, God! We'd better alert the Humber Bridge Authority so they can close the bridge to traffic.'

As predicted, the radio crackled once more with the news they had dreaded.

'He's parked on the Humber Bridge Country Park and he and his passenger, a young teenager, are on foot making their way to the Eastern pathway. The Humber Bridge Authority have already closed the Bridge, sir. I've sent an officer round, but the suspect is ahead of us. What are your instructions?'

Taverner thought about his hostage training. 'Look, on no account rush at him or surprise him or the girl might well end up in the Humber. I'll try and get a trained negotiator out. Armed response officers are on their way, but we have to use crisis resolution first. So, I repeat, take no action and await further instructions.'

Five minutes later, Wildblood drew into the Country Park and came screeching to a halt alongside other police vehicles. The bridge was lit up and looked spectacular against the night sky. Taverner peered into the distance at the huge structure and thought he could see the outline of two figures stumbling towards the centre of the bridge on the footpath. He spoke urgently into his phone to keep Sykes updated.

'We have a very serious situation, sir. Matthew Lawson has Lauren and he's taken her onto the Humber Bridge. I need a negotiator here as soon as possible.'

'Right, I'll get on to it. I'll ring you back in five minutes.'

Taverner and Wildblood had no choice but to sit and wait. As he looked out at the bridge and imagined Lauren's terror, he reflected that it was the longest five minutes of his life. He thought back to his training which was a while ago, willing himself to remember the steps.

'It'll be alreight,' said Wildblood, watching him closely. 'He used to be a man of God, remember that. He'd have to overcome many more psychological barriers than our usual crims to harm her.'

Taverner nodded, thankful that his Sergeant had just spoken out loud his own thoughts. It made him feel slightly better about the situation. Still, desperation could do strange things to a man, he knew, and they shouldn't get complacent.

He was startled by his phone ringing. He snatched it up and jabbed at the buttons.

'Taverner here.'

It was Sykes. 'It's bad news, I'm afraid. There's an idiot in Whitby holding his wife and kids hostage, so a negotiator is there, someone else is dealing with a domestic in Scarborough and the other officer is on leave.'

Damn, that was not what he wanted to hear. 'What about using someone from Humberside Police? It's their jurisdiction by rights.'

'I've already tried and it's a no go. There's no one available, they're all out on jobs. There's an officer in South Yorkshire but we can't get hold of him. I've left an urgent message. That's the best I can do. I know you've done your training and even if it's out of date, I'm afraid it will be down to you, Taverner. If I can get hold of the other officer, he can be on hand to give you advice.'

Taverner's heart sank. He had completed the course a few years ago and could remember most of it. Softly, softly, respect, engage with the suspect, find out what he wants and talk through his options, humanise the hostage and talk up the perpetrator's future, give them a way out, something like that anyway. He fought the panic that threatened to wash over him, yet this was the job, and he would just have to get on with it. He remembered what Wildblood had said about Matthew being a man of God and decided that that was an angle he could definitely use. He took a deep breath.

'OK. I'll keep in touch but let me know if the negotiator rings you, in the meantime. I'll keep you updated.'

'Mind you do. And Taverner, good luck.'

Taverner signed off. 'Did you hear that? I can't bloody believe it. No negotiators, one possibly in South Yorkshire but not answering his blasted phone. So, it's down to me.'

Wildblood touched his arm. 'You can do it, guv. I have every faith in you.'

If only he did.

'Thanks. Right, best get to it then.'

Both of them climbed out of the car and went to talk to the Armed Response Unit. Taverner spoke to the Tactical Firearms Commander and it was agreed that Taverner would attempt to make contact with Matthew and that Authorised Firearms Officers, AFO's would surreptitiously go to the footpath opposite to where Matthew and Lauren were and standby. With that, the doors of the vehicle opened and a stream of black clad AFO's appeared and ran towards the entrance to the western pathway, smoothly and stealthily. Wildblood handed Taverner body armour which he hastily put on, adjusting the velcro straps so it fitted tightly. He fiddled with his headset. He looked up at the inky black sky and into the stars wishing he was tucked up safely in bed like any other sensible person. Then he thought about Lauren's terror and his focus sharpened.

'Do we have Matthew's phone number?'

Wildblood nodded and handed him a piece of paper with the number written on it.

He took a deep breath, punched the numbers into the phone and waited.

'Yeah.'

'Matthew. It's DI Taverner here. We met before.'

'Right, what the hell do you want?' He heard a muffled high pitched cry, presumably from Lauren.

'Just calm down Matthew. I just want to check that Lauren is alright and you and me are just going to have a chat. I know you're upset, and you think that everything has gone wrong, but there is a way back' He paused and heard his breathing slow. At least he was listening which was something.

'I'm going to come up to where you are, slowly, no rushing and no surprises, because we need to sort this out. OK?'

'Piss off!' The phone clicked and then there was silence.

Shit! Maybe he had pushed him too far too soon.

Matthew and Lauren were lit up by the lights on the bridge and he turned at the noise of a helicopter complete with search lights circling overhead. They would also have the thermal imaging equipment in place, not that they needed it. They knew only too well where Matthew and Lauren were. In hindsight, it was probably the noise that had panicked Matthew. Taverner felt adrenalin surge through him as he dialled Matthew's mobile again. The phone rang out. In the distance, he could make out the silhouettes of the firearms officers hiding behind the concrete pillars on the opposite side of the bridge. After about 2 minutes, it was clear he wasn't going to answer.

326

Wildblood frowned. 'What now, sir?'

'I'm going to have to go up there. He's maybe worried about the helicopter and wondering what they are planning. I need a megaphone.'

Wildblood disappeared into the back of her vehicle and produced one. Thank God that they routinely carried a lot of equipment in their cars.

'Be careful, guv.' Wildblood touched his arm.

Taverner nodded and began walking purposefully towards the steep steps that led to the Eastern pathway of the bridge. The steps led to a narrow path with a rail about 1metre high that prevented pedestrians from falling over the side and into the grey sea of the Humber Estuary. He took several deep breaths once on the footpath and tried to compose himself. The temperature had dropped considerably next to the water, there was a faint scent of diesel and sea salt, and rain began to fall softly. He pulled up his collar against the elements, screwed up his eyes so he could make out the two figures huddled against the rail. They were towards the middle of the bridge where the water would be at its deepest, he realised, if they did jump into the water. Given the distance, it was highly unlikely that anyone would survive such a jump. Don't think about it, he told himself sternly. He took more deep breaths and lifted the megaphone to his mouth.

'It's DI Taverner, Matthew. I'm on the bridge and I'm just going to approach slowly, so we can talk this through, man to man.' His voice exploded out of the funnel and into the night sky. He saw the larger figure of Matthew move jerkily and heard a faint sob from Lauren.

'I'm just going to come a bit closer, Matthew, just so we can talk. Just take it easy.'

He edged forward until he was about thirty feet or so away. He heard Matthew shout a warning and he stopped stock still. His eyes scanned the figures ahead and he waited for Matthew to relax. The light faded and became more opaque as the heavens opened. The rain began to pelt his skin and started to run down his neck. Damn. It would make the AFO's job that much harder, as the visibility would be considerably poorer, not to mention the acoustics. The sound of the downpour was deafening. He had to get Matthew talking and hope that the weather would change.

'I'm just edging a bit closer,' he called through the megaphone.

Matthew yelled what could have been, 'stop' but it was hard to tell with the sound of the rain.

'OK, Matthew. We need to talk about a way out for you and Lauren. I know you're a good man, a man of God, but enough harm has been done already. Just let Lauren go, she's just a kid, just fourteen, she has her whole life ahead of her. Imagine if she was your daughter, Matthew. I know you're angry and upset but don't take it out on her.' He let his words sink in and looked down into the grey waters.

'I'm coming closer, Matthew, so I can hear you...'

He waited for some sort of response from Matthew, saw no movement, so edged forward. As he approached, he made out the taller figure of Matthew, his hands around the throat of the smaller figure of Lauren, her face obscured by her hoodie. Matthew's eyes were trained on Taverner, his body rigid with tension. Lauren was sobbing, terrified. He was about twenty feet away now, and the rain had stopped to a lighter drizzle. Thank God. He put the megaphone down, deciding to shout instead.

'Come on Matthew. There's a way back from this. I can understand how you feel but I know you don't want to harm Lauren. Don't make things worse than they are. Just let the girl go and everything will be better…'

Matthew was sobbing now but it was hard to make out the words.

'I never meant to hurt her…'

'Who?'

'Emily…'

'I know, I know.'

'I just wanted to talk to her, that's all…'

'You thought you were just doing right by your lad. I get it. Now what I want you to do is let Lauren go, she's just a kid, Matthew, and needs to return home. Now what's going to happen is I am going to come forward and get Lauren. Her parents are desperately worried, and I know you don't want to cause them any more pain.'

Matthew looked anguished and uncertain. Then almost as if in slow motion, he made out the outline of Matthew as he started to climb the rail. Shit. Matthew looked down at the murky, grey water beneath the bridge. He had his arm around Lauren's neck, and he bent his head and spoke urgently to her and she began to climb on to the lower rung of the railing too. Christ, no! Taverner felt his heart racing as panic set in. Taverner edged nearer and nearer.

'Don't do it Matthew, let's get you down. We can resolve this. If you didn't mean to harm Emily, you'll be looking at manslaughter, a sentence of ten years max, you'll be out in five. It will go quickly. But Lauren had nothing to do with it. She's not even needed as a witness, Matthew, do you hear. Nathaniel confessed; we know everything. He'll go to prison too and he'll need you, Matthew. You'll need each other to rebuild your lives. You can't let Nathaniel down.'

Matthew took this in, his face contorted with anguish and then loosened his grip on the girl.

'You're lying!'

'I swear, I'm not. It's true.'

Matthew looked wildly about him and then his head slumped forward. He looked utterly dejected. He knew it was over. Taverner edged closer holding out his hands as Matthew threw the girl towards him. He scooped her up and pushed her out of harm's way. An AFO appeared in the corner of Taverner's line of vision, his gun trained on Matthew's chest.

Taverner motioned for the officer to stay still and took a deep breath.

'Come on, it's over, Matthew. You're a man of God. Even though you think you've lost your faith, it's there somewhere. And God hasn't lost faith in you. Remember that.'

Taverner held his breath as Matthew slowly climbed down from the rung, his head lowered.

'That's it, now raise both your hands and walk towards me. No sudden movements.' Matthew stared at the gun man, as though he had only just noticed him, raised his hands and walked forwards as more officers appeared, shouting commands. Taverner let the armed officers arrest him as he gathered a sobbing Lauren up and walked back along the pathway. The girl felt sodden and fragile, like a tiny, frightened bird.

'It's alright Lauren. Everything's going to be fine.' She shivered and clung to him as they made their way along the footpath. He looked back to see Matthew being forcibly handcuffed and led away and he realised he had been holding his breath. The stars twinkled overhead as though in approval. Jesus. It had been close. Matthew had almost jumped and taken the girl with him. It had been a near miss. It was over and as the adrenaline began to subside, he felt like he could sleep for a week.

They made their way back along the pathway and followed the steps towards the car park. Lauren was led away by waiting paramedics. She'll be OK, he realised, she was a survivor.

'You did it, boss!' Wildblood grinned and then hugged him. 'God, I really thought he was going to jump at one point...'

Taverner smiled. 'Me too.' He sighed. He felt elated now, satisfaction tempered with a vein of sadness for the devastation and misery Matthew had caused to Emily, Lauren and their families. All to protect his son's football career. He remembered Emily's distraught parents. At least he had something to tell them now. He would visit and break the news in person, it wasn't the sort of thing you could do by phone.

Wildblood took his arm. 'Christ, you're freezing. Come on, let's get you out of those wet clothes, wrap this up and get some sleep. I'll drive you back. We can think about what we're going to do afterwards on the way. There is a life beyond this, you know, and we mustn't waste it. We need to think about the future. I fancy a holiday somewhere interesting like the Algarve, me, Rob and the twins.'

Taverner shivered as he slipped off his sodden suit jacket and pulled on a vast fluorescent standard issue coat, not stylish, but at least it was warm. His teeth began to stop chattering. Wildblood was talking for England as she drove, he knew relief and adrenaline did that to you sometimes, whereas he just felt exhausted, as though he had nothing left. She was right though. Investigations were so absorbing you hardly had time to clean your own teeth, eat or sleep whilst you were in the thick of it. There was still an awful lot of work to do to ensure a successful prosecution, a vast raft of forms, witness statements and forensic evidence. Any cock ups could still jeopardise the case. Still, he could now see a way through it to the other side. Now it was time to think about ordinary things, relationships, family.

'What will you do, guv?'

He didn't even need to think about it. 'Well, sleep then I'll probably arrange to meet my mother…' He also remembered the beer mat with Milly's phone number on it. He intended to ring her too.

Wildblood nodded. 'Good. You could meet her at the Minster and go for a coffee, or how about an afternoon tea at Betty's. She'd love that.' She looked at him intently. 'You are still going to meet her, aren't you?'

Taverner looked at his colleague, she was sometimes tactless, outspoken and did not suffer fools gladly, but there was no one he'd rather have on his side when the chips were down.

'Yes, of course. I just need some time, I'll get this case sorted and then I'll contact the adoption agency.'

'You mind yer do. It's important.'

332

It was only when he was just about to fall asleep having replayed the bridge scene a hundred which ways in his head, that he realised he had forgotten something important. It nagged away in the recesses of his mind. He dimly realised that things weren't quite resolved, but he was so tired he drifted off without remembering what it was.

Chapter 35

Taverner had remembered as soon as he woke up. It was the lock of hair that had been placed under the plant pot. He contacted Forensics and left an urgent message. The case wasn't complete until he knew who the lock of hair belonged to. The laboratory personnel were analysing the sample and cross referencing it with any other Mispers in the hope of a result, and the relevant teams were also looking at the pictures on the SD card. Until, they had the results back, then he was still on tenterhooks, and it had been agreed that the wider team were not told about this development, unless it was relevant. For now, it was time to thank the team. The celebrations had been loud and noisy. Even Sykes had offered his congratulations to Taverner and the detectives and gave him £100 towards the kitty for the bar but declined to join them.

'Well, didn't I always say that you can never trust a member of the clergy…' he had added, having no compunction in taking credit for the arrests. The team's facial expressions ranged from incredulous to disgust, with Haworth having to suck in his cheeks to prevent himself from laughing out loud. But no-one really minded, they all knew the truth. The party promised to be raucous and the mood was high. They made their way to The Old Starre Inne, Stonegate, one of the oldest pubs in York, as the team were determined to show him around the best watering holes in York. Taverner took in historic building and made his way through the snickelway and into the courtyard and then the inn. The pub has wonderful views of the Minster and was rumoured to have been used in the civil war as a hospital and mortuary for the wounded. It also boasted a wide range of real ales much to Ballantyne and Haworth's delight. They wasted no time in getting a round in.

Haworth thrust a pint of real ale at Taverner. 'Thought you'd like this, it's Allendale Pennine Pale.'

Taverner tasted it and was pleasantly surprised. 'Not bad. I suppose this place is haunted too?'

Haworth nodded. 'Oh aye. There's rumoured to be a poltergeist, lights being turned on and off, chairs moved and that. There are the ghosts of two black cats, an' all.'

Taverner was not surprised. Everywhere seemed to have ghosts in York.

'I just wanted tae say I weren't sure about yer to begin with, but you're one of us now,' explained Ballantyne, his top lip still decorated with white froth from his pint.

'He's not one of you, yer Scottish windbag, but he is one of us, a proper Yorkshire man,' continued Haworth. 'And a damned fine detective, despite the cat piss tea and falafel.'

'He is,'added Cullen. 'We'll soon teach him to talk proper and drink proper too. He'll be ,'hey upping' and 'appening', and be 'nithered' along with the best of us.'

'Nithered?' Taverner laughed. He had picked up a lot of the local sayings but not that one.

'Freezing, you're always saying it's cold up here, but we say 'nithered.'' She cuddled up to Patel who looked rather embarrassed.

He clearly hadn't been ready to declare their burgeoning relationship to the whole office.

Taverner noticed the developing relationship between the two officers and wondered if he would be forced to separate them. He hoped not. Patel was a great officer and Cullen was shaping up under the eagle eye of Wildblood.

'Aye he will,' replied Haworth. 'I feel bad for Sheffield though, losing their best winger. I didn't realise it were him, he's proper talented, that Nathaniel Lawson, with great pace.'

'Serves him right though,' Wildblood added darkly. 'Not much call for those skills where he's going. He's toxic now, so can't see any team touching him even when he's released.'

They contemplated Nathaniel Lawson's fate and the lengths his father had gone to, to protect his burgeoning football career. Matthew was likely to plead guilty to manslaughter, but that might be a long shot since he had followed Emily with a large weapon, the wrench, in his hand. The prosecution would certainly press for a murder charge given the premeditation this action implied.

Taverner felt quite giddy and delighted at finally being accepted by the team. It felt wonderful. A speech was called for.

'Well, I couldn't have done it without you lot. Thank you, Ballantyne and Haworth for bringing your experience to bear on the case and your humour, Patel for your outstanding technical skills, Cullen for sterling work research skills and Wildblood for your attention to detail and nose for bullshit. You have all worked amazingly hard. I have never felt so proud to be a fellow Yorkshireman. Thank you for your welcome and I look forward to solving more cases with you. But above all we have justice for Emily.'

They all raised their glasses and the stamping of feet and clapping of hands was deafening.

The next day, Taverner was feeling a little fragile and did a couple of hours work going through the evidence. It was coming together nicely, but he still hadn't heard back from Forensics about the lock of hair that was left outside his house. He was just going to chase it up when James King, the lead officer, came to give him the results in person, his expression oddly grave.

'I just wanted to talk to you about the lock of hair you brought in for analysis and I have some enlarged stills from the tech lads from the SD card here for you to look at.'

Taverner snapped to attention. He wondered if they'd had a match, maybe it was from a Misper. Perhaps, another girl from the literacy group, someone who had escaped Emily's attention.

'OK.'

'I thought I ought to talk to you face to face, it's just a bit irregular, that's all. I have spoken to DCI Sykes too.'

That really got Taverner's attention.

'Why is that? Is the hair human?'

'Oh yes, it's certainly human.'

'What then? Do we have a match?'

James nodded.

'Erm, well, you know we have samples of DNA and fingerprints of all police officers so we can rule them out, well, we have your DNA and fingerprints and we've checked it and double checked it. Look, there's no easy way to say this, but the hair sample does match someone. It's yours, so I thought I'd better tell you personally.' He sucked his teeth and avoided Taverner's eye.

'Are you absolutely sure?'

'Yes, I have tested and retested it against your most recent sample…'

'But it can't be mine, it's blond for a start.' Taverner pointed to his dark locks, utterly perplexed.

'Yes, well.' He looked wildly about him, keen to avoid Taverner's eye. 'But there is one explanation. It could have been taken from when you were younger, a boy, even as a baby, I suppose…'

Taverner gasped. Oh my God! Of course. It had to be from her, his mother, for who else could possibly have a lock of his hair as a baby?

'And the photos?'

King handed over an A4 envelope. 'See for yourself.'

'Ah, fine, thanks for telling me,' he replied coolly, wanting to send King away so he could be alone with his chaotic thoughts and examine the photos in private.

King merely smiled and aware of the enormity of what he had revealed, walked away as quietly as he had arrived. Taverner's emotions lurched from joy to horror to joy again. He had put the whole identity thing to the back of his mind as he struggled to investigate Emily's murder, but now he could take some leave and find the woman who had given birth to him, but what was amazing was that she had somehow known he was here in York and she clearly knew where he lived. She had found him first. With shaking hands, he opened the envelope hoping that an image of his mother might appear. There were three prints in total which showed the same figure dressed in dark trousers, coat and hoodie with the hood up, to show them kneeling in front of his house, but their features were blurry and indistinct. The others were no better but showed them walking away in one, and further down the driveway towards the field. It was impossible to tell if it was a male or female, or even guess the person's age. How disappointing! Christ, he needed to talk to someone. He wondered if Wildblood was in and took the steps two at a time towards the main office. She was at her desk gathering up her coat and bag.

'I'm just on my way out to get a sandwich, do you want one?' She took in his expression. 'What's up boss, you look quite pale. Are you ill? Look, walk with me and we can talk on the way.'

He followed in a daze. 'Forensics have got back to me about the hair someone left at my house and I have the blown up photos from the SD card.'

'And? Whose is it then?'

Taverner ran his fingers through his hair in an abstracted manner. 'Well, that's just it, it belongs to me...'

Wildblood's mouth opened to a wide O shape.

She took one look at Taverner's face and ushered him outside with her.

'Come on, let's have a coffee and a chat, somewhere private.' Taverner followed her out into the street, his hands in his pocket, his expression wild. It was bitingly cold and Wildblood wrapped her scarf tightly around her neck and pulled up her collar against the wind. A while later they were ensconced in Ma Baker's, Wildblood sipping a cappuccino and Taverner a cup of Earl Grey. Wildblood had treated them to brownies too, though Taverner had lost his appetite.

339

'So, what did Forensics say exactly?'

'Just that they had checked and double checked the hair sample and cross checked it with other samples and then included my DNA but found there was a match! I couldn't believe it. King double checked it and got the same result.' Taverner looked elated yet confused at the same time, like someone who'd arrived home to discover a surprise birthday party when he'd thought everyone had forgotten. 'I mean it must be from my mother. She must have kept a lock of my hair before she gave me up. She must know where I live. To think that she came to my house! I just don't know why she didn't knock on my door?' He shook his head, baffled. 'I mean, why didn't she?'

Wildblood sipped her drink and studied the man opposite. His expression was bewildered, so vulnerable and dejected that she had to fight the urge to stretch her hand over the tabletop to comfort him. It meant so much to him, she realised.

'Well, the way I see it, is that she kept the lock of hair for all these years, so the first thing is that it were so very important to her. Then, she found out where you lived, which is another hard thing. I reckon she just bottled it at the last minute, didn't dare knock on your door; that's all. You know how nervous you'd be meeting her, well, she'll be the same. In fact, a lot worse because she will think that you'll blame her for what happened. I mean, for all she knows, you might be really angry. You might even hate her.'

Taverner brightened and thought for a moment. 'God, of course. Yes, I'm sure you're right. I hadn't thought of that.'

'And the photos?'

Taverner passed the envelope over the table. Wildblood frowned as she examined them all closely.

'And of course, the other good thing is that we don't have another victim,' she added absently as she studied the images.

'Yes, you're right, of course. I'm very pleased about that.' He studied her. He truly was, but now he was consumed with emotion. 'Anyway, the photos are too grainy to reveal much, sadly.'

Wildblood looked up at him. 'Hmm, I suppose.' She spread the photos out in front of her and pointed to the wide angled shot. 'Looks like he or she escaped via the field at the back of your house, though. Look, they're heading towards the fence. I wonder where they were going? Is there a footpath behind your place?'

Taverner suddenly stared at the photo for a minute or two and laughed.

Wildblood scowled. 'What?'

'Did I tell you about the gypsies that moved into the field behind me?' He looked at his calendar on his phone. 'The gypsies left just after the lock of hair was planted. It must be significant.'

'So, the person in the photos might belong to that particular group of gypsies? You could be related to 'em?' Wildblood looked alarmed. 'Would that bother you, if yer were?'

Taverner grinned. 'No, of course not, but to think my family might have been living behind me all the time!' He sipped his drink and the colour came back into his cheeks. He looked at her thoughtfully. 'If it's a man in the photos, then it could be a male relative, a brother or something, even my father...'

Wildblood considered this. 'So, you don't know who he is either?'

341

Taverner shook his head. 'No, my mother wouldn't say apparently.'

They contemplated this for a minute or two as Wildblood finished her brownie, then looked longingly at Taverner's. He was too revved up to eat and silently passed the plate to her.

Wildblood took a bite and pulled out her phone. 'Speaking of gypsies, listen, I've been thinking that Maggie Malone, our psychic cum fortune teller, was actually quite accurate, all things considered. I mean she knew about your adoption, the dragon and parasol in the Geisha Club, and she came up trumps with the hierophant card.'

'Oh yes, the hierophant card? What does it mean again?'

Wildblood showed him the picture on her phone of a mystical looking man in flowing robes.

'It's a wise man or advisor. Another word for hierophant is a cleric.' She nodded to emphasise the point. 'Strange when the murderer turned out to be an ex-vicar, isn't it? Makes you think.'

'I suppose. Maybe, she just got lucky.' But in his heart, Taverner knew there was more to it than that, like her reference to his friend who went missing. 'She also picked out the moon card and a page one.'

'Yeah, I looked those up too. The moon means deception amongst other things and the page one was something to do with a young man who was immature in his relationships, acting younger than his years. Nathaniel maybe? Dunno about you guv, but I'd say she was spot on, wouldn't you?'

'Pretty well, we should use her in the future, perhaps?'

'Maybe. I'm not sure Sykes would approve, though. All the more reason to do it I reckon.'

342

Taverner laughed. God this day was really turning out to be most bizarre. His mother had found him, and she may or may not be a gypsy, or at least someone in the family was. And he was seriously thinking of consulting a psychic with tricky cases.

He looked at her. 'Look, you remember when you said you'd come with me when I meet my mother, you will, won't you? I mean, I'd ask my dad, but I don't think it would be fair on him…'

Wildblood shook her head exasperated. 'Gi' over, course I will. You don't even have to ask. Gypsy or not! Honestly!'

As they made their way back to the station, it was late afternoon, and the light was fading. All around them, people were making preparations for Christmas, most houses had brightly lit fir trees festooned with baubles, tinsel and fairy lights. This Christmas would be different and Taverner found he was looking forward to it. Last year, he and his father struggled to celebrate without his mother's warm presence, and had muddled through the whole day, just about, but this year he might have many other people to celebrate it with. The biting cold had given way to the faintest sprinkling of snow, which reflected the light, giving the street a magical glow. He found he was really looking forward to the future. Safe in the knowledge that his real mother, his flesh and blood, was near and ready to meet him, he felt his spirits soar. Wildblood shivered besides him and stamped her feet against the cold. Since coming to York, he'd complained endlessly about the freezing temperatures but today, on one of the coldest days of the year, he didn't feel it. Right now, he thought he would never feel the cold again, ever. It really did feel like he had come home.

Message from Charlie De Luca

I hope you liked **Coming Home**, this mainstream detective fiction book set in York. Many eagle-eyed readers will have noticed that DI Taverner and DS Wildblood appear in my last two racing thrillers, **Making Allowances** and **Hoodwinked.** The idea to develop them came from writing those books and wondering how the two characters could develop. It is set in York because this is one of my favourite places and really needs no introduction. However, I am still writing racing thrillers and my next book '**Fall From Grace'** is due in spring 2021. As ever, I would be grateful if you could leave a review. It takes hardly any time but is so important for indie authors like me. Thank you in anticipation.

Charlie De Luca was brought up on a stud farm, where his father held a permit to train National Hunt horses, hence his lifelong passion for racing was borne. He reckons he visited most of the racecourses in England by the time he was ten. He has always loved horses but sadly grew too tall to be a jockey. Charlie lives in rural Lincolnshire with his family, various pets and even has a couple of ex-racehorses in residence too.

Charlie has written several racing thrillers which include: **Rank Outsiders**, **The Gift Horse**, **Twelve in the Sixth**, **Making Allowances** and **Hoodwinked**. These are also available in paperback.

You can connect Charlie via twitter; @charliedeluca8 or visit his website.

Charlie is more than happy to connect with readers, so please feel free to contact him directly using the CONTACT button on the website.

www.charliedeluca.co.uk

Printed in Great Britain
by Amazon